Five Tries to Get It Right

Kathryn Dodson

Renegade Reads

Contents

1.	Chapter 1	1
2.	Chapter 2	7
3.	Chapter 3	10
4.	Chapter 4	18
5.	Chapter 5	23
6.	Chapter 6	29
7.	Chapter 7	33
8.	Chapter 8	37
9.	Chapter 9	43
10.	Chapter 10	50
11.	Chapter 11	53
12.	Chapter 12	58
13.	Chapter 13	61
14.	Chapter 14	70
15.	Chapter 15	82
16.	Chapter 16	85
17.	Chapter 17	91
18.	Chapter 18	99
19.	Chapter 19	103
20.	Chapter 20	107
21.	Chapter 21	116

22. Chapter 22 119

23. Chapter 23 126

24. Chapter 24 131

25. Chapter 25 138

26. Chapter 26 144

27. Chapter 27 153

28. Chapter 28 163

29. Chapter 29 168

30. Chapter 30 173

31. Chapter 31 183

32. Chapter 32 188

33. Epilogue 190

Afterword 193

Acknowledgements 194

About the author 195

Chapter 1

Lydia

Lydia paused at the door to the hospital room and took a few seconds to compose herself. Thirty minutes of lying to get in and then sneaking down the halls as if she didn't belong had left her breathless. The friend on the other side of the door would need her calm and pulled together.

She peeked around the corner. Seeing Kate, her dark hair splayed against the stark white hospital bed, IV attached to her arm, wrecked Lydia. She would not lose one more person she loved. Not like this.

She crept into the room. Kate's eyes stayed closed, and Lydia hoped she slept. Dark circles remained visible despite the obvious layer of concealer. Only Kate would arrive at a hospital with a full face of perfectly applied makeup, except for the red-orange smudges around her mouth. Coco by Chanel. Kate's signature lipstick.

Kate's eyes opened, mahogany wells boring into Lydia. "How did you get in here?"

"I told them I was your sister. And I'm pretty sure they asked you about it, so it shouldn't be a surprise," Lydia said. The indignation in Kate's scratchy voice had hurt, but Lydia had a job to do.

"I wanted to be left alone." Kate looked toward the far wall where two large windows looked out over Malibu and the Santa Monica Mountains. Her voice projected anger, but the tears forming in her eyes gave her away.

"Why did you do it?" Lydia barely kept the pain from her own voice. "You can't kill yourself."

"How did you find out?"

"Mitch called. He called me after he called the paramedics." Lydia watched Kate's eyes drop at the mention of her ex-husband. Crimson rose on her cheeks, making her look more alive than ever. Thank god.

"Did he tell you?" Kate looked up, her gaze searing into Lydia's.

"That Hadley is pregnant? Yes, he told me." Mitch and Kate had divorced a year earlier. Six months ago, Mitch married Hadley, and now they'd started a family. "That can't be why you did this. You didn't even want kids."

"Well, neither did he, back in the day." Kate practically spat the words.

"So, you thought you'd attempt suicide because your ex-husband is happy?" The words sounded mean, but Lydia needed to understand the why behind this situation. The Kate she knew, had known for forty years, would never have done this.

"Well, that was just the latest bit of bad news on a shitty day that capped off a shitty, month, a shitty year. Hell, it's all downhill now."

Lydia pulled over a chair and sat next to her friend. She reached for her hand atop the blue and white checked blanket stretched across the bed. "Do you want to talk about it?"

"I already talked to the shrink." The heavy sigh deflated Kate, collapsing her into something fragile.

Lydia held on, hoping for more. She squeezed Kate's hand but kept her mouth shut.

"You'll know soon enough anyway. The board of directors at Indulge fired me." Kate looked straight at Lydia as she spoke, but her eyes were an empty room. No emotion. No sadness. Nothing.

The shock of the announcement pushed Lydia into the back of her chair. How was this possible? Kate had started the lingerie company decades earlier. The business had made Kate wealthy, especially when the pandemic hit right after Indulge had come out with a line of beautiful but comfy loungewear. Kate sourced and manufactured all Indulge garments in the US, so the company had avoided the pandemic's supply chain crisis. Lydia had tracked the media stories that called Kate Cameron a genius. None of this made sense.

"Kate, they can't fire you from your own company."

"I took the company public. Remember? Stockholders own it now." Kate no longer met Lydia's eyes. Instead, her head lolled and her voice flatlined. "Do you remember how happy I was when Greg Stavos decided to invest in the company? Well, he staged a coup. He said the company needed to go in another direction. Most of the board members went with him. They voted me out."

Lydia held on to Kate's hand like a lifeline. That company had meant everything to her friend. It had been her baby, her pride, her identity. Having it suddenly ripped from her might have left Kate believing she had no future. Lydia found some comfort in this, because as much as Kate hurt now, with a little time, she would recover. Or she'd find the will to fight back. And Lydia would help. No one had died. This wasn't permanent.

Before she said anything, a loud rap sounded at the open door. Lydia turned to see a white-jacketed woman sweep into the room.

"Hello, I'm Dr. Bhavnani. How is our patient doing?"

Kate looked up at the woman with the same vacant stare but said nothing.

Dr. Bhavnani sighed, then turned to Lydia. "Are you family?"

"Yes, I'm her sister. Lydia." Why not continue the lie? Kate might as well be her sister. They'd been inseparable since grade school. Well, maybe not inseparable. Not lately. Not really since they'd been in their twenties. After that, families, jobs, and life had made their visits less frequent. But Kate would always be her best friend, and every time they got together, they seemed to pick up their conversation, and their friendship, mid-sentence.

"Nice to meet you." Dr. Bhavnani nodded at Lydia, then turned to Kate. "May I share your medical information with your sister?"

Kate shrugged, then nodded. What had happened to the animated, fast-talking Kate? And more importantly, how would Lydia get her back?

"We admitted Kate this morning after an overdose attempt. She swallowed multiple oxycodone-acetaminophen tablets after consuming a bottle of red wine. Fortunately, paramedics arrived before the tablets dissolved. She was administered naloxone by paramedics to combat the opioid, and we pumped her stomach when she arrived."

The matter-of-fact manner combined with the big words made everything sound equally horrifying and like no big deal. Kate stared sullenly at the doctor, as if the words bounced off her.

"What does all that mean?" Lydia finally asked.

"Well, because she got in here quickly, there shouldn't be many ill effects from the medication. We would like to keep her here under observation for twenty-four hours. A psychiatrist has evaluated her, and we recommend she start therapy immediately. Ideally, she would have her first appointment set prior to leaving the hospital."

"Okay," Lydia said. She appreciated a direct solution. A phone call, the beginning of therapy, a path back to health.

"As her family member, I'd like you to see that this happens."

"Of course, anything it takes to keep her safe." This, Lydia could do. She'd arrived in a panic, not knowing how to save her friend, but the doctor had given her a roadmap. Lydia would help Kate set the appointment and carry out any other tasks the doctor suggested. Of course, one look at Kate's annoyed face indicated a more difficult path forward.

"We are always concerned about repeat suicide attempts. Kate's home should be cleared of unnecessary drugs and other items she might use to harm herself."

Kate crossed her arms and exhaled. The doctor lifted an eyebrow at Kate's angry stare. Lydia needed to tamp down the tension between these two.

"I'm sure this was a one-time thing. Kate received some terrible news this week and struggled to get beyond it. I'll do anything I can to help." And just like that, Lydia had someone to take care of again, right when she really needed it.

The doctor exited the room, leaving Lydia with a sheaf of documents on resources and instructions. Kate pulled her blanket up to her chin and closed her eyes.

"Are you feeling okay? Can I get you anything? Lydia asked.

"I want you to leave me alone. I want everyone to leave me alone." Then, in a smaller voice, "I want to go home."

"Everything's going to be all right." Lydia almost cooed, as if Kate had transformed from grown-up to child. Taking care of Kate might be a new role for Lydia. She'd have to bring the perseverance she'd brought to other challenges. She had to. She loved Kate.

Kate had always seemed the more mature of the two, even though Lydia was a few months older. Kate got her driver's license first, had sex first, went to graduate school, started a company. Hell, her life was totally put together compared with Lydia's. Now Lydia needed to step up.

"Nothing is going to be all right. Ever." A flash of the old Kate lit the room. Angry. Bossy. But the empty, hollowed-out look in her eyes was brand new.

"You can get through this. I'll help." Lydia patted Kate's arm.

"Just leave." Kate's tone had a coldness Lydia hadn't expected.

"No." Not when she had a job to do. She'd hold out until the bitchy Kate retreated.

"Well, look who decided to finally grow a spine."

The comment sliced through Lydia. She hadn't been the outgoing one, the one who was bold and brave. The truth hurt, but today wasn't about her. "You're being mean because you're hurt. I'm here to help."

"No. I'm being mean because I don't want your help."

A fierce anger ripped through Lydia. "Well, too bad. I'm not going to let you kill yourself. I already lost Joe last year. I'm not going to lose you too." Twenty-three years of marriage, and she'd found Joe on the sofa, thinking he'd passed out from one too many beers. Again. She might have left him there for hours, started dinner, graded papers. Except he wasn't snoring. When she'd investigated, she discovered he wasn't breathing. She'd never tell anyone the first thought that jumped into her mind: freedom.

She'd quit her job teaching school the following week. Instead of long days melding into longer weeks, months, and years until she died, she could start over. Her life didn't have to be boring, it could be wonderful, the way she thought Kate's was. Of course, twelve months had passed, and she'd yet to change anything about her life. She'd told herself she had to help Sophie, her college-aged daughter, recover from her dad's death. And now Kate. She had to help Kate.

"This is completely different. Joe had a massive heart attack. He didn't try to kill himself," Kate said.

"I don't care. Death is death. Now, how do I get into your condo? I need to clear out any drugs and dangerous objects like the doctor said." Lydia tried to keep from crying, but the sobs came anyway. Great, gulping, ugly sobs took over. How would she deal with Kate trying to kill herself? The panic of learning about her friend's hospitalization and the rush to help had subsided, but it left Lydia with the full force of what Kate had tried to do.

She sank back into the chair and let herself cry. She couldn't look at Kate. Her tears felt selfish—she should be here for her friend, not have her own breakdown. But she'd barely held it together lately. Joe had died, Sophie had gone to college, and Lydia had retired, all in just over a year. She thought she'd finally have freedom but now spent each lonely day in a dumpy house, afraid of moving in any direction at all.

She thought without Joe stuck to the sofa and a job to tie her down, she'd transform into the person she always imagined she'd be. But somehow, she'd gotten stuck herself, not sure what to do next, how to take that first step into the rest of her life. She hadn't changed into someone better. Only now she was lonely as well as disappointed. Everything about the future sucked when you were alone. It would never have occurred to her to take her own life, but she understood not wanting to face another boring, lonely day. Poor Kate.

The tears slowed. Lydia found a box of tissues and wiped her eyes. Finally, she turned to face Kate. Blank eyes looked back.

"Let me try to help you. I have absolutely nothing going on in my life, and I would love to spend some time with you."

"I don't want help. I want to fucking leave this place." Despite the cursing, no passion accompanied the words.

Somehow, that steeled Lydia. Kate wouldn't make this easy, but Lydia had a few skills of her own, namely dogged persistence. She'd managed to be married to Joe for twenty-three years, and she'd spent the last fifteen not kicking him out despite his reluctance to find a job and desire to drink all afternoon. Plus, she'd learned a bevy of skills for dealing with unruly people over decades as a schoolteacher. She'd find a way to handle Kate too.

"I can help you get out, but you've got to work with me a little. You know what the doctor said. She doesn't want you going anywhere if you're a danger to yourself. Can we agree to partner on this?"

"Fine." Kate's dull voice barely even registered resignation.

Lydia would take it. Kate needed help, and her own life needed purpose. They'd get through this together.

Chapter 2

Lydia

Lydia let herself into Kate's condo. As always, the view of the Pacific Ocean across a wide sand beach drew her toward the wall of windows. The plank flooring with its knots and whorls made the modern space cozy. That, and the plump blue velvet sofa atop a white shag rug that caressed her bare feet like cashmere.

Standing at the window with the afternoon sun warming her face, she gazed down upon tan bodies strolling the ocean walk. After that, nothing remained but raw-sugar sand, mesmerizing blue ocean, and an azure sky streaked with clouds.

Kate had so much. A beautiful view, the quirky cafés and celebrated restaurants of Venice Beach a short walk away, more money than she knew how to spend. Lydia had none of those. One hundred miles south and twenty miles east of the ocean, her one-story home could fit inside Kate's condo, not to mention the hemmed-in views of dreary neighboring houses with peeling paint and overgrown yards. Her home sat on a suburban cul-de-sac, in an unremarkable city, a reflection of Lydia's uninspired life.

She'd always envied Kate's life of glamor. Posh hotels, fancy business trips, fashionable clothing.

"Stop." She spoke out loud, and the word rang through the empty space. She'd had a good life. A great one. She had a wonderful daughter and had spent her career teaching elementary school students, just as she'd planned. And at least her husband hadn't left her for another woman, although there'd certainly been times when she'd wished he would. Enough of this wallowing. She was here to help Kate.

She grabbed an empty bottle of wine lying sideways on the coffee table and a cut crystal glass stained with dried wine. It looked like blood. Those were the only items that marred the pristine room. The kitchen looked unused, and every surface gleamed. Lydia's kitchen had never been this clean. Although Lydia didn't have a weekly cleaning lady.

She opened every cabinet and drawer, but other than the contents of the wine fridge and a cabinet filled with booze, nothing looked dangerous. Nevertheless, she hauled the block of wood that sheathed sharply honed German knives down to the underground parking garage and set them in the trunk of her car.

She drove to the nearest Target, no easy feat in L.A. traffic, and purchased boxes and bubble wrap. Back at the condo, she wrapped up every bottle of alcohol. By the time she'd finished, nothing else fit in the trunk of her car. She thought about driving home and leaving the booze and knives there, but it would have meant hours in the car. The day had exhausted her, and she hadn't even started on the bedrooms.

She went through the guest bedroom and bath first, even though she doubted she'd find anything that needed to be removed. Finally, she entered Kate's bedroom. So very little appeared wrong. An empty glass and emptier prescription pill bottle rested on the nightstand. The bed's pillow and comforter were slightly mussed, as if someone had lain atop them.

A baby blue tote with Prada emblazoned in gold sat boldly beside the nightstand, a stack of papers bound by a silver clip protruding from the depths of the bag. Lydia reached for the papers. **TERMINATION AGREEMENT** sprang off the page, and she shoved them deep into the bowels of the bag. It might be impossible for Kate to kill herself with paper, but this was clearly the most dangerous item in the apartment. She didn't want the bag in her car in case it got stolen, but it couldn't stay in this room.

She stowed the bag in the empty bottom drawer of the guest room's dresser. The heft of the bag meant Kate's laptop resided there as well as the so-called agreement, but she'd wait until Kate asked for it.

Fuck that man and his agreement. Lydia returned to the master bedroom and slid open the cabana doors that opened to the balcony and the ocean beyond. Moist air straight off the ocean blew into the room, cleansing it of all that had happened there.

Despite the cool breeze, fury seethed under Lydia's skin. Kate's dismissal from her own company burned. Her friend was practically the only woman she knew who hadn't been screwed over at work, until now. Lydia had thought Kate immune to the perils that affected so many she knew. She stood on the balcony, facing the sand, waves, and nothingness beyond. Kate's loss echoed through her heart.

She inhaled the fresh air in long, slow breaths. The breeze calmed her, flowed through and seemed to cleanse her as well. Where had this wind originated? Hawaii? Japan? Australia?

She and Kate had visited Australia once, back in their twenties, when they traveled together at least once a year. They'd gone over Christmas, and the country had been warm. The temperature, the ocean, and especially the people.

They'd promised to keep traveling, but they only took one more trip after Australia. Lydia wished they'd never stopped, wished she could ride this breeze to someplace far away and far more interesting than Kate's lost job and the lonely house in the suburbs Lydia called home. They needed to start over.

Chapter 3

Lydia

Kate looked much better when Lydia returned to the hospital the next morning. The dark circles under her eyes remained visible, especially now that the makeup had worn or washed off. But the whites of her eyes had lost the pink tinge of a hard night, and the vacant look had softened to tired.

"Please, Lydia, tell the doctor you made an appointment with the psychiatrist."

"But I didn't." Lydia tried to combat Kate's pleading with a firm voice.

"I know you didn't, but I want out of here."

"Then let me make the appointment."

"Absolutely not. This is my life, and I choose not to see a psychiatrist. Do I look crazy to you?"

"You are in the hospital because you tried to commit suicide. Looks have nothing to do with it." Jeez. It was like talking to a fifth grader.

"Maybe I just need some time to process the job loss."

"What does that mean?"

"It means I don't want to see a fucking psychiatrist."

Lydia sat back and crossed her arms. They'd reached an impasse. She understood the desire to leave the hospital. She hated them. People went there to die. Like her mother when she had cancer. Of course, Kate had tried to die at home. Joe had succeeded.

"How am I supposed to know you're better? What if you go home and try this again and succeed next time? I'll have to live with that guilt forever."

"That's dramatic." Kate shook her head.

"You don't think trying to kill yourself is dramatic? What is wrong with you? I'm here to help. I understand that you're not happy, and you've been dealt some pretty terrible blows, but you've got a lot of life ahead of you. I do too. You know, you're not the only one who's had to deal with a lot recently."

"Has something else happened?"

The interest in Kate's eyes at the comment made it worth having to share her daughter's news. "Sophie left for Semester at Sea last month."

"You're kidding. That's so sudden. Isn't she a communications major? Why that program? I didn't even know she liked boats." Kate's comments hit Lydia like darts hitting a board.

"They had a last-minute spot. She barely had time to pack. Hopefully it won't set her back on her major, although when I asked, she said she didn't care." Lydia's ears burned with shame. She hadn't told anyone why her daughter preferred to live on a traveling boat than stay at her college near home. "Sophie says I'm smothering her. She doesn't appreciate my calls, texts, or visits, even when I'm delivering her laundry."

Kate's eyes grew big and sparkled for the first time since she'd been admitted. "That little bitch." She hardly got the last word out before she started giggling.

"It's not funny. She takes one damn Intro to Psychology course, and now she's saying I've become codependent since Joe's death, and she needs some time away from me."

Lydia watched Kate trying to hold back the laughter, but every time she stopped, a new giggle burst forth. Soon it infected Lydia as well, and she couldn't keep herself from laughing. Even though she really wanted to cry.

"We are such losers." Kate said, trying to catch her breath.

Lydia saw the tears streaming down her friend's cheeks and wondered whether the laughter or her situation caused them. "Speak for yourself. But we do have to figure out how to start over from here. Let's do it together."

Kate stilled. Then she wiped her eyes. "Fine. Let's do that. Let's get out of here and go plan something."

"I don't think you should be alone. Would you like to stay with me in Escondido? The change of scenery might do you good."

"Well, um. That's a nice offer. But wouldn't it be easier if you stayed with me in Venice Beach? We can walk to great restaurants and shops. I mean, at least until we've planned something more permanent." Kate pushed the button to call the nurse.

"I don't have any clothes up here." Lydia stood and walked to the window. They needed to think this through, have a plan. Kate moved too fast for Lydia, maybe too fast for her own mental health. They hadn't even talked about if Kate still wanted to kill herself, or how long Lydia should take care of her.

She didn't think she could handle Kate on Kate's own turf, but she couldn't imagine Kate in her Escondido home. If only they had some middle-of-the-road compromise. A hotel might work, but where? And a hotel would cost money. Money Lydia definitely didn't have.

If only time would rewind and take them back to their twenties when, somehow, they'd managed, even though neither of them had a ton of money back then. What they did have, they spent on travel. Life then had been uncomplicated, an adventure, not something she'd had to grapple with and plan for on a daily basis. At least that's not how she chose to remember it.

"How can I help you?" an unfamiliar voice said.

Lydia turned to see a man in scrubs approach Kate.

"Hi, Kyle." Kate's chipper voice had changed one-eighty degrees. "I'm ready to check out now."

"Oh." Kyle's eyebrows arched in surprise. "Has Dr. Bhavnani been in yet? She'll need to approve your discharge."

"Actually, it is my legal right to leave." Kate still had a smile on her face, but her voice had become a knife edge. "If Dr. Bhavnani is unable to discharge me in the next five minutes, then I'll be on my way."

"But you've still got an IV." Kyle shifted nervously as if he couldn't decide whether to stay and talk some sense into Kate or make a break for the nurse's station and bring in reinforcements.

"Yes, would you please take this off me?" Kate lifted her needled arm.

"Um. I need to go find a supervisor."

"Five minutes. After that, I do it myself." No trace of a smile remained. Kyle broke for the door.

Lydia caught a glimpse of the future, and it didn't look good. "You railroaded that guy. Is that what you plan to do with me?"

"What? No, of course not. You're my friend. I just really need to get out of here." Kate almost looked sincere, but Lydia had seen through it to the calculating mind at work.

Lydia shook her head. She couldn't do this. More than anything in the world, she wanted to help Kate return from whatever dark place she'd entered. She wanted her friend to overcome the hurt life had shoved her way and move on. Hell, she wanted that for herself.

But Kate didn't want to try. Instead, she used her forceful personality to manipulate people rather than ask for help. They couldn't even decide where to stay.

"I can't do this." Lydia crossed the room, stopping briefly at the chair to grab her bag. She wanted to flee, not only to escape the responsibility of dealing with Kate but to avoid examining the emptiness in her own life that Kate's incident had provoked. But she wasn't the type to run away. She helped people through things. Dependable Lydia. Boring Lydia.

She turned at the door. "I'm sorry. I need some fresh air. You are one of the most important people in my world, but if you're not going to be open and honest with me about what you're going through and what the future holds, then I can't do this. I'll be back in an hour. If you're still here, we can figure out a plan together."

She saw the protest on Kate's lips, the argument that would stop Lydia and persuade her. But Lydia wouldn't wait around for that. She walked out the door.

Lydia sped down the hospital corridor and slipped into the elevator before the doors closed. Outside, she stepped into the bright sun under a blue Santa Monica sky. She crossed the street, wanting to be as far from the pressure of the hospital as possible, and headed toward the ocean. Finally, she could fill her lungs. She inhaled deeply, then coughed up car exhaust and salt air.

She passed a place called Tehran Market. Her peek through the open glass doors pulled her in further. It might have been the cleanest store she'd ever seen. Tile floors the color of lead drew her deeper into the interior. Wide aisles neatly packed with containers of nuts, beans, and dried fruits led toward a brightly lit produce area with a rainbow of colors beckoning. She passed rows of olives and pickles, then cookies, followed by candy, then stacks of long flat lavash.

She'd stepped into another part of the world, hidden behind a Santa Monica storefront. The aroma of charcoal-grilled meat wafted by. In the produce section, dates glistened, and she wanted to run her fingers across the velvety skin of the peaches. It was as if the world had stopped, and she'd been granted a reprieve from everything she didn't want to face. Travel had been like that once.

She strolled through the fruits and vegetables, palming the nubby skin of a tangerine, then making her way past box after box of greens she didn't recognize. She looked down the aisles, pondering where to go next. Row after row of spices, some in bottles, some in bags, filled each endcap.

On the far wall, a metal case stretched the length of the store. She wandered over, passing a glass-fronted freezer full of white and yellow ice creams. The metal case beyond greeted her with vats of pickles, olives, and preserved lemons. She walked past the meats and prepared foods, finally reaching containers filled with her favorites: baba ghanoush, hummus, tzatziki, tabbouleh. Her stomach rumbled. She grabbed a container of each and a package of lavash.

She'd only been gone twenty minutes, but returning to the hospital seemed a better choice than finding a park. She pictured herself sitting alone on a bench, binging on food flavored with far-flung adventure. It was the alone part that bothered her. That's how she ate every meal these days. So, she turned toward the hospital and Kate.

Lydia wondered if she'd find an empty room. Maybe one splattered with blood from where Kate had ripped out her IV. But when she turned the corner into her friend's room, nothing had changed. Kate lay in bed, IV attached, looking glum.

"Look what I've got." Lydia pushed the roller tray halfway over the bed. Then she pulled container after container out of the bag, opening them as she went and releasing the aroma of garlic, herbs, and spices into the sterile room.

"What's all this?" Kate didn't seem excited, but Lydia would take curious over uninterested. For now.

"There's the greatest market across the street. It has all kinds of incredible Middle Eastern food. It was all I could do not to buy out the entire store. It reminded me of the first time we explored the market in Madrid, and we purchased so much we had to drag the grocery bags back to our apartment."

"Smells good. How are we supposed to eat it?"

"Ta-da!" Lydia whipped out the lavash. Then realized she should have gotten plates, napkins, maybe serving spoons.

"Fine." Kate opened the bag with the flatbread and pulled off a corner. She studied the containers, then dipped the bread in the baba ghanoush. "Beats the hell out of hospital food."

"I miss our trips. Those are some of my fondest memories," Lydia said. She ripped off her own piece of lavash and dragged it through the hummus. So smooth and creamy. Completely unlike the stuff they called hummus at a normal grocery store.

"That's a great idea. Let's go someplace exotic like we used to." Kate took another piece of bread, this time running it across the hummus, then pressing it into the tabbouleh. It came out studded with the mix of parsley, mint, and bulgur wheat. She popped it in her mouth and even gave a little groan of pleasure.

Relief washed through Lydia at the site of her friend eating, enjoying food. It filled her with happiness, and possibility. "We could do that. We could go back in time, revisit a place we loved in the past. We could start over."

Kate coughed at the comment, almost choking on the tzatziki she'd shoved in her mouth. "That's a tall order. There are so many things I would change if I went back in time. I'd rethink getting married and starting a company."

"You don't mean that." She couldn't mean it. It was one thing to think you'd made a few mistakes, but something entirely different to wish you'd traveled a different path. Everyone had always envied Kate. If she thought she'd screwed up that badly, Lydia certainly didn't want to review her own pedestrian decisions.

"Maybe. Maybe not. Listen, you were right earlier. I need your help. And I haven't exactly been open or honest." A swell of emotion visibly swept through Kate, reddening her skin and bringing tears to her eyes.

"Oh, honey. It's going to be okay." Lydia rolled the food out of the way to reach for Kate. The IV stand and table blocked her path, only allowing her to put a hand on Kate's shoulder. This place with its hospital smells, beeping machines, and rotating faces would not help Kate get better.

A lone tear rolled down Kate's cheek. "It's been really hard, and I can't see how it will ever improve. I wish I could start over, do everything differently. But we don't get second chances, not at the big stuff. I'm fifty-two and the future is bleak. I'm too old to start over."

"Well, you can't say that. Because if you're too old, I'm too old."

"But you don't need to start over. You've got Sophie, and you just retired. You've worked hard to get to where you are. I worked hard and am in the opposite place from where I expected to be. My life is bleak. No job, no marriage, nothing. I hate it."

Bleak. What a word. Lydia pictured a vast, charred desert. Her life didn't feel like that. Instead, she faced a forked path. One side, the shadowy dark one, held nothing but loneliness: a daughter who actively tried to escape her mother's outstretched arms, a stale house where she wore a path between the bed, the kitchen, and the chair facing the TV.

But the other side held promise. Green fields and outdoor parties. A life restarted and filled with someone who brought her love and joy. Surely it was possible. But that path curved and dipped out of sight. How the hell did one get from here to there?

She scooted her chair as close to the bed as possible. She reached for Kate's hands and held them both in her own. "Kate. I need your help. I don't want a future where I'm lonely and bitter. It scares me. Please help me figure my life out. I'm lost."

When Kate didn't respond, the room grew heavy with desperation. How would they find their way out of this dark place?

Finally, Kate chuckled, shaking her head. "I don't think I'm the best person to help. After all, I just downed a bottle of pills because I hate my life." Kate squeezed her hands hard, pinching Lydia's fingers.

"But you're the only one I have left." Determined not to cry, Lydia retrieved her hands and waved them in front of her face. It was bad enough that she'd burdened Kate with her own problems. She'd come here to help, not whine about her life. The need to keep Kate safe, for Kate's sake and her own, grew like an insatiable hunger. "I can't lose you. I just can't."

"Fine. Let's get out of here and make a plan. Let's go someplace far away."

"Yes!" Lydia grabbed the idea. "Let's really do it. Let's go back to one of the places we visited when we were young and hopeful. Maybe we can recover some of that energy. We can go home, well, to one of our homes, and start planning. Depending on airline fares, we might be able to go next month."

"There is no way I'm hanging around L.A. for the next month. Or Escondido. Why don't we spend one night at my house and one night at your house and then leave? We can just pack and go."

Lydia's heart sank. She'd never have the money to buy last-minute plane tickets to any of the places they'd visited in their twenties. At least she wouldn't have the money unless she stole it from her retirement savings, and she already worried about that lasting long enough. Her pension would never allow that type of travel. How embarrassing to have to admit that.

"I can't go that soon. It would be too expensive. But I promise I'll investigate fares as soon as we're out of here."

Kate snorted. "Don't worry about money. I'll buy the tickets. My buyout plan left me a very rich woman." Bitterness oozed through the words.

"Well, that doesn't sound fair."

"Lydia. Nothing in life is fair." Kate's anger faded to resignation.

A rap sounded at the door, and both women turned to see Dr. Bhavnani barge into the room.

"I hear you are ready to go home." The doctor looked down at the clipboard she carried.

"Yes. I'd like to leave right away."

"Have you made an appointment with a psychiatrist?" The doctor looked first at Kate, then turned to Lydia.

"We're working on it," Lydia said, hoping the doctor bought her lie.

"Sometimes, people think they are capable enough to help their loved ones overcome mental illness." Dr. Bhavnani focused on Lydia. "This is rarely the case. And the guilt family members feel when things don't work out can be hard to handle. Professionals have years of training, experience, and access to medication that can help a patient recover."

Lydia grew hot under Dr. Bhavnani's gaze. She wondered whether leaving with Kate would be a mistake, potentially a terrible one.

Kate cleared her throat. "I believe this is my decision. I want to leave now."

Dr. Bhavnani turned back to Kate. "All right. I will sign your release. But I strongly encourage you to seek therapy as soon as possible."

Once the doctor left the room, Kate visibly relaxed. That seemed positive. But deep down, Lydia worried that their plans might not be enough to save Kate. Or herself.

Chapter 4

Lydia

"Can we go for a walk? I spent so many hours in that hospital bed that I feel like I haven't moved my body in weeks." Kate stood in her condo drinking a glass of water.

Lydia couldn't think of a better thing for them to do. Nature and exercise had a positive effect on the psyche, after all.

They headed outside and turned left onto the path along the ocean. Occasionally, a breeze brought a little cool air to an unusually hot afternoon. On one side, a broad expanse of ecru sand stretched toward blue ocean. A wall of multimillion dollar condos and houses flanked them on the left. Ahead, sailboats glided by on their way into the marina or out to sea.

Lydia wanted to curl up in the warm sand to nap and blissfully forget everything that had happened over the last two days. But she'd made her choice. She had helped Kate out of the hospital and into the rest of her life. And the responsibility fell to Lydia to make it a long and happy one.

"So, where should we go on our trip?" Kate walked with her arms crossed, her voice more resigned than excited.

"If we actually want to start over, the further away, the better. It will give us more perspective." Once upon a time, each adventure abroad had changed the women. That's what they needed now, and the bigger the change the better.

"Well, take your pick. I guess it started our junior year abroad in Madrid. Do you count that?" asked Kate.

"Definitely. Then we went to Amsterdam for graduation, then learned to scuba dive in Bonaire."

"That one was awesome."

Lydia laughed. "You would remember it that way. You spent a good part of that trip between the sheets with our scuba instructor."

"He was hot." A wry smile passed Kate's lips.

Kate's smile brought one to Lydia as well. Perhaps they should choose Bonaire, a place of good memories for Kate. Unless remembering how great her life had been would make her sad. If only Kate's emotional distress came with a user's guide.

Kate dropped her clenched arms and her stride opened up, forcing Lydia to keep up. Just talking about these trips seemed to make Kate feel better. This had to be the key to helping her. Once Kate got beyond these recent blows, she'd have a chance to find happiness again.

"Australia for Christmas was fantastic. And then we ended up in Costa Rica for a month, my personal favorite." Lydia offered up her preference.

"Only because of the hot surfer," Kate teased.

"It wasn't only because of Robert. I loved the volcanoes, the hot springs, and the beautiful beaches." If she'd ever made a wrong decision, it was leaving Costa Rica.

"Robert. I'd forgotten his name."

"Not me." Had the yearning come through in her voice? He'd been the first guy she'd ever loved. Maybe the only one. No, that wasn't true. She had loved Joe. It was just a different kind of love.

Kate reached out and grabbed Lydia's hand. "You do need a vacation."

Lydia nodded, her thoughts trapped in the past. They walked on until they reached the marina. Tan bodies glistened on the nearby volleyball courts and the city faded away as they reached the point where beach and ocean met. The whole world stretched before them. They could go anywhere. "So, which place do you want to visit the most?"

Kate gave a long, defeated sigh. "Honestly, I don't give a shit. Just pick one. Or pick all of them. It doesn't matter."

"Well, we can't go to all of them. I can't afford that." Lydia stared across the ocean, unable to meet Kate's eyes. It embarrassed her to be this far along in life and still have to worry about money.

"Oh, Lydia."

"Do not feel sorry for me." Shame burned through her.

Kate stopped and pulled Lydia in front of her. "I do not feel sorry for you. You've got a kid in college. Your husband died unexpectedly. I don't feel sorry for you at all. But don't let money hold you back. Let me pay for this. The only thing I've got left in my life is money."

Stuck somewhere between mortification about her own circumstance and sadness that her best friend believed she had nothing but money, Lydia couldn't speak.

"Please." Kate's voice cracked.

"You've got me in your life. You've got me. That's not nothing." Lydia surged forward and wrapped Kate in her arms. Tears spilled from her eyes. Her poor lost friend, unable to see how much love stood right in front of her.

"I'm sorry." The desolation in Kate's voice made Lydia think of barren plains and howling wind. She needed to pull her friend back into a world with songbirds and flowering trees. Or to the here and now where slick-skinned volleyball players dove into sparkling sand and the love of a best friend screamed to be embraced. Somewhere deep in her soul, Lydia knew she had as much to gain from Kate needing her as Kate did. She had her own lonely places from which she yearned to escape.

Maybe she should accept Kate's offer. If it kept them together and enabled Lydia to help her friend heal, perhaps that reason was worth the handout. And she'd have the opportunity to restart her own life.

"Okay. You can pay for things, but I'll try to save us money where I can. We were pretty frugal the first time around."

"Oh no you don't." Kate pushed back and looked her in the eye. "We are not staying in hostels and I'm definitely not flying coach. I don't think you understand. When I say I've got a lot of money, I mean I've got a fuck ton of money. Remember, I took Indulge public last year. I made a fortune. All those assholes who kicked me out of my job, they paid heavily for that privilege."

Lydia expected the familiar twinkle in her friend's eye at the cuss words. Instead, she saw resignation. She'd bring Kate's fire back, for both their sakes.

"Fine. But let's not go too posh. I want to get out there and meet interesting people. This is going to be a fresh start."

"Rich people aren't interesting?"

"Well, I wouldn't say no to finding a rich husband, but it's not my number one goal." She giggled at her joke. Although . . . First, she'd help her friend, but that didn't mean she wouldn't keep her eyes open for the right guy. She'd found him once on a trip.

"Come on, let's finish this walk so we can start booking flights and a place to stay." Lydia turned and pulled Kate back down the path toward the condo. "So, which of our trips should we revisit?"

"I told you, I don't know. Pick them all for all I care." Kate's lackluster voice dampened the mood.

"Well, if you're going to be that decisive, maybe I will. A week in each destination," Lydia joked.

"Fine."

Lydia's mind spun. What a ridiculous thought. Traipsing around the globe like, like what? Like middle-aged women with too much money and time and not enough going on in their lives? The idea fascinated her. If they spent a week in each place, would that be enough? Enough to meet people and perhaps begin again?

"It is possible," Lydia said. She'd meant to mention how ridiculous the idea was. But they'd be exposed to so many people, have so many opportunities to forge a new future.

Kate gave her a sidelong glance. "You'd do that?"

"It's not like I've got anything going on here."

"Same."

Lydia's feet trudged forward while her mind exploded with possibilities. Should they really do this? It would be horrifically expensive, but Kate didn't seem to mind about the money. Kate had always been generous. With money, yes, but also with her time. She'd had Lydia and Sophie over for days on end. Not Joe, not in years. Lydia's constant complaining about him and the one time he'd reacted badly after Kate had offered him a job had meant keeping them separate.

But she didn't have to dwell on those issues anymore. She wished the last years with Joe had been different, but she had to let them go. Returning to the haunts of her youth might make Lydia feel even older and wearier than she did already. But she was tired of her life, not physically exhausted.

She wanted something exciting to happen. Hell, deep down she knew she wanted to fall in love again. She longed for romance, wanted someone to sweep her off her feet just like in her favorite novels and movies. If she started over and built a future with someone new, that would bring her joy.

Over the past year, her future had become something to dread, one lonely night after another until she died. She'd wanted to date again, but she despised the idea of online dating sites. The local dating pool included people who knew Joe, and she'd never overcome the awkwardness of that. She didn't even like where she lived. They had bought the best house they could afford in a decent school district. What if she could choose anything going forward?

She stopped, overcome by the thoughts whirling through her brain. "Let's do this. Let's really do this. We can spend a week in each place. Think of all the people we'll meet and all the experiences we'll have. We loved traveling like this when we were younger. I'm so excited about it."

"I'm glad." And Kate did seem glad.

Not happy maybe, but at least not quite as dead as she seemed earlier. Lydia smacked her own forehead. Not dead. She couldn't even think with language like that. She had to find a way to bring the vivaciousness back to her friend's smile. Kate had been fierce in business and in love. She'd always been there for Lydia. Now, it was Lydia's turn.

Chapter 5

Lydia

Lydia rubbed her eyes. They watered from staring at the computer screen for so long. "This is going to cost a fortune," she called out.

"Oh, my god. I'm so tired of hearing you complain about money. Here." Kate slapped an American Express platinum card onto the desk. "Use this and stop looking at prices. Something should be done with all this money."

Lydia wondered at the comment, hoping Kate hadn't slid in a threat to spend her money since she might not need it later. Dead people didn't need money. But the purpose of this trip, renewal, would show her how to get her life back and build a new future.

A few clicks later Lydia froze, unable to push purchase. Thousands of dollars, thousands, just for the first plane ticket. "Are you sure about first class? I'm happy sitting in coach. They even have premium economy on this flight."

Kate stormed into the living room. "Buy the damn first-class tickets. And I want to stay at the Ritz in Madrid. Two rooms." She put her hands on her hips and stared Lydia down. "It is very expensive, and I don't want to hear a single complaint."

"Oh, I remember walking by the Ritz on my way to the Prado. It's in a phenomenal location." She'd ambled down the shady streets of Gran Via past the multistory wedding-cake white building frosted with decorative scrollwork. She'd never even considered peeking inside, protected as it was by uniformed doormen. But she had seen the posh people entering and leaving. The fashion in Madrid rivaled Paris, with the Ritz the epicenter of the rich and well-dressed. She couldn't imagine fitting in at the Ritz and would definitely have to up her clothing game to stay there.

Lydia glanced at Kate, who now slumped against the doorway. Dressed in black yoga pants, a black tank top, and a gray hoodie, the once sharp dresser now radiated apathy instead of energy. "Are you sure you're ready for the Ritz? From what I remember, that outfit's not going to cut it."

Kate smirked. "I've got a closet full of appropriate clothing. But you're right. I'm not sure I'm up to that much effort. I'll leave it up to you." She turned away from Lydia.

Kate's momentary zeal disappeared, and she left the room, shoulders humped. For a second, Lydia considered going after her. Unfortunately, she had no tricks to bring her friend out of the doldrums. Better to stay at the computer and pull the travel rabbit out of the hat.

Lydia sighed, burdened with the responsibility of finding just the right place. She brought the computer back to life with a click.

"Don't go cheap!" Kate yelled down the hallway. "Remember, luxury and location."

Lydia smiled at another spark of anger from her friend. My how things changed. Luxury had been the opposite of their college experience. They'd first landed in a home with a woman and her two grown children who shared the small apartment. They'd arrived in the dead of an especially cold winter, and the smell from the space heater in their tiny room had given them both such bad headaches that they'd complained to the school. Luckily, they'd been relocated to an apartment shared by two Spanish students.

The freedom of being set loose in a foreign country with no adult supervision at twenty years old remained one of the best experiences of Lydia's life. It had been hard, and she hadn't spoken Spanish well enough to get by when she'd first arrived. She learned to smile, point, and survive.

She'd always said she'd return to Spain and explore all the places she hadn't gone. But Joe hadn't been much of a traveler, unless it involved sports, and then Sophie was born, and her motivation for travel vanished. Babies are wondrous and completely exhausting. There's so much to learn, to organize, to pack—there's hardly time to think of one's own needs and desires. And then years go by, and desires become faded memories. Something about entering the Iranian market had flipped that burner back on, and it raged inside her now, making her desperate to board a plane and travel someplace far away.

Fine, if Kate wanted to go first class all the way, then that's what they'd do. No more wasting time. She looked at the airline tickets on the screen. She'd originally set them for a week from today to give them plenty of time to prepare. She changed the dates, found the first-class tickets she wanted, and pressed purchase. They'd leave the day after tomorrow.

Excitement thrummed through her like a drug. She went on a binge, buying hotel rooms, airline tickets, a bike tour of Madrid followed by a canal cruise in Amsterdam. She had intended to return to California before continuing their trip, but in her lust-fueled buying spree, she realized that didn't even make sense. She had no trouble finding a flight from Amsterdam to Bonaire, part of the Dutch Caribbean Islands.

The hotel they'd stayed at in Bonaire no longer existed, but she found a fabulous beach club right off the marina. She hadn't been scuba diving since that trip, but they'd have to go again, as it had been such a big part of their adventure.

She'd thought flying from Bonaire to Australia would be ridiculous, but she found a connection and hit purchase again. Her hands trembled as they left the keyboard. She'd spent more money in the past hour than she'd spent in years. She closed her eyes and slowed her short quick breaths. Had excitement or terror fueled her shopping spree? Maybe a combination. This trip was a last-ditch effort and a new beginning rolled into one.

Finally, she reached the last destination. Costa Rica. Her favorite. This time, her heart pulled her there. Memories of learning to surf and the tanned strong body of the most incredible man she'd ever met tugged at her.

She typed Tamarindo into the keyboard and found the beautiful beach town had changed almost beyond recognition. They'd only had a few accommodation choices thirty years ago, but today, resorts lined the white sand along the beautiful bay. She wished it were the way she remembered it, but wishing wouldn't make it so.

She found a resort with a wide swath of beach access relatively close to where they'd rented rooms before. She'd have to reset her expectations with this trip. It wasn't about going back in time, it was about moving forward.

Packing seemed to lift Kate's spirits. She became, if not excited, then determined, as if she had a puzzle to solve. She brought two rolling bags into the living room. The same size and shape, the first had Patagonia etched across it in navy on a teal background. On the second, the same word in light blue lettering sprawled across brown fabric manufactured to look like leather.

She laid the bags on their sides, unzipped them, and then jumped back as if she'd been bitten. She pressed her fingers into her temples as if to keep her head from exploding.

The sharp movements startled Lydia, who had curled up on the blue sofa as she looked up restaurants in Madrid on her phone. "What is it?"

"It still smells like him. I was going to let you use this one, but I can't be around it." She bent down to rezip the offending bag.

"I've got a suitcase. I've even still got my old backpack from when we were twenty."

Kate turned, hands splayed on either side of her face, her look now incredulous. "Please tell me you're joking."

"Of course not. Why would I joke about that?" Not everyone could afford to buy new luggage for every trip. Not everyone wanted to. "It's up in the attic."

"When was the last time you used it?"

Lydia's ears seared with embarrassment. "When we went to Costa Rica."

"That was thirty years ago. Bags have gotten so much better. You'll be amazed at how much you can pack into one of these. But first . . ." Kate grabbed the bag by the handle and marched out of the condo.

Sometimes her friend really did seem to be losing it. Lydia wondered if she should follow Kate out the door. Mitch leaving and the ensuing divorce had come as a huge surprise to Kate. Lydia too. She'd always thought of them as a near perfect couple. They'd never had kids. Not that it mattered really, although it would have given Kate another reason to live when everything went dark. Joe was the reason Sophie existed, and Sophie was the reason Lydia had held on to him for so long.

Kate returned, her hands empty.

"What did you do?" Lydia asked.

"I threw it away. I don't want anything related to that man in my condo."

Lydia thought about telling her that they might have at least taken it to Goodwill. It looked almost new. But one look at Kate's face and she kept her mouth closed. Her friend needed her support right now.

"I wish . . ." Kate's eyes filled with tears. She took a deep, shaky breath. "When he called to tell me they were pregnant, I could tell he was terrified. But that didn't mask the sheer joy in his voice. We were married for decades, and I'd never heard him like that. It is such a shock to think you have a happy life, a happy marriage, and then you wake up one day and it's all been a lie." Tears spilled, and she wiped them away with her sleeves.

"Was that when you took the pills?" Lydia asked. "He sounded so worried when he called me. He told me he'd called 911."

"No. He told me a couple of weeks ago. I didn't take the pills until I was fired. I drunk-dialed Mitch because I knew it would hurt him, and I really wanted someone else to hurt too. The board wouldn't have cared. Hell, they might have given me a standing ovation."

Lydia rose halfway off the couch, but Kate put her hand out, stopping her. "No. Let me get through this." Lydia sank back down.

Kate dried her eyes, then stood over the lone remaining bag and slipped her phone out of her pocket, working it intently. "Do you want baby blue or black with pink straps?"

"What are you talking about?"

"I'm buying you a new bag."

"You don't need to do that. I told you I have a suitcase."

"Do you have anything like this one? This size? Something this durable?"

"I have the green rolling case I took when we went to Palm Springs for the weekend." She hated the defensiveness in her tone, but really. What she had was fine.

"You mean the green one with the duct tape on the seam and the tiny wheels that make all that noise when you roll it?"

Lydia wanted to crawl under the numerous throw pillows on the sofa. Joe had thought the duct tape was ingenious, he'd even prodded her to thank him and tell him what a great job he'd done. She had to use it after that, but now she saw the suitcase through Kate's eyes. "Black with pink sounds nice, but I'm paying for it."

Kate looked up from her phone. She stared at Lydia for a long minute, her nose reddening and her eyes becoming watery. "I owe you so much." Her voice broke. "You got me out of the hospital and brought me home. You're the only one who cares about me. I can never repay that debt. Please let me pay for this."

Oh, god. She had to quit pushing Kate. Her friend looked so vulnerable, as if she still stood on the precipice of despair. "Fine. Thank you."

After a few minutes, Kate put her phone aside. "Done. I can go pick it up tomorrow while you're in Escondido."

"But you're going with me." That was the deal. It would take most of the day for Lydia to drive home, pack, and return. Their flight to Madrid left the following day. She didn't trust Kate enough to let her stay by herself that long. Not yet. Not when she still didn't truly understand what had caused Kate to attempt suicide. And certainly not when she didn't know if Kate still leaned that direction.

"Why don't you just go, and I'll stay here and pack." Kate's voice was light.

But Lydia didn't trust it. "I'm not comfortable with that."

Kate put her hands on her hips and stared at her. Lydia wasn't sure if she'd start arguing or crying, but something was coming. She looked like a cat stuck in a carrier.

"So, you're not going to leave my side for the next month? I don't have any autonomy?"

"I'm sorry, but not yet." Lydia had taken responsibility for her friend. She had to make sure Kate didn't have the opportunity to harm herself.

Kate deflated in front of her. "Fine." She turned and left the room with an angry step.

She reminded Lydia of Sophie as a teenager when she seemed constantly angry or sad and always argued about restrictions. Lydia had managed to keep her safe, and she'd do the same for Kate.

Chapter 6

Lydia

It wasn't like Lydia had never been in a first-class lounge. She had, once. She and Joe had used miles to fly from Los Angeles to Kansas City for a football game. While not her idea of an ideal vacation, she'd convinced him to stay downtown, and the revitalized area had lots of cute restaurants and sports bars.

Lounges had definitely upgraded since her last visit. Kate pulled her rolling bag straight to a cozy nook with four alabaster leather chairs. She set her shoulder bag on the chair beside her, effectively taking over half the space. Lydia followed her lead.

"I'm getting a glass of cabernet. Can I get you anything?" Kate asked the moment Lydia had settled.

"I'll have the same, please." She worried a moment about Kate drinking. After all, she'd downed a bottle of red with the pills she thought would kill her. Lydia had dealt with Joe's drinking as well. Once, she thought she'd set an example and removed all the liquor from the house and told herself she'd quit drinking too. When she told him her plan, he'd finally gotten his ass off the couch. He walked straight out the door and came back thirty minutes later with a case of beer and a warning not to treat him like a child. After that, she'd have a glass of wine when she wanted one, and she commented a lot less on his drinking.

Lydia surveyed the lounge. A few patrons wore suits and diligently typed away on laptops, clearly the businesspeople of the group. She spotted two sets of families, one with one child and another with four children. Who would pay first-class prices for kids? Although, why not if you have the money?

The rest of the lounge's occupants didn't clearly transmit their purpose. Vacationers, celebrities, who knew? She turned her attention to the food bars. Of course, she noticed the desserts first. A three-tiered platter overflowed with an impressive selection of cakes, tarts, and cookies.

She noticed a salad bar, healthy yet boring, and a cabinet with hot food, although she couldn't tell what it held from where she sat. Along one wall she spied an impressive selection of cheeses, meats, fruit, and olives. Her stomach grumbled. That's where she'd go the second Kate returned.

Just then, Kate swooped into her vision, offering her a glass of garnet-colored liquid. Lydia took a sip. Divine. Definitely not Two Buck Chuck.

"I read you shouldn't drink too much on an international flight because you can get dehydrated." The article Lydia had perused mentioned everything you needed to do to hit the ground running. She'd found earplugs and a sleep mask at the local drugstore and hoped to sleep through most of the flight. They'd arrive in Madrid at eight in the morning, and she wanted to be ready to roll.

"Fuck that," said Kate. "I plan to get drunk as shit, then pass out and not wake up until the wheels hit the ground. Just like we used to."

"There's no way this old body can survive a day of sightseeing after a night of drinking. We were twenty when we went to Madrid. I wish I could go back to those days." Longing clutched at Lydia's heart. They'd been so young and bright-eyed. If she'd only had today's knowledge back then. Maybe she would have made different choices.

"God, I don't. The last thing I want is to live my life over."

"But why? I loved things back when they were fresh and new." Lydia thought a moment. "Well, I don't actually want to relive my life. I want to start over. That's what this trip means to me, and I hope to you too. We can start the second half of our lives on this trip."

"That's a pretty Pollyanna view. Sorry, but I seriously doubt you're going to live to be one-hundred-four." Kate cocked an eyebrow at Lydia, then glanced down. "I just want the future to be over."

Lydia stared at her friend, stunned at the words that flew out of her mouth. This had been a terrible mistake. She needed to stand up and roll her bag out of the airport. But to give up and leave all these hopes and dreams behind, she at least needed the last word. "Way to go. First, you insult my attitude, then you insult my age, and you end up scaring me to death. I can't do this. You do need therapy." She begged her legs to stand, to walk away, but they ignored her.

"Stop being so dramatic."

"Screw you." Lydia stood. "I want you to live, to be happy. But I don't know how to get you there. I don't even know what's wrong. I mean I know about Mitch and the company, but you're not the kind of person who lets people beat them."

Kate's sigh was so heavy it seemed to sink through the floor to the center of the earth. "Please sit. I can't fight anymore. I'm sorry I was mean."

Lydia sat. Not to forgive, not yet. But she honestly had nothing better to do. "Tell me what's going on. I can't help if I don't understand what's running through your head." Why had she waited so long to have this conversation? She shouldn't have let Kate leave the hospital without delving into the why behind her suicide attempt. Except that Kate had seemed so sad and alone, and it had triggered her own similar feelings.

"Okay. But can you not judge me or try to talk me out of how I feel?"

"Of course," slipped out of Lydia's mouth before Kate had finished talking. She took a deep breath. She needed to be here for her friend, listen to her. She nodded.

"I've had a great life, even given the past year. I don't have anything left to accomplish." Kate held up a hand. "Let me finish."

Lydia nodded again. She'd been about to break in, to stop what Kate was saying. She vowed to stay silent until Kate had her say.

"I'm just done. Tired. Over it. I don't want to try anymore. It's time for me to take my ball and go home."

Lydia waited a breath. This time Kate nodded at her.

"There is no home where you want to go. There's nothing. You won't exist," Lydia said.

"That sounds peaceful."

"Well, I can't lose you. I just can't."

"Lydia, this isn't about you."

"Please don't kill yourself on my watch."

"This isn't your watch. It's my life. You need to go out there and do exactly what you said you'd do, restart your life. Go live the second half with all the joy you can find. But I need you to understand that I can't follow that path."

Tears sprang to Lydia's eyes. "I can't stand thinking about life without you. And I know that's about me and not you, but I can't help it. We've been friends since elementary school. My life sucks too. You're one of the only good things left." A sob escaped.

Kate drained her glass of wine. "Drink up. I'm getting more for both of us."

While Kate trekked to the bar, Lydia wiped her eyes with a napkin. She'd hatched this travel plan without really thinking it through. Now what? She should probably refuse to board the plane and instead convince Kate to see a therapist. Only she knew Kate wouldn't. She'd try to kill herself again. Maybe she should be committed to some facility, but that went against everything she knew about her friend.

The best course seemed to be forward. If she extracted a promise from Kate not to kill herself in Madrid, maybe she could start chipping away at her friend's hurt. Maybe in a new location, and in time, Kate would regain her will to live. Hell, regain her personality. They'd take it destination by destination. If it became too much, Lydia would be honest with her and tell her they needed to return home. It was the best she could do.

This time, when Kate handed her a glass of wine, Lydia took a long sip, downing a third of it. "Promise me you won't kill yourself in Madrid. That's the only thing I ask. If you can't make that promise, I won't go."

Kate looked at her, glass awkwardly raised as if she'd wanted to toast, but had reconsidered.

"It's only a few days, less than a week by the time we arrive." Lydia vowed again to stop talking. This was Kate's decision and Lydia needed to let her make it.

"Fine." Kate brought the glass to her lips and downed the whole thing.

This was going to be one hell of a trip.

Chapter 7

Lydia

"Oh, my god! They have lie-flat seats. I've heard about these." As much as she'd argued against the business class tickets, Lydia's curiosity had been in overdrive wondering what the fancy cabin would actually be like.

"Act like you've been in a plane before." Kate took the seat next to Lydia. Their expansive seats sat in the middle of the wide jet.

Lydia beamed. Kate's seat faced hers and the back of the plane. They had their own little island in the middle of the aircraft where they could chat all night if they wanted. She'd already thrown the no-drinking rule out the window, might as well toss the rest of it and pretend she was twenty again. Kate returned her look with a sour face. They were off on a grand adventure, and the wine put a rosy glow on the trip.

Lydia rifled through her bag for her bottle of water and her Kindle. She saw the soft pashmina wrap Kate had lent her for the trip and pulled it out as well. As she stowed the bag in the overhead bin, it seemed surprisingly heavy. It didn't have much left in it. Some granola bars and a bag of nuts, another bottle of water, a guidebook, and an emergency change of clothes.

One final heave and the bag slipped fully into the bin. Success. Lydia swung around and right into a broad chest. She looked up at the man she'd run into. His graying hair and kind blue eyes behind wire-framed glasses didn't match the muscular body.

"I'm so sorry." Why did her voice sound so breathy?

"It's all right. Close quarters here. Do you need help with anything?"

"No. I'll get out of your way." Lydia stepped into her pod and watched the man easily swing his carry-on into the overhead bin on the window side of the plane. He pulled off a bright green half-zip jacket, and his T-shirt shimmied up with the jacket, revealing a nicely muscled back disappearing into perfectly fitting jeans. She felt a hot flash coming on.

"Lydia, stop staring at him." Kate's exasperated voice must have carried halfway through the plane.

Lydia dropped into her seat and shot an embarrassed look at Kate. The wine might have been a mistake.

"Hi, I'm Keith." The man offered his hand to her. "We're going to be next to each other for over eleven hours, we might as well get to know each other."

"Lydia. Nice to meet you." She turned back to Kate, aware of the grin stretching across her face.

"Ma'am, would you bring my friend a glass of champagne?" Kate asked a passing flight attendant and then gestured in Lydia's direction. "Oh, and I'll take one too."

Grumpy friend to the left of her, hot guy to the right. Lydia sank into the comfortable seat and accepted the proffered champagne. She appreciated how flight attendants had changed from her first flights abroad. These women resembled her—a few wrinkles, a little thick around the middle. She had no doubt they would easily fling open the emergency doors should something happen. She also appreciated that they brought an endless supply of champagne, warm nuts in a porcelain dish, and a salmon dinner. If not sumptuous, it surpassed what she cooked at home.

Unfortunately, Kate shook her head every time Lydia pointed out the delicious food, wonderful drinks, plush pillows, and everything else that seemed like a brand-new discovery. She even raised the privacy screen between them once, the frosted glass cutting Lydia off mid-sentence.

Fortunately, Keith proved to be a wonderful conversationalist, even though she had to lean forward and peer around the plastic curve supporting her seat to see his face. The champagne made her bold enough to flirt with him a little, just a quick wink or a thoughtful gaze.

The champagne made Lydia chatty. When Keith put his headphones on to watch a movie, Lydia decided she needed to talk to Kate about her goals for the trip. Well, the goals beyond keeping Kate from killing herself. She rapped on the glass between them, the knocks ringing through the cabin.

"Be quiet." The glass slid down. "We have to share this cabin with other people and that noise is obnoxious."

"I want to talk about the trip. I hope I find someone on our travels. A love interest, maybe a future husband." She hadn't voiced this desire out loud before. The wine may have loosened her tongue, but the idea had taken hold from the first mention of travel. She wasn't the type to live alone.

Kate rolled her eyes. "You just got out of a twenty-three-year marriage. Why don't you try finding yourself instead?"

Lydia considered the comment. "I have found myself, and I'm better off sharing my life with someone. I think you are too."

"There is no way in hell I will ever marry again. I can't believe you'd actually consider it. I mean, your last few years, maybe even the last couple of decades with Joe, weren't exactly fabulous."

The comment twisted her excited buzz about this trip into something painful. She teetered between fury and desperation. If she didn't stop drinking, she might cause a scene. She handed her champagne glass to a passing flight attendant.

"How can you say that?" she angry-whispered to Kate.

"I'm the one you called when he embarrassed you at an event or passed out on the sofa. How many times did you complain to me about Joe's drinking? And he hardly held down a job the last eight years. I mean I don't want to speak bad about the dead . . . well, actually, in this case I do. That man put you through the wringer. You deserved so much better."

Lydia reclined her seat, wishing she could slink away from the entire conversation. The last decade had not been good. Joe lost his job as a warehouse manager after complaining for years about how companies wanted to replace workers with technology. Technology he refused to learn. She remembered his anger when they'd wanted him to attend community college courses to learn a new inventory management software. He'd cursed his boss, changed jobs, and within six months the new company wanted him to learn the same system. She'd come home exhausted from work and have to listen to his frustrating stories.

Three companies in a row fired him, and she doubted he put much effort into looking for work after that. Usually, he still wore the same pair of shorts when she came home as when she'd left. The one time she'd brought it up, his angry yelling almost shook the foundation, and it mortified her that the neighbors had overheard. No one needed that kind of confrontation.

After that, he quit hiding his drinking, even from Sophie. Mother and daughter had tried to get him to stop. They'd even gone to an Al-Anon meeting. That had been a terrible experience for a sixteen-year-old. So much crying. So many sad stories. Sophie had begged her to never go again.

So, she did what she'd always done. She bucked up and took care of things. Lydia had worried so much about money back then. If Joe had contributed even a little those last few years, hell, maybe she could have afforded the first-class seats on her own or could have sent Sophie somewhere other than a state university. Instead, she'd supported her husband for what felt like the second half of his life. And it's not like being out of work meant he helped more around the house. Nope, not Joe. He watched TV on the couch all day, started drinking at noon, and after a while, only left the house to play the public golf course with friends.

The old, ever-present anger swelled in Lydia. That part of their life together really pissed her off. But since he'd died, and with Sophie off at college, she missed taking care of someone.

She raised her eyes. At least she had Kate to take care of, for now. She wanted to help her get better more than anything. And maybe, by the end of this trip, her own life would be back on course.

"Things weren't perfect with Joe. They probably aren't with any man. But I don't want to be alone the rest of my life."

Kate's gaze raked across her skin as if trying to find the place that would pierce her soul. A gynecological exam would be more pleasant. "So, you want to find a new man on our exotic travels and then take him back to your two-bedroom ranch house in Escondido and live out your days?"

No, that sounded horrible. That life she'd lived already. "I want a big life that's full of adventure this time around. I've been a wife, a mother, a teacher. Instead of repeating my life, I want to live a new one. And part of that is finding a partner."

"Well, we're not even five hundred miles from Los Angeles and you're already flirting with Keith here. Is this how it's going to go?" The sparkle had returned to Kate's eyes.

Lydia shrugged. Why not? Keith had kind eyes, appeared to like chatting with her, and had a great bod. She peeked around her seat at him.

"Sorry, I'm gay." He shrugged.

Lydia whipped back around and hid in her seat, her cheeks about to burst into flames. Kate's full-throated laugh echoed through the cabin. The joy of hearing her friend laugh, even at her expense, made it all worthwhile.

They hadn't even touched down in their first country yet. Surely with Kate by her side, they'd both end up in a better place.

Chapter 8

Lydia

Lydia steered the bicycle down a packed dirt path lit with dappled sunlight. She worked at keeping her pace even, having already crashed into the Danish teenager on the bike in front of her. She'd thought the bike tour would be a fun way for her and Kate to reacquaint themselves with Madrid, but it turns out the old saying is wrong. At least for her, *it was just like riding a bike* didn't exist.

She did blame the teenager a little. He'd squealed to a stop to look at a peacock, and Lydia had ridden into his back wheel. Fortunately, Kate had less trouble on the bike and managed to steer around Lydia instead of causing a major pile up.

Lydia glanced up and spied Álvaro, the tour director, as he waved his hand and slowly pulled his bike to the side of the path, gesturing for them to do the same. She carefully negotiated the stop, then looked up. A huge glass building loomed above them. It looked like an oversized greenhouse, if greenhouses had ornate ironwork and what must be hundreds of clear glass plates.

"Huh, I don't remember seeing this when we lived here," Kate said, expertly pulling her bike next to Lydia's.

"El Palacio de Cristal was built in Madrid since 1887." Álvaro raised his long arms and circled his wrists, his signal for the ten bikers on his tour to park their bikes and gather around.

"Well, I guess it predates us by a few years anyway," Kate sniped.

Lydia hobbled toward Álvaro on unsteady legs. Now she understood why cyclists wore those pants with the padding. Still, she enjoyed the exercise, sunshine, and fresh air, and hoped Kate liked it as well. Besides, Álvaro impressed her with his knowledge, not to mention his Spanish good looks. His long dark hair flowed over his shoulders, and his beaked nose fit in perfectly with his angular face and thin body. And she could have drowned in the depths of his brown eyes. Seriously, she needed to switch from reading romance to heartier fare. The one she'd devoured on the plane had been a little spicier than she'd expected, and now she couldn't get seduction off her brain.

"This building is now part of the Reina Sofia Museum. The exhibit today is called 'Mirrors,' and we will spend fifteen minutes enjoying it. Please follow me." Álvaro turned and sauntered toward the building, immediately surrounded by a contingent of four young Italian women. They'd hung on him like groupies from the moment the tour started. They'd butted in line to make sure they rode closest to him and drew all his attention every time the tour stopped. Of course, he didn't seem to mind.

Lydia and Kate followed the group into the airy building which appeared to float instead of being anchored to the ground. The brightness inside almost blinded them. Hundreds of mirrors hung from the structural iron bars, and more reflected up from the floor. All at different angles, they shot shafts of light across the open space. Some mirrors, as tiny as teardrops, dangled close to their heads, swaying in the air stirred up by the visitors.

Unfortunately, the largest mirrors, soaring upright from the ground like in a funhouse, showed truth instead of distortion. Lydia's yoga pants were not flattering. Nor were her plump upper arms. She inhaled harshly, trying to pull her belly toward her spine.

"Oh fuck." Kate stood smack in front of a huge eight-foot by eight-foot mirror. She looked exhausted, with dark circles beneath her eyes and gaunt cheeks.

Lydia pulled her away. "This exhibit is torture."

They fled toward an edge of the building where they looked outside and saw the sun glinting off a small pond. Better to gaze upon the surrounding gardens than the barbaric exhibit. On the way over, they'd passed the Italian women preening in front of mirrors. Their short shorts and crop tops already left little to the imagination, but the way they adjusted their clothing to emphasize perky cleavage or ran their hands along flat bellies made Lydia want to throw something at them.

"You have to get me out of here. I can't look at myself right now." The desolation had returned to Kate's voice.

"I'm sorry." They shouldn't have come. Lydia pulled her friend toward the door. She'd thought outdoor exercise would be good for Kate's mental health, but she'd never imagined this house of horrors.

"Esa exhibición es brutal," said a middle-aged Spanish woman exiting the building before them.

"Sí." Lydia followed the woman out the door. Brutal perfectly described the experience.

An hour and a half later, they turned in their bikes just off the Plaza Mayor. As they crossed the grand space surrounded by buildings from the 1700s, Lydia wondered if she'd ever walk normally again. No more bikes.

"Let's stop for lunch. I'm starving," Kate said.

"I promise, we're going to eat in a minute. I've found someplace wonderful." She led Kate out of the plaza and around a corner. In front of them stood another iron and glass building, this one darker and more inviting.

"If there are goddamned mirrors in there, I'm going to kill you," Kate snarled.

Lydia laughed before pulling her friend forward. "No, it's a market. They've got all kinds of great food. And wine."

Lydia opened the door. Stalls selling an enormous variety of foodstuffs surrounded aisles teeming with people, tables, and displays.

"What the hell is that?" Kate stood in front of a seafood vendor. She stared at the ugliest creature Lydia had ever seen. The enormous fish, if it was a fish, had a humongous head with frighteningly curved and pointy teeth. Its tail had been suspended, so it looked like it had been stopped mid-dive, about to devour the person in front of it.

"Gross. Keep moving." Lydia prodded Kate.

Fortunately, the next display showed dozens of varieties of tapas: meats, cheeses, and seafood atop slices of fresh baguettes. An olive seller followed, then a cheesemonger. They worked their way further into the market. The sights and scents delighted Lydia. Despite the crowds, they found seats at a community table in the center of the market.

"You stay here, and I'll go bring back a selection of food," Lydia said.

"Let me make a quick stop first. Stay here and save our seats." Kate disappeared into the crowd almost as soon as she'd finished talking. Soon she returned, carrying two glasses of sparkling wine.

"Ooh. Delicious." The crisp dry wine suffused with bubbles refreshed Lydia.

"Spanish cava. Do you remember how much of this we used to drink when we lived here?"

"Totally. I'm surprised there's any left." Lydia giggled, then left in search of food.

Ten minutes later, she returned with a tray laden with delicacies. Spanish tortilla, fried calamari, padrón peppers, a selection of cured meats—all of which she placed on the table. "You drank my wine."

"Indeed. And mine. I'll be right back with more." Kate jumped up and disappeared again.

She returned quickly and handed a glass to Lydia. "Cheers. And thank you for bringing me here. This is fun."

"I'm so glad." Lydia couldn't remember the last time she'd felt so good. Maybe it was the fresh air from the bike ride, or the excellent food and wine, but probably it was seeing Kate happy. They'd had some good times in this city, and while they and the city had changed in the intervening years, some of the former magic remained.

"I don't remember this place at all." Lydia surveyed the market. Families, tourists, and a smattering of young people who looked Spanish ate and drank and talked. On her first visit to Madrid, middle-aged and older women filled the markets and negotiated loudly with the fruit and meat sellers. Cleaned up and refined, this market catered to a different crowd.

"I don't remember it either. Although, we usually only came to this part of town at night to visit the cave bars or go to Joy Esclava." Kate slugged back the rest of her wine.

"Oh, my god. So many nights we danced until dawn at Joy. I wonder if it's still here."

"I'm fifty-two years old. Even if it's here, I'm not going to a disco."

"We'll see. Although I doubt it's still open. The city has changed so much since we lived here. Can you believe how many pedestrian streets they have now? And the buildings all look so clean." They'd seen a spiffed-up version of Madrid on their bike ride. Lydia loved thinking of the city renewed.

"I kind of miss the grimy version of Madrid. It felt more exciting back then, a little dangerous. I wonder if they still have hash bars."

"Oh, my god. You are not going to a hash bar. Seriously? And you think you're too old for a disco?" Lydia started giggling, maybe from the cava. Something else she hadn't done for far too long. Years of tension released themselves from her back and shed onto the floor.

"I'm going to find more cava." Kate popped up from her seat.

"Find some dessert too." Lydia didn't miss Kate's eye roll as she turned away. At least it showed emotion, something other than the hollowed-out husk of a woman in that hospital bed.

Lydia had planned daily adventures, hoping to keep Kate too busy to dwell on her problems, at least until she got a little time and perspective. So far, her plan had paid off.

She gathered the paper containers with the detritus of their lunch and tossed them into a nearby bin. What else in her own life needed to be tossed aside? She liked flying first class more than she had expected. And the fancy but not over the top hotel had a bed like a pillow, a lovely breakfast buffet, and excellent coffee. She could get used to this—traveling without a budget—hell, traveling at all. She didn't regret her life. She didn't. Not one moment. But perhaps this second half would be a little grander than the first.

Kate returned, a glass of pink cava in each hand. She plopped down on the bench and handed one to Lydia.

"No dessert?" Lydia asked.

"Hang on." She reached a hand in her pocket and pulled out a box.

Lydia opened it and found four perfect strawberries dipped in dark chocolate. "Oh, they look amazing."

"They'll go especially well with the wine. Happy?"

"Definitely." Lydia took a sip of cava, then a bite of strawberry, letting the tart and sweet flavors combine. She could definitely become accustomed to a champagne and strawberries lifestyle. But first, she would take care of her friend. "Okay. After this, I thought we'd tour the Prado. Then we can go back and rest a bit before the flamenco dinner tonight."

"Oh, Lydia. I don't want to do all that stuff. Why don't you go without me?" Kate's sigh heaved with invisible weight.

"But I'm doing this for you. You should stay active."

"I didn't bring you along to be a cruise director. I just don't have the energy for all your plans."

"You didn't bring me along at all. This was our deal. You didn't want to stay in Los Angeles and see a psychotherapist, so we decided to go on this trip. Think of this as your recovery." She'd meant the words to sound hopeful, but they came out stale. Lydia dreaded this part. If she made a mistake, how much would it set Kate back?

"You are not my counselor, you're my friend. And I promised you I wouldn't try to kill myself here, so you're off the hook. You definitely don't need to schedule my days so I don't have time to wallow or find a gun or sharp knife." Another eye roll.

"How can you even talk about that? We need to get the old Kate back, the fierce one who would never take shit from anyone."

"I never want to see that version of myself again. Never." Kate stared straight at Lydia as if daring her to respond.

Hopelessness embraced her in its constrictive hug. She shouldn't have taken on responsibility for someone else's problems. The only way Lydia knew to help was the last thing Kate wanted. The tears came unbidden, welling up in her eyes and threatening to fall. She turned her head, hoping Kate wouldn't notice.

"You can't cry. Listen, I need some time to rest, and the last place I want to be is the crowded Prado. I want to sit in the chaise lounge on the patio of my hotel room. It's a beautiful day. I'd like to read, or sleep, or both, in the fresh air. I do not want to traipse around and exhaust myself." Kate didn't reach out to Lydia but remained stiff and in her own world.

"I was just trying to help." Lydia ran a hand under her eyes, sweeping away the unwanted tears.

"I know. It's just too much right now. At least for me. You should go do all that stuff. I'll be fine. Remember, I promised."

Lydia had to let it go. In fact, the morning had exhausted her as well. Maybe she'd go crawl under the covers, since her room didn't have a patio, and try to forget all the things she'd done wrong. Not that she hadn't tried. She had. She always tried harder than anyone else. With her husband, with her daughter, with Kate. That's what she really needed for the future, far more than money or a soft life. She needed someone to meet her halfway. Not Kate. Kate had always been a great friend, she just needed to survive this rough patch in her life. And Sophie hadn't meant to hurt her mother. She only wanted to establish her independence.

Lydia needed a man who would meet her halfway, maybe even more than halfway. She would never settle again. Of course, she still had to find this mystery man, but surely, he was out there. She inhaled deeply, then let the breath out in a long, cleansing exhale. She would make this work. She needed to be patient with Kate, and with herself.

This was a new beginning for both of them. It wouldn't always be easy. The second day after a long international flight had always been tough, even when they were young. In their fifties, maybe they needed a little more rest. Fine. It's not like they had to return to jobs or kids or husbands. They could take all the time they needed and do it right this time.

Chapter 9

Lydia

The bartender delivered her café con leche without a word. The mermaid from the Starbucks across the street glowed at Lydia, and she raised her white ceramic coffee cup in salute. She had tried coffee before coming to Madrid her junior year but had always hated it. Spain had been the first place where coffee tasted the way it smelled, heavenly. Even better, it was served in the same bars she'd closed down the night before, usually by a mustachioed older man who must never sleep.

Faint sunlight crept through the large plate glass window, and she swiveled on her barstool to watch the barman cut a wedge from a round potato and egg tortilla. He placed it between a section of baguette and set it before her. Pure decadence.

The strong coffee and carb-heavy breakfast pulled memories from her. She'd probably never been in this particular bar, but with its tile floors, chrome fixtures, and marble bar top, it mirrored many dozens of others spread throughout the city.

No other country, at least none she'd visited, did bars quite as well as Spain. People nipped in for a quick breakfast on the way to work or school. They stopped by late morning for another shot of caffeine, or perhaps something stronger, and returned in the afternoon for a glass of wine or beer, always accompanied by a small plate of olives, potato chips, or some other delicacy. She could live here. Why had she never returned?

"Algo más?" the bartender asked.

She thought about what else she wanted. Maybe to sit on this stool for an hour and figure out her life and Kate's. Maybe she needed another jolt of morning brew. She asked for another café con leche and a coffee and tortilla sandwich to take away.

She'd left Kate sleeping at the hotel. Of course, she only knew this because she'd taken one of Kate's room keys when they'd first arrived and checked in on her before she left the hotel earlier that morning. Since their bike trip and market feast two days earlier, Kate had barely left her room.

Lydia had canceled their tour of El Escorial, a monastery outside of Madrid. She'd missed going during college, and now she'd miss it again. Although why she'd want to visit a place inhabited by celibate men was a question she hadn't spent much time on.

She looked at the barman as he put a to-go cup and a foil-wrapped sandwich in front of her. Twenty years older than she, he had a few strands of hair pasted across his bald head and a heavily salted mustache. Definitely not her type. Dating felt like the great unknown. Was she still attractive? Could she flirt with a man? Thirty years ago, that had been second nature, but now her waist had thickened, and her skin had dulled. Not that there had been a time in her life when she'd particularly liked her looks.

Ugh. She had to quit dwelling. Kate had to quit dwelling. If this trip was supposed to be some magical elixir for age and depression, they needed to start the search. It was time to get her friend out of bed.

The autumn sun gently warmed Lydia's shoulders as she sat at a table in the Plaza Santa Ana. She'd finally pulled Kate from bed at ten-thirty that morning, and for hours they'd wandered the streets of Madrid. They'd passed the yellow building that once housed their school, the Hollywood Burger they'd visited on the regular when they needed a taste of home, and Plaza Dos de Mayo, a once seedy neighborhood that had been upgraded in the intervening years.

Lydia vaguely remembered Plaza Santa Ana from her youth, but like everything in Madrid, it looked far better now than it had back then. The beautiful buildings surrounding the plaza appeared fresh and clean. Before, a dingy soot had shrouded Madrid's buildings. Now, a play area had overtaken one side of the plaza, and the banning of automobiles left more room for the umbrellaed restaurant tables that stretched toward the center of the square.

They'd ordered large salads dotted with Spanish cheese, dried apricots, and nuts. That had also changed. Spain had morphed from a country that served overcooked soups and stews or weakly imitated French cuisine into a culinary powerhouse. Lydia hadn't had a single bite of food she didn't consider extraordinary, including the salad. Of course, it paired well with another caña, the small glasses of beer ubiquitous across Spain.

That was the thing about this country. They didn't down pints or bottles. Civilized drinking meant a few ounces of beer or wine in a small glass, accompanied by a morsel of food. Back in her twenties, she'd learned to drink all day on this schedule, especially if she included time for an afternoon siesta. She'd expected to enjoy Madrid as she had before, but the trip had thrown her into a world much improved from the one of her memories. Better food, prettier city, but that same sense of possibility.

"Today feels like the beginning of something wonderful." She raised her glass to Kate.

"Ha." Kate snorted from across the table.

"Come on, Kate, you've got to feel it. This old city has had a facelift, and she's better for it."

Kate's gaze swept the plaza. "It truly amazes me how much the city has changed. Even the air seems cleaner. The beer tastes the same though." She lifted her glass and gazed at the amber liquid before downing it in one gulp. "Too bad everything doesn't improve with age."

"But maybe it does. I've been thinking about this a lot today. I'm so much older than when we first came here, yet when I look in the mirror, I'm no more disappointed than I was back then. In fact, I think I look okay for my age. I used to hate the mirror." She dropped her hands to her lap so Kate wouldn't see her work them. How could she admit to something that had tortured her for so many years? And it's not like she ever wanted to be a ravishing beauty. But still, mirrors, photos, reflective surfaces had always replied to her question with *not good enough*.

"I used to be fine with mirrors." Kate's voice flatlined. "At least until my husband left me for someone younger and more beautiful."

Ouch. "You were more beautiful than Hadley when you were her age. And you're more accomplished than she'll ever be." Lydia tried for cheerful, but truly, the situation sucked. Joe might not have been the greatest catch in the world, but at least he didn't leave her.

"Don't lie. I never looked like Hadley. She's practically attorney Barbie with those big blue eyes. And big other things." Kate cupped her hands in front of her chest.

"But those aren't real. And didn't she stop practicing law?"

"Yes. Because she's having Mitch's baby."

Although the conversation never led anywhere good, Lydia couldn't help her response. "You never wanted a baby. Not even before you met Mitch. Besides, were you really happy with him?"

"I certainly thought so." Kate paused, as if putting thought behind the automatic response. "I thought we had a great life together. Exotic vacations, nice dinners out, good sex. I didn't expect it to end."

One lone tear made its way down Kate's cheek. Lydia could almost see her wrapping herself in steel, girding herself against the pain. She wanted to force her friend's thoughts toward something new.

"I really need a man." The words erupted out of Lydia, born from the loneliness she saw in her friend, and the loneliness she'd carried for years.

"Ha!" Kate's sharp snort caused two more tears to drop from her eyes. "Why? You just escaped Joe."

"It's how I feel. You may not want a partner, at least not yet, but let's play it like we did in our twenties. I was always looking for a husband, and you were just looking for fun." She couldn't keep her smile back. They'd both had plenty of fun back then.

Kate returned the smile, or maybe it was a grimace. "You look fantastic. You shouldn't be afraid of mirrors, but maybe you should focus on fun this time around. I'll probably sit this one out."

"A mirror's got nothing on you either." Lydia reached for her friend's hand.

Kate placed her hands in her lap but stared straight into Lydia's eyes. "When I look in a mirror, I see what's shattered on the inside."

She might as well have plunged a shard of reflective glass into Lydia's heart. A familiar sense of overwhelm engulfed her. She should have gotten Kate professional help. She wanted her friend happy, or at least not devastated, more than anything in the world. "Do you want to go back to the hotel?"

"No. I want to stay here in the sunshine. I want to have another glass of beer with my friend. And then maybe one more. It's beautiful here, and warm. In the hotel room, I'll try to drown myself in the bed and sleep until I wake up in a different world. And there are far too many mirrors."

Lydia raised her glass and clinked it against Kate's, a familiar gesture. On their first trip to Madrid, they'd sit outside for hours on the weekends, drinking, sharing snacks, and people watching.

As the afternoon wore on, young parents arrived to visit the play area with small children in tow. Tiny girls chased boys who pursued them back in a game they would never outgrow. Older women paraded around the perimeter of the plaza. And men, one after another, sat at the tables on the patio and ordered a drink. Most of them opened laptops. A young blond man read Ernest Hemingway, a sure indication of a tourist. A man at a table near theirs opened one of the tabloid-sized newspapers still sold at kiosks throughout the city. It had a big red banner across the top, and the front page featured a soccer player.

He stayed at his table for a while, and every time he turned a page, he glanced up and caught Lydia staring at him. She didn't mean to, he just looked so Spanish. His glossy black beard had more than a little white sprinkled in, and his olive skin and heavy brows contrasted perfectly with his ocean blue eyes. He had relaxed into his chair and opened the paper wide as if he sat in his living room instead of a crowded cafe. She noticed a low grumble in his voice when he ordered his second cerveza.

"Put on your big girl panties and go over and say hello." One eyebrow arched high as Kate stared into her friend's eyes. "Or maybe I'll tell him you have a crush on him. I seem to remember doing that for you a time or two."

"Stop it," Lydia whispered. "I think he understands English." She'd noticed him glance her way at Kate's words.

"For god's sake, you're not twenty anymore. Go talk to him."

"I want to be courted."

"What the hell? Tell me you haven't been reading *Jane Eyre* again."

Lydia shook her head before standing and heading to the inside portion of the restaurant. She'd needed a restroom break anyway, and she didn't want to continue that conversation. She needed to do everything right this time. When she and Joe met, they'd been set up by friends who thought they'd be a good match. Maybe because of that, she'd believed it.

This time, she wanted love to unfold naturally, without any pressure from well-meaning friends. Her own heart, not some book, made her long for romance. As good as things were the first time around, she wanted something better this time.

She found the steep set of stairs that led down to the restroom. This she remembered from her youth as well. Now, wearing espadrilles, the stairs challenged her. How did all the older people in this country negotiate the treacherous paths to Spanish toilets?

The wall above the sink held a large framed mirror. She washed her hands and splashed a little water on her familiar face. She'd never be a great beauty, but she looked friendly, something far more important to her. The burgundy wrap dress with tiny pink and white flowers scattered across it looked fantastic. Kate had made her buy two of the dresses, each a different pattern, at the mall in Santa Monica. Lydia had balked at the price, but looking at herself now, she might never wear anything else. They gave her thick middle a waist, and her boobs looked fabulous.

Could you drink yourself pretty? Maybe she'd needed the vacation, but she hadn't looked this good in years. Even the gray in her chestnut hair looked like highlights in this lighting. The boost of confidence drove her back up the stairs and out into the sunshine. She gave the handsome Spanish man a big smile as she passed his table.

"Welcome back," Kate said. "I took the liberty of ordering another caña de cerveza."

"We're going to get drunk if we stay here all afternoon." Lydia hoped Kate wouldn't bury her feelings in alcohol the way Joe had. The familiar guilt of wanting to control someone else's drinking while still enjoying a glass herself started to rise. But sitting in a gorgeous sunlit plaza, Lydia didn't want to say no and didn't want Kate to have an excuse to return to bed.

"And that sounds like the perfect afternoon," Kate said.

Lydia had planned on them visiting the Reina Sophia Museum to see Pablo Picasso's Guernica, but the painting would be there tomorrow. The mellow glow of the afternoon could be perfectly enjoyed from her current location. She sat back, raised her glass, and let the schedules and plans float away.

"Good afternoon, ladies. I hope you are enjoying Madrid."

Lydia opened her eyes. Had she dozed off? Blue eyes in a tanned face stared at her. It was the man from the other table.

"Well, hello," she said. She glanced to her side and caught Kate's wry smile. "We are having an excellent time. I'm Lydia."

"My name is Jordi. Are you from the United States?"

"Yes, we are. This is Kate. Would you like to have a seat?" Lydia waved her hand toward the empty chair he currently leaned across. He flashed her a glimpse of dark chest hair. The afternoon suddenly warmed.

"No, I'm afraid I must return to work. But I was hoping you would join me at **Cervecería** Alemana, across the plaza, this evening." He gestured toward one of the beautiful buildings lining the plaza. "It is the building with the wooden front. It is a very traditional Spanish bar, and it is said that your Ernest Hemingway visited often. Perhaps you will join me for dinner after that?"

Half dread and half dream come true, the invitation shocked Lydia into silence. She glanced sideways, but Kate's smirk said she wouldn't ride to the rescue. "We'd love to join you," Lydia said before the gap in words became awkward. "What time should we meet you?"

Jordi looked at his watch. He had a real wristwatch with a leather band instead of relying on a phone. "Let's say eight o'clock this evening?"

"Excellent. We'll see you then." Lydia watched as he turned away, his newspaper tucked under his arm, and strode across the plaza. She appreciated the always slim cut of Spanish denim in new ways.

"I haven't seen you wear that smile in a long time," Kate said.

"Did that really just happen? He was gorgeous." A thrum of excitement pulsed through her chest and spread all the way out to her fingers and toes.

"That totally happened, and I'm not going to be around to spoil your fun."

"Do not make me do this alone. Please." Lydia would beg if it meant Kate would accompany her.

"He's clearly only interested in you. He didn't even look at me."

Lydia studied her friend to see if the words held some deeper hurt. Kate seemed fine. She even looked hopeful, if that were possible. But Lydia wanted to play it safe.

"Listen, I haven't been on a date in decades if this is even a date. Please go with me. We don't know anything about him, and I don't want to be stuck with someone who's a real jerk. Or an axe murderer."

"He hardly seems like an axe murderer. How about I go to the bar with you? But if you like him, you're on your own for dinner."

The waiter arrived with two fresh glasses of beer. "Would you like anything else?"

Lydia asked for the check. "Let's finish these, then wander for a while. I don't have the stamina to drink all day anymore."

Kate took her glass and finished in one long swig. "Why don't we head toward the palace? I can't imagine a better way to see it than slightly tipsy."

Lydia followed suit. Once they'd paid up and set off for the Palacio Royal, she grabbed Kate's arm and pulled her close. The anticipation of meeting Jordi and concern for her friend threatened to tear her in two. She concentrated on taking one step at a time, hopefully pulling herself and her best friend into a better future.

Chapter 10

Lydia

The bar had dark wood accents, white marble-topped tables, and an entire wall filled with liquor bottles. They'd arrived early and positioned themselves where they had a view of the door. Lydia ordered a red wine, while Kate asked for a vodka, double. The lanky waiter with long black hair and dark electric eyes raised a refined eyebrow, then smiled at them before turning to pour their drinks.

"What do you think of him? He could be your type," Lydia said. She thought about recommending a less severe drink, but Kate wasn't Joe. She'd never had his trouble with booze.

"Definitely. But he's also twenty years younger than me."

"So?" Lydia's blood raced with excitement and the world seemed new again, just like she'd hoped it would. "Who's to say we can't be young again, just like the city renewed itself?"

"You keep harping on that, but time doesn't lie." The bartender set their drinks in front of them, and Kate took a healthy sip before thanking the man.

He smiled back and asked the requisite questions about where they were from. He said he'd always wanted to visit California and see movie stars. His eyes lit bright when Kate told him she knew Matt Damon and Ben Affleck. She did. She'd helped finance Project Greenlight, which they'd created to fund small-budget indie films. He hovered until an older waiter grumped a few harsh words in his direction.

"See, I'm right. Everything can be new again."

"That's not new. Name dropping celebrities so a young person will pay attention to you is one of the oldest tricks in the books—or haven't you been to Hollywood?

"You're not name dropping; you know them. And you've led a fascinating life. A guy would be lucky to have you. Really, Kate, this can be the start of a new future. Don't you want to leave your rotten ex-husband and job trauma behind?" She wished she could share with Kate the optimism running through her blood like a cocktail. Lydia had opened herself up and manifested a date. She'd never believed in that particular brand of optimism so prevalent on the internet. *I just wished for a million dollars and lo-and-behold, it arrived.* But you definitely had to believe in the possibility of something good happening.

Kate threw back the rest of her vodka and signaled the waiter for a refill. "Listen. I'm glad you see this as a chance to start over. You need that. I'm not trying to be harsh, but you didn't have such a good go of it the first time around. But you have to understand, I did."

Lydia searched for a response. Not everything had gone Kate's way either, or else she wouldn't have tried to kill herself.

Before she responded, Kate continued. "I had everything. The husband I wanted. I created the company I wanted. Became disgustingly wealthy. Took exotic trips around the world. Have celebrity friends. I'm done. I did it all already. Why would I want to start over when I can't possibly do better than I did the first time?"

Lydia wanted to draw that venom out of her friend the way you would a snakebite. It had polluted her veins and darkened her outlook. It was poisonous enough to kill.

"Hello, ladies. I'm so glad you made it tonight."

Lydia turned into the blue eyes of Jordi. "Hi. It's good to see you again. Why don't you order a drink?" She sidled toward Kate to give him room at the bar. "Are you okay?" she mouthed to her friend.

"I'm perfectly awesome. Have fun on your little date."

"Do not leave. I will not let you leave like this." She leaned forward to whisper in Kate's ear. "He means nothing to me. You mean everything. Let's go back to the hotel and talk."

Kate stopped for a moment, then threw her arms around Lydia in a hug. "I'm exhausted. I'll go back to the hotel and rest. Believe me, the last thing I want to do is talk. My brain needs a rest, not to mention my feet. You dragged me all over Madrid today."

Lydia pulled back from the hug to look into Kate's eyes. "Are you sure?"

"Yes. You stay out and have fun. Please. I'll see you at the hotel after your date. Don't do anything I wouldn't do."

"That leaves my options pretty open."

"Exactly." Kate winked, then turned away and headed out the door.

"Your friend is leaving?" Jordi asked.

"Yes." Deep down, it troubled her to watch Kate walk away, but she probably did need to rest. After all, this had been the first time she'd been out all day instead of spending a good portion of it in bed. In the morning, she'd help her friend. They would leave Madrid soon and make their way to Amsterdam. Maybe the hope Lydia had found in Madrid waited for Kate in that city.

"Salúd." Jordi raised his glass of wine to her. She raised hers as well, clinking one garnet-filled goblet against another. The blue of his eyes in his dark face caught her off guard again. Eyes to drown in. But no. She wasn't ready to lose herself yet. She wanted to bask in the appreciation she found there. She wanted him to desire her, to flirt with her, court her, but nothing more. Not yet. Tonight, she would dip a toe into the lust of pool blue eyes and find a part of herself she thought she'd outgrown. Then she'd return to the hotel and the friend who needed her. They had four more places yet to explore. She could take things slowly.

Chapter 11

Kate

Outside the bar, Kate turned and walked until she'd passed the brightness streaming out the plate glass windows. Then she rested, her back against the wall of the building. Would Lydia come after her, or would she finally be on her own? She waited two minutes. Five. Ten. She wanted to leave almost as much as she wanted to stay and have her friend talk her out of the night ahead. Finally, she turned and walked away.

The dark cloud that had grown inside her for months now amassed its storm. She leaned in, letting the desperation rage around her, pierced by lightning strikes of self-loathing. She sank into its comforting trap. She didn't have to work when the storm held her in its grasp, didn't have to be perfect, didn't have to prove her worth, because clearly that didn't exist. She was so damn tired of trying.

These spells had always been a companion, but earlier in her life they flashed hot and bright before disappearing completely. As a teen, she'd screamed at her mom once that she wanted to kill herself. Her mother made her promise she'd never take her own life as long as she was alive. But her mother had been dead for a decade.

Kate had kept the promise easily and learned to better hide that side of herself. After the storm loosened its grip, she could look at it as no more than an embarrassing incident. She was totally normal, most of the time. And most of the time, she shoved these incidents down deep, refusing to acknowledge them.

She became so adept at hiding the storms that no one but her mother and her ex-husband knew. Mitch excelled at convincing her to take a nap, or a shower, or to eat something when they happened. He hated that part of her, especially when she hit herself or knocked her head against the wall. Despite that, she found relief in being able to show someone her messy insides and exposed him to them more often than she should have. The storms seemed to lessen as she aged. But he left anyway. She would never go through that again.

If only she could convince Lydia to let her go. She was proud of everything she'd accomplished, but she was also done. Tired. Unwilling to start over. It had been a good life. It was enough.

She wouldn't break her promise to Lydia, but leaning against a cold Madrid wall, she decided, again, that she'd had enough. If she couldn't die by her own hand, perhaps she'd entice some nefarious character to help her.

She headed toward Plaza Colón. She'd crossed it daily on her walks to school a million years ago. In the early nineties, the square had been a concrete slab of brutalist architecture lined by expensive shops. It also had an underground bus stop and metro station. The combination of money and transit made it a hub for bad deeds. She'd seen the prostitutes at night. Crossing the plaza in the mornings, she'd find half-smoked blunts, broken bottles, and stains. That rough atmosphere appealed to her now.

She stopped at a corner bodega and bought a small bottle of sherry. She hated sherry, but its cloying sweetness never failed to get her drunk. She smiled as she took a sip from the bottle hidden in a paper bag. She'd been many things in her life, but derelict was new.

By the time she arrived at Plaza Colón, she'd downed over half the bottle. She hated the taste, which only challenged her to keep drinking. Booze as punishment. She'd never been a huge drinker, but she had used liquor as a tool many times. A glass or two of wine helped her relax after work. A snifter of fine scotch or bourbon gave her an air of sophistication in evening business meetings with men who invariably thought they had something to teach her. She'd used it to wash down the pills that hadn't worked on that ugly night.

Tonight, she used sherry. It tasted *feo*, ugly, exactly matching her mood. She wouldn't break her promise to Lydia, but not because she wanted to live. She wished Lydia would let her go, would understand that it was okay to have lived your best life and then be done. The future held nothing for her. Not anymore. The pillars of her life had been demolished. Her marriage. And far above that, her identity. She wouldn't start over. She was done.

But Lydia had shown her one last thing to take care of before she went. Her best friend had shown up for her when Kate prayed no one would. She would repay that act of kindness.

She hadn't understood Lydia's financial situation, not to mention her mental one. The first came with an easy fix. The second, who knew, maybe tonight in the bar, Lydia would take the first step toward the twin dreams of love and marriage. Although Kate hoped not. She wanted more for her friend. Lydia's insistence that she needed a man for fulfillment—or happiness, or whatever else—bothered Kate. Even before her marriage fell apart, she understood that she alone was responsible for what she achieved and how she felt. Lydia needed to learn that lesson before she ended up in another loveless marriage she'd never have the heart to leave.

Of course, Kate couldn't demand Lydia change any more than Lydia could demand that of her. Maybe they would just hold each other to the basest of promises. I won't kill myself in Madrid. You won't end up married before you've traveled to five countries and figured out who you are on your own.

Kate smiled to herself before taking another deep swig of the vile liquid. Of course, Kate would do her best to break the spirit of the rules, if not the promise itself. Wasn't that why she'd picked sherry and Plaza Colón? If she punished herself enough, death would become a relief.

The lights of the plaza rose before her. Still mainly concrete, they'd tried to add a few nature patches to make the area more welcoming. A water feature and a few plants didn't help the aesthetic much.

Kate wandered through the surprisingly empty plaza. She passed two men deep in conversation on a park bench. A few people strolled the nearby sidewalks, but the area no longer emanated danger like a bad cologne.

She sat on a concrete riser and finished her bottle. A woman on a bench nearby muttered to herself with the vacant stare her mother had worn at the end of her life. And Kate's grandmother before her. Alzheimer's. Just one more ugly part of the future she wanted to avoid.

Kate looked away from the woman. She'd prefer a knife or a gun to that demented path to death.

Madrid used to be a dangerous place at night, at least in a few areas. She'd come here hoping to keep her promise to Lydia and still end up dead. Not that she necessarily wanted pain or torture. Deep in her bones, she wanted to no longer exist, no longer worry, no longer try. At whatever cost. She'd already tried the easy route, pills. She didn't want to fail again.

She rose from the bench. Fine. She'd have to try harder to attract something treacherous enough to threaten her. Trying hard, working her ass off, had been her whole life anyway. A lot of good that had done.

She pulled out her phone and found the nearest open bodega. Great, she could beeline from there to Retiro. Rougher neighborhoods probably existed, but she didn't know how to find them. Retiro, a big central city park, had to have something shady happening.

She kept the new bottle closed until she got to the park. The first bottle sloshed around her guts and threatened to come back up. She practiced walking smoothly to try to calm her stomach. She imagined a book on her head and not letting it fall, a game from childhood rumored to help beauty pageant contestants. She giggled at that, imagining what her smooth walk must look like to anyone sober.

She finally made it to the park's lake. During the day, the football field of water teemed with swan boats filled with tourists. Tonight, the calm surface reflected moonlight. She hovered near the tree line at the edge of the wide path, looking for whoever else might be out for an ominous stroll. She thought she heard voices but saw no one.

A wave of nausea overtook her, and she vomited into a bush. Good. Just what she deserved. She walked further into the park, to an area dark with tree cover. She left the path, climbing over a low ornamental barrier. Then she slid down against the trunk of a tree and opened the new bottle of sherry. If the police or some other authority patrolled the park, they'd be unlikely to find her here. For someone with ill intent, she'd be an easy target.

She forced herself to drink. Tears slid down her face, but she didn't care, didn't even bother wiping them away. Life was too much, it had become too heavy. She hated herself, hated every mistake she had made. She used to make good decisions, but it had likely been years since that had happened. Her mental decline centered on a list of things gone wrong.

Once upon a time, she'd thought taking her company public was the smartest decision she could make. Instead, it had opened the door to shareholders, men, who thought they knew how to run the business better than she. Kate had always believed she'd outwit them and outlast them. At least until they'd fired her. She'd been so naïve.

The tears blurred her eyes, or perhaps the alcohol had stolen her sight. It didn't matter anyway. Every direction she looked showed nothing but regret. She brought the bottle to her lips, drained it. God, she hated sherry. She slammed the bottle down, heard its crash. Leaned her head back against the tree and tried to forget all the shitty things in her life.

Kate jerked awake and quickly leaned over to her side and threw up. Once she finished heaving, she rolled her body to the other side. Her hands touched dirt. Where the hell was she? She shivered in the cold night air and clambered to her knees. She reached out and used the tree to help her stand, then threw up again.

The night came at her in waves of memories. Sherry. Wanting to die. Lydia.

What time was it? She located her bag, somewhat soiled, and wiped it on a tree. Then she pulled her phone out. Twelve fifteen a.m. Lydia would be scared to death. Unless she was still with that guy. One could hope.

She staggered toward the path and fell climbing over the low fence. How could her head already be pounding when she still felt drunk? She was so fucking sorry. She couldn't do anything right. She hadn't been able to kill herself. Now, not only had she not been accosted, not to mention murdered, but no one even robbed her. Even though she'd gone to the most dangerous place she could think of and passed out with her purse beside her. Fuck. She couldn't catch a break.

"I'm going to fucking live forever," she shouted at the sky. Then she started crying.

By the time she made it back to the hotel, the tears had dried. She'd survived one more crappy night in a lifetime of mistakes. She walked into the posh lobby, bedraggled and filthy, a true walk of shame.

Lydia jumped up from a lobby sofa the moment Kate walked in. "Oh, my god, you're alive." She burst into tears.

Kate didn't know what to say. She'd disappointed her friend. She'd disappointed herself.

"Where were you? I've been terrified." Lydia grabbed Kate by the shoulders, gave her a little shake, then wrapped her in a hug. "Oh, my. You stink."

"Yeah. I need a shower."

"Come with me."

Lydia led Kate to the elevators. It felt like returning to jail.

Chapter 12

Lydia

Lydia woke the next morning with the hollow feeling of not getting enough sleep. The cozy foam-topped mattress and fluffy white comforter made it difficult to climb out of bed, but she did anyway. She second-guessed not going to bed with Jordi, but wanting a man so badly made her feel desperate. Dissatisfaction with herself coursed through her like a low-grade fever.

Before she left the hotel, she checked on Kate. A mop of dark hair peeked out from covers that gently rose and fell with her breath. Lydia closed the hotel room door softly behind her, despite wanting to slam it so hard the building shook.

She hit the street almost blind with rage and the sense that she needed to flee far from everything her life had become. She huffed past cafes, not stopping for coffee, and passed monuments, plazas, and beautiful buildings without seeing them. She wasn't sure where this anger had come from. Her fury with Kate for scaring her matched her disappointment that their lives had veered so far off track. Her frustration that she hadn't taken things with Jordi further provoked her, and now she'd never see him again. Always the good girl, her own needs always coming last.

Atop a hill next to the Royal Palace, she briefly stopped and searched for a direction to pull her forward. She turned right and trotted down an enormous staircase to the formal gardens behind the palace. The garden struck her as harsh, with every plant trimmed within an inch of its life to maintain the exact lines some garden god demanded. She fled again, first into a slightly wilder garden, and then back into the bustling streets of Madrid.

She'd walked for miles, her breath coming quick and shallow the entire time. Her energy burned into the pavement beneath her feet and the air surrounding her, but never seemed to lessen. Why was she here? Where was she going?

She broke the questions into smaller bites. Why had she agreed to this trip? Actually, why had she instigated it? How had she ever thought she'd be able to help her disturbed friend? Why did she ever think flitting from country to country would solve her own problems? Her anxiety grew with each unanswered question. Step after step after step.

She'd enjoyed her time with Jordi the night before, at least until things turned awkward. She hated the way she'd acted like a schoolgirl with a crush. She'd giggle, he'd take her hand, kiss her fingers. They didn't know each other yet had become caricatures of a fawning, in love couple on a date. Even at the time it seemed ridiculous, although the wine kept her flirty.

After dinner, they'd had a digestif at the bar, Chinchón, a licorice-scented drink she'd loved in college. He invited her back to his place. His arm had snaked around her waist possessively. She'd loved sinking into his embrace. He smelled like spice with a tinge of smoke, and she wanted to listen to his deep voice forever. All night, he'd behaved like someone suave but caring. It took her that long to realize he just wanted to get laid. They could have reenacted a scene from thirty years ago, the charming Spaniard setting his sights on the easy American. Hadn't she outgrown that?

When she told him no, she needed to check on her friend, he tried to convince her. He brushed his lips against her cheek, squeezed her hip. She'd almost said yes. She only needed to turn her body into his and let go of every reason she had for saying no. She could have let loose the swirling warmth inside her, but it had been too long. Her friend needed her. They would leave soon. She wanted a relationship. The reasons to say no overpowered the spark of desire that hadn't burned hot in too many years.

Anger swirled around her as she walked. Her feet grew sore, her breathing more labored, but she couldn't stop if she had no answers. She approached a huge building, the Atocha train station. She knew it well. If she stepped inside, she could be on the coast in two hours. Maybe she should leave everything behind. But that wasn't an answer. She'd already run halfway around the world and hadn't made any progress at all.

She turned away from the station. Across the wide street, she spied a building full of the inspiration she needed. The Reina Sofia glowed in the morning sun. They'd talked about visiting the museum time after time but had never made it. Finally, she had somewhere to go.

She waited her turn in line, then asked the ticket seller where to find Picasso's masterpiece, Guernica. She'd read about the painting for years, and while she'd learned it had been on exhibit in Madrid when she'd lived here, she'd never seen it.

She trudged up the marble stairs to the third floor, her legs shaking from their earlier exertion. A large courtyard divided the building into four wings, and the painting occupied a room on the opposite side from the entrance. She took her time, stopping to look at incredible works by Georges Braque, Joan Miró, and Salvador Dalí. Then, she turned a corner, and the painting stole her breath.

Over six feet tall and twice that in width, the enormous black and white painting drew her toward it. At first, she could only see a jumble of arms and legs and faces. A horse screamed from the center. People dying, life ripped apart and strewn across the canvas the same way the bomb the painting memorialized had torn through the town of Guernica during the Spanish Civil War. Books would never tell the story the way one piece of canvas filled her heart with knowledge.

Then her eyes lit upon two figures on the right side of the painting. A mother holding a dead child. The mother's cry, mouth open and screaming toward the sky, echoed through Lydia's bones. Tears flowed silently from her eyes, for the mother, for wars, for the incalculable callousness of humans bent on destruction.

A man with a British accent approached and asked if she was all right. She nodded, her eyes fixed on the painting. He offered her a tissue from a small cellophane wrapped pack. She looked at him, noting his balding head and kind eyes behind wire-rimmed glasses.

"Thank you," she said, taking a tissue.

"It's a powerful painting."

"It really puts things in perspective." All the stupid shit she'd worried about when she left the hotel that morning vanished. What first-world problems. Being unhappy or lonely wasn't a tragedy. It was life. She and Kate had the ability and the means to fix their problems. So many in the world did not. Yes, she'd love to find a partner to share her life with, but that shouldn't be her only goal. She'd spent decades helping children learn, she wasn't supposed to focus only on herself. Once this trip was done, she'd set her sights a little higher.

"Would you like to have a cup of tea or a coffee?" the man asked.

Lydia smiled at the man, warmed by the request. "You seem like a wonderful person and any other time I'd love to. But this morning, I've got a lot to do." Like go get her friend and figure out what was next. Like permanently pulling her gaze from her navel, or her daughter's, or Kate's, and getting on with a meaningful life.

Chapter 13

Lydia

The next morning, they boarded a jet bound for Amsterdam. Lydia hadn't spoken to Kate about her revelation in the Reina Sofia. Kate looked exhausted and embarrassed, so she let the moment slide. Now, they had two and a half hours side by side in an airplane, and the time had arrived.

"Let's talk about what happened the other night."

Kate turned toward her, eyes wide, perhaps in shock. Lydia put on her understanding face, the one she'd used with elementary school children. She needed to be open and open-minded, while still making sure they had the tough conversation.

"Here? In the airplane? Where other people can hear us?"

"I doubt anyone cares about our conversation." The woman holding her dead child in the painting flashed before her eyes. "And if they are interested, I don't care. This is about me, at least part of it. I had an epiphany yesterday. I've been way too focused on things that don't matter. I used to spend my whole day helping kids learn. That work is important. And while I want to be happy, shining a light on my loneliness, or anything else bothering me, can't be the only thing I worry about over the course of a day." She'd been working on her speech, wanting to share her news in a way Kate would take seriously.

"So, you're saying I should stop moping around and, I don't know, do something different?" Kate's voice returned to the flat, scary tone from the hospital.

Lydia took her friend's hand and laced their fingers together. "No. I think you have a serious problem that needs professional help."

"Then why are we going to Amsterdam instead of going home?" Kate stared straight ahead, her voice untrusting.

"Because I can't drag you home without your agreement. We need to have this conversation. You have always been the smartest person I know. You get to decide what you need." She squeezed Kate's hand. "And if you don't know what that is, that's okay too. But it probably means you do need to talk to a professional who can help you figure that out."

Kate turned her head to the window, and Lydia followed her gaze. Bright blue sky stretched above white clouds seemingly forever. Below them, people went about their lives, struggled with their own problems, and hopefully found peace, if not happiness. Guernica lay somewhere below them, decades after the bomb. Life went on.

Kate turned back to Lydia. "Can we take it one day at a time? I'm not ready to go back. At least here, I'm not surrounded by constant reminders of everything that went wrong."

"Of course," Lydia said. Wanting to take it slow sounded like the most honest response she'd had from Kate. "But you can't put me in that position again. Promise you'll get help before it gets that bad."

"Promise." Kate's voice came out in a whisper. Lydia hoped she hadn't lied.

Today, she would trust. Lydia settled back in her seat, declining the offer of wine from the flight attendant. Kate would sort through her problems, and Lydia would focus on being happier and figuring out a worthwhile future.

As they walked out of the sliding doors of the airport, an enormous bright red food truck drew Lydia toward it. "Poffertjes! We have to get some." She hadn't had the tiny Dutch pancakes in years, and when she had tried them in America, they never had the fluffy yet slightly crusty quality of the ones from her memories.

She purchased a paper cone overflowing with them and found an empty bench. Kate followed, rolling her suitcase up to the bench and taking a seat. Lydia tilted the cone in her direction. Kate pulled out a powdered-sugar-encrusted pancake just as a gust of wind blew by.

"Damn, there's going to be sugar everywhere." Kate said, shoving the treat in her mouth.

"There will be. That's part of the fun." Lydia bit into a pancake, causing another snowfall of sugar. It melted on her tongue, bringing intense flavor and happy memories. "Do you remember the first time we had these at that little wood and glass restaurant by the river?"

"That place was straight out of a fairytale." Kate smiled and plucked another cake from the bag.

The dark circles under Kate's eyes had tinged blue. She looked like she'd lost weight on the trip, yet all she did was sleep. Lydia might not have much influence over the dark circles, but she could encourage her friend to eat more. "I've booked us on a pizza cruise tonight."

"What the hell is a pizza cruise?"

"You'll find out soon enough." Lydia laughed, excited about a whole new city to explore. They took a train into the center of town, then stashed their bags at the Marriott. Not nearly as fancy as their Madrid hotel, Lydia had booked it because of its ideal location across the street from a canal and within easy walking distance of parks and museums.

"Where are you taking me?" Kate asked as they headed back out the lobby doors.

Lydia had insisted they let the bellman take their luggage to their rooms. Their flight had only been two hours, and Lydia didn't want another day of Kate in bed. Lydia paused for a moment and almost stifled the mothering urge. The waiting around bored her, and surely, Kate would do better out in the fresh air.

"Let's go explore. The sun is shining, the afternoon is warm, and we haven't seen this city in decades." Lydia grabbed her friend by the arm and headed toward the city center.

"Watch out!" Kate hauled Lydia back from the edge of the intersection where she'd stood a second before. A man flew by on a bicycle, angrily ringing his bell.

"What the hell?" Lydia struggled to keep her balance.

"Look down. You were standing in the bike lane."

A wide, double row of brick-colored paint snaked its way down the sidewalk. "That guy almost killed me."

"And that would be a particularly shitty way to go." Kate bit down on one side of her lip but couldn't keep the other from curling into a smile.

Lydia stood still, her heart racing, probably from the bike. She'd tried so hard to avoid the word kill, or dead, or suicide. "You would know." She held her breath, praying the joke would cut the tension between them and not cause Kate to fling herself into a canal or throw herself in front of a bus.

Kate's eyes had gone big. "You made a joke! Oh, thank god. Can we please go back to being normal friends now?"

"I hope so. But that's up to you."

"Fine. How about we both try not to die in Amsterdam?" The light had turned, and Kate looked both ways, then crossed the bike path and intersection. Lydia followed, caught up in a group of people where the tall, conservatively clad Dutch easily stood out from the tourists in neon and baseball caps.

She caught up with Kate midway across the bridge. Kate leaned over the stone railing, peering into the gray-green water. Lydia joined her just as a boat emerged beneath them. A dozen incredibly loud American women in tiny dresses raised glasses to one another, while a young man clad in orange stood behind a makeshift bar. One of the women wore a tiara and a sash.

"Fancy bachelorette party," Kate said.

"You think? They're a long way from home."

"Perhaps the fiancé is Dutch. They look so young." Kate shook her head as the boat motored away.

"They're probably in their mid to late twenties. We were younger than that when we came here."

"True," Kate said. "Probably not our smartest move."

"What do you mean?" Lydia hoped Kate's dour disposition hadn't returned after such a short absence. "Come on, let's keep walking. I think there's a little plaza if we turn right after the bridge."

"Don't you remember how awful that trip was? We met those cute guys at that bar, and they'd told us about a great party," Kate said as they crossed the street, then took a set of stairs that led to the canal's edge.

"Oh, no. I'd forgotten all about that. We followed them to some seedy part of town, and then they stole our money." Lydia had been terrified. Kate had wanted to fight. The fishy smell of the warehouse district suddenly wafted past, seeming far more real than a memory. That frightening night, Lydia had stared into a graffitied brick building with broken windows. A shadow moved inside. Then one of the guys, the one she'd been flirting with, asked her for money for a cab. He was lost. She'd stupidly pulled out her wallet. He grabbed it and ran. Simultaneously, his friend had pulled Kate's purse from her shoulder, breaking the narrow strap.

Kate had run after him screaming. Lydia had followed, fleeing the spooky building and not caring if they caught the guys. She barely kept Kate in her sights, speeding around one corner just in time to see her friend disappear around the next. Finally, she caught up with her. Kate held her bag in her hands, shouting every cuss word known to man. The guy had stolen her wallet but left the purse behind.

Fortunately, the front desk clerk at the hotel had held their passports. Lydia had two travelers' checks in her suitcase, which they converted into enough cash to get them through the trip. Barely.

"That was the worst. It took us so long to find our way back to a decent part of town. I was terrified. Why didn't I remember that?" A sliver of the fear from that night slipped up Lydia's spine, despite the warm afternoon and cute, table-strewn plaza they'd entered.

"I think that's your gift. You see the good in people and situations."

"And ignore the bad?" Yes, she tried to be positive, but Kate's comment sounded like a dig. Probably another complaint about Lydia's marriage.

"It's your best quality. I'm not always the world's nicest person, yet you've put up with me for decades now. Speaking of the time passing, can you imagine being a kid here now?" Kate pointed to a couple of teens at the next table immersed in their phones. "We'd have GPS in our cell phones, not to mention a digital wallet with cash."

"I'm sure there's some new hustle today. We'll have to be careful." Lydia hated hearing her schoolteacher's voice come out. She sounded like a little old lady.

"I'm not positive we'd be considered targets today. Although, if I happen to see one of those guys, I'll kick his ass."

"God knows you tried to thirty years ago. They were just faster than you."

"I had on sandals. Remind me to wear running shoes when we go out tonight."

Lydia laughed, but she wished she had her friend's fearlessness. She promised herself to have a bigger life now that she had a second shot. That would mean putting action ahead of worrying for once. Using that philosophy, she probably should have slept with Jordi. A warmth tugged at her insides at the thought of undressing him. She needed more courage.

They crossed another canal, this one lined with houseboats and tall, narrow homes on either side. "Let's go this way," Lydia said, turning onto the street beside the canal. She didn't know where it led. Refusing to look at her phone for directions, she took a small step toward fearlessness. She didn't have anywhere to be until the pizza cruise hours from now. She had time to get a little lost.

"Honestly, that was an awful trip." Kate had stopped near one of the houseboats, seemingly wallowing in that long-ago vacation. "Do you remember spending the night at the Chicago airport because the flight was delayed? And then when we got here the hostel didn't want to honor our reservation because we'd missed the first night."

"That hostel smelled terrible, like the building itself had BO. I'm surprised we didn't come home with bedbugs or some horrible disease." Lydia shuddered at the memory.

"Yeah. After that, we promised ourselves we'd never stay in a youth hostel again." Kate tramped on from the houseboat. "I certainly never have."

Lydia hadn't either, but mostly because she'd traveled so little. She wanted to change the subject. "Let's stop for a coffee at this cafe." Lydia pointed at a building with a green awning and wooden chairs and tables pulled to the canal's edge.

They requested a table by the canal, and Lydia closed her eyes and enjoyed the sun's heat on her face. Roses bloomed nearby, and their sweet aroma perfumed the air. Something unlatched in her shoulders and lower back, and she sank into deep relaxation. "I like Amsterdam better than last time. I like myself better than last time too."

"Wow. I definitely don't feel that way. I was a little badass back then, ready to take on the world."

Lydia opened one eye and looked at her friend. "You're still a badass."

"No. That person is gone." Kate didn't sound sad at the loss, just frank.

"I think there's still a badass in there. She's been run over by a truck and needs to recover, but she hasn't disappeared."

The waitress brought them coffees and the tart Lydia had ordered when the waitress mentioned it was the special. It looked like a piece of red velvet cake. Just saying yes to something without asking questions became another small step toward bravery. Small things would lead to bigger risks. She would learn to be fearless.

Kate wouldn't have lost her fearlessness, something that had been so ingrained in her personality. She had to understand that. Lydia looked at her friend. "I want to be like you when I grow up, or at least in this next phase of life. I want to be fearless."

With that she picked up her fork and took a big bite of cake. Why the hell not? No more saying no to pleasure. If she gained a pound, so what? Yes, she desired a man, companionship, but she'd never put up with someone who criticized her weight again. Especially not when he did it from the couch, resting his beer can on an ever-growing belly.

The flash of anger surprised her, and she shoved another piece of cake in her mouth. Definitely red velvet. She sipped her coffee but suddenly wanted wine. She waved a hand at the waitress and asked for a glass. "Do you want one too?" she asked Kate.

Kate looked stunned but nodded. "Why on earth do you want to be like me?" she asked once the waitress retreated. "You do remember I just tried to kill myself. I didn't do that because things were great."

"You don't see yourself the way I do. You've always taken big risks. After college, I got my teaching certificate and went into a job I knew would be stable until I retired. You had about a million jobs, retail, working in a bank, you even had a stint at a chamber of commerce. You lived in a shitty apartment with three other girls and learned everything you could. Then you launched your own company. That took balls, my friend. And it totally paid off."

Kate shook her head. "It wasn't like that. I was desperate most of the time. Well, desperate and having fun. But I would never go back to that life. The last thing I want to do is start over."

"You don't have to. You've got money. You can do anything you want in the world."

"Money without passion is nothing."

Lydia shoved her cake toward Kate. "Eat. This is delicious, and you're getting too skinny." She took a sip of the recently delivered wine. Crisp and bright, it reminded her of all the things she wanted in her life. Something about the cake or the wine or even the air in this city filled her with desire for things she hadn't tried.

"Passion." Lydia's mind dumped words into her mouth as she tried to convey her swirling thoughts. "I've been thinking a lot about that, and not only as it relates to guys. I was a good teacher. I have skills and experience, and I'm not ready to give up contributing to the world just because I've retired. We are so privileged. I need to give something back."

Kate used a fork to swipe frosting off the cake. "Okay. So, you want to be fearless, and you're passionate to give back."

"Yes. And I want a man."

"Why?" Kate sucked the frosting from the fork.

The memory of Jordi's kiss flashed through her, zinging her with the same electric shock she'd had when their lips touched. When he'd slipped his tongue inside her mouth, she'd pressed herself into him, her body craving his heat. It had ended there. She'd been too timid. His smooth moves had both attracted and repelled her, probably because she'd thought of him as a potential life partner. But what if she'd been braver and had only thought of him as someone for a fun night? "I think I need to get laid."

Kate, mid-drink, sputtered her wine and then had a coughing fit. "You are the last person I thought would ever say that."

Lydia didn't want to admit she'd missed out on this part of life. "I loved Joe, God rest his soul, but we didn't have the most passionate marriage. At least toward the end."

"You were married over twenty-three years. How much toward the end?"

"I don't want to talk about it. We weren't like you and Mitch. You guys were always holding hands and kissing." Lydia realized her mistake too late.

"Yeah, well all of that was a lie. He'd make love to me, then go see his little mistress."

"How long do you think he was with her before you got divorced?"

"I really don't want to get into the details. I did once, back when I cared. Now, I'd prefer to never think of them again."

Lydia wished she hadn't steered the conversation in this particular direction. Time to reverse course. "I almost wish Joe had had an affair. He might have learned something."

Kate, wine at her lips again, snorted, spraying the liquid across the table. "Would you quit being hilarious while I'm drinking?"

But Kate wasn't angry. She'd laughed. And although Lydia didn't love being the butt of the joke, seeing her friend laugh brightened the world a little. She'd been brave and shared an embarrassing story. She took a deep breath. It felt good to talk about Joe. She'd often defended him in the past, at least when others complained about him. Today, somehow, sharing the truth made her lighter. "Honestly, when I kissed Jordi, I had stirrings I haven't had in decades. That man knew how to kiss a woman."

"Did you sleep with him?"

"No, but we did kiss when he walked me to the hotel." Lydia's cheeks ached from her hard smile. "There was tongue."

"Oh, my god. You really do need to get laid. Why didn't you invite him up to your room?"

"That just seemed, I don't know, so slutty. I mean, he wasn't looking for a relationship."

"You are over half a century old. Be a slut while you still can. Seriously Lydia. Go have amazing sex. I'm certainly not going to judge you, and you don't even have to worry about getting pregnant."

Lydia burned with embarrassment, but also with excitement. She could have sex. Just sex, without turning it into some plan for the future.

Kate whipped out her phone. "This is great. You've got a lot of things you want to accomplish. Let's start a list. Number one: take risks. Number two: do some good in the world and put your knowledge to use. Number three: have sex. Anything else?"

"Find a man."

"I think that comes under *takes risks*, not *accomplishments*."

"Maybe it's both. I want a long-term relationship, but that may take a little time. Maybe good sex can come before then. Do you remember Robert, the guy I met in Costa Rica? We had great sex. I'd like to have that again, even for a single night. But I also don't want to live the rest of my life alone."

Kate set her phone on the table and leaned back in her chair. She peered at Lydia, cocking her head like a parrot about to speak. "So, you want great sex, and you want a man. But they don't have to go together. How bad was it with Joe?"

Oh no. She couldn't go there. "He's dead, we shouldn't talk ill of him."

Kate shook her head. "You left the South when you were eighteen, but sometimes you still sound like you walked out of Anderson, South Carolina, last week. I'm not speaking ill of him. I'm talking about you. Sex is a two-way street. Pleasure is a two-way street. Did you have that?"

Lydia closed her eyes. If only she could close her ears.

"Honey, when was the last time he went down on you?"

"1996. During the Atlanta Olympics." Eyes still closed, she felt around for her glass of wine. She managed to find it without knocking it over and drank the rest without opening her eyes. She heard birds chirping nearby, but nothing from Kate. She opened one eye. Her friend looked at her with—pity? Confusion? Lydia opened her other eye. She might as well accept it, the way she'd accepted the crappy sex until eventually they hadn't even done that.

Kate straightened and picked up her phone again. "Okay. I'm moving getting laid up to number one on the list."

Lydia nodded and signaled for the check. She needed to leave the table and walk off this embarrassment. She could change. She would change. But she wasn't the only one who needed new goals in life. "Kate, I want you to come up with your own list. Just three things. We've got Amsterdam and three more countries after that. Let's figure out the rest of our lives. I'll take risks, do good, and find a partner. Will you at least think about what you want?"

Kate rose from the table. She looked nervous, like she wanted to bolt. "I want to help you achieve your goals. Can that be enough for now?"

Lydia stood and gave her friend's hand a quick squeeze. "For now."

Chapter 14

Lydia

Lydia followed Kate into the coffee shop. The interior design existed somewhere between art nouveau and Alice's rabbit hole. Wavy green and brown banquettes lined pink textured walls. Multicolored velvet tuffets topped barstools, and a tall blond with a smile on his face waited for them behind a rose-colored marble bar.

She had never understood why they called hash bars coffee shops in Amsterdam, but this place carried that nonsensical theme to a new level. Still, for some reason, the trippy atmosphere calmed her nerves. Kate had convinced her to give it a try, and what with her new risk taking and all, Lydia had agreed. She wanted to explore, not just the world, but her own boundaries.

She took a seat beside Kate at the bar, where the bartender—drug dealer?—explained the wide selection of marijuana and related products. Kate focused wholly on the young man, while Lydia watched their interaction. This guy was Kate's type, tall, blond, great body, good smile. He had more angles to his face than Mitch, but for that and twenty years, he might have been a carbon copy of Kate's husband. Ex-husband. Over many years, many boyfriends, and a healthy number of one-night and vacation-long stands, Lydia had never seen Kate with anyone but a tall blond.

The young man turned and took something from a shelf behind him. He had a great ass. Lydia shook her head. Ever since that kiss with Jordi, her body had been on fire. She'd tried to satisfy her needs herself, but it only made her hornier. Just thinking about sex made her run her hands along her dress, ostensibly smoothing the fabric, but delighting in the warmth of her skin and wishing for the caress of other fingers.

She shook her head again. She needed to pay attention. Who knew what kind of trouble Kate would get her in tonight? Not trouble. Fun.

The man's long fingers smoothed a white paper, and Lydia's cheeks went warm. Then he rolled a joint.

She hadn't smoked a joint in decades. In high school, she and Kate had sat next to a stoner in world history class. He'd invited them to a party at his house one Friday night. The party ended up being just the three of them. He rolled a joint and offered it to them. They both tried it and spent hours giggling and talking about things Lydia never would remember.

The next morning, Kate had announced that most potheads weren't smart, so they shouldn't hang around them too often. So, they didn't. They'd imbibed a few times over the years, but mostly they'd been drinkers.

It had surprised Lydia when Kate demanded they visit a coffee shop. Kate told her she'd used edibles back in California. Lydia hadn't tried them. Of course Lydia hadn't tried them. She never tried anything. Until today.

She reached for the joint Kate offered and took a long slow draw, filling her lungs with fragrant smoke. She verged on the edge of coughing, but that moment passed, and she let the smoke settle in her lungs before releasing it into the air.

"You've become a pro at this," Kate said. "Have you started smoking?"

"No, not in ages. But I want to fully embrace this experience." She definitely wanted to fully embrace something. Her body felt alive, and for the first time in many years, she craved a man.

The bartender left to serve two customers who had entered the shop. Lydia surveyed the wavy benches as they stretched toward the back of the building. Two skinny guys who looked like the punk teens of her youth huddled along one curve in the wall. A single man sat in a leather chair a little further back. His peridot green eyes met hers.

Heat crashed through her body. She felt caught, as if he saw through to her emotions. She dropped her eyes but couldn't keep herself from looking back up. He had wavy brown hair graying at the temples and a trim beard. He held his joint in a large hand.

She kept her chin down but let her eyes wander up. He gazed back at her. She gave him a half smile, then turned her attention back to Kate. "What the hell is in that stuff? It's making me horny."

"You've been talking about sex since we got here. There's only one cure for that." Kate winked at her.

"Given what happened last time we were here, I don't think either of us should follow a guy anywhere."

"You're right. That really scarred me for a while." Kate took a drag from the joint. "We shouldn't have trusted those guys, but when I got back home, I couldn't trust anyone. I think we both broke up with our boyfriends after that."

"I remember. The experience made us choosier."

Kate picked up the joint again and inhaled. "Did it though?" she said after exhaling. "We both deserved better guys than the ones we got."

That statement didn't quite fit, like a too-tight sweater. "Maybe we found the right guys for where we were in our lives. I needed someone like Joe when I married him. Maybe you needed Mitch too. You guys had a lot of good years together."

"How did you need Joe?"

"I think I was nesting then. I wanted to have a kid. He was the first guy I dated who wasn't terrified of having children. I got to live the fantasy of my youth, being a wife and mother. I loved those years." Lydia reached for the joint. She'd cherished raising Sophie, watching her turn from adorable and precocious into a strong woman making her way through the world, even though it meant leaving her mother's side. She wouldn't have given those years up for anything, but she didn't want to relive them.

"I guess Mitch and I had some good years too." Kate's forlorn voice wavered in the smokey air. "We did some amazing things together. He supported me when I started Indulge. Once it found a little success, we took wonderful trips—New Zealand, the Red Sea, Cambodia. I loved that time in my life."

Lydia held the smoke in her lungs, then exhaled a mellow breath. "I think I'm getting high."

"That's the goal." Kate wiped a tear away.

"Is it making you sad?" Lydia's brain relaxed into a solemn rhythm. She could see Kate's torment but didn't feel it. The marijuana kept her a step removed from the emotions that normally would have buffeted her. It muted her urge to step in and help.

"My life makes me sad. I am despondent about the future. I wish you could see inside my brain. I've led this truly incredible life, achieved every goal. I finished early, and I don't want to wait around for another twenty years as things slowly get worse." A tear rolled down Kate's face, but her breathing stayed calm.

"What if you've got more good times ahead, and you just can't see them yet?"

"Like what? I've literally accomplished every goal I've ever had. The only things left are watching my ex-husband have children with someone younger and prettier than me, watching those jackasses destroy the company I spent my life building, and waiting for Alzheimer's to show up the way it did for my mom and grandmom."

An odd combination of mellowness and wisdom rolled through Lydia like a wave. She touched her friend's hand. "You could get laid and have phenomenal sex."

Lydia watched the one second of shock hit her friend's face before Kate started laughing. "Oh. My. God. We have got to get you a man. You honestly can't think about anything else." Kate dissolved into giggles and passed the bug to Lydia.

Lydia laughed so hard she feared falling off her stool. It had been years, decades, since she'd totally let loose like this. She hadn't known how much she'd needed it. The constant tension in her shoulders and back disappeared, and she imagined floating off the stool instead of falling from it. "We should have done this years ago."

"I love you," Kate said, wrapping Lydia in a hug. "I want to make things good for you before I go."

"You're not going anywhere. You promised."

The bartender appeared in front of them. "How are you ladies doing? Would you like anything else?"

"No, this stuff is great, far better than the pot I've tried in the US." Kate said.

"Well, I hope you'll take that word back to the States with you. Tourist business is down significantly since American states started legalizing cannabis."

"Fascinating. There aren't many experiences like this in America. It's so much more industrial and less social. The dispensaries I've been to are a weird cross between a pharmacy, a fast-food joint, and a hippy crystal shop. People enter, buy their drugs, and leave as quickly as possible. Most people prefer getting high in their homes."

"Coffee shops are about the experience. This is a great place to try new things," he said.

"Yeah, my friend here is totally into trying new things." Kate nodded at Lydia.

"Yep," Lydia said. A happy glow lodged in her core. It made her smile and filled her with warmth. Why hadn't she tried this before? Why say no when yes felt so good? She giggled at the question, and her eyes searched out the green-eyed man.

He caught her glance, smiled at her. She held his gaze for a second before she returned her attention to Kate.

"How do you advertise and differentiate your product?" Kate asked the bartender.

"Give me the joint." Lydia had no interest in the shop talk Kate would likely engage in for the foreseeable future. Once an entrepreneur, always one. In fact, that's something

Kate should do in this next stage of her life. She could help small businesses, maybe bring them the kind of success she'd found with Indulge.

She took another drag and let her eyes wander down the bar again. The man looked down at something in his lap, probably his phone. That started her giggling. What if it wasn't his phone? She tapped Kate on the shoulder. "Oh, my god. I am so high."

"I know. Isn't this great? Much more fun than a pizza cruise." Then she turned back to continue her conversation with the bartender.

Lydia had loved yesterday's pizza cruise. They'd traveled through the canals at night, and so many of Amsterdam's tall, narrow houses glowed with indoor light and no curtains. She had briefly glimpsed into the lives of others as the boat passed by. The spaces gave off a warm and sophisticated vibe. She'd spied art on the walls and gleaming kitchens.

It had made her wish for different things. If someone had peeked into her living room a year ago, they'd have seen a television on the wall and Joe sitting on the beige sofa with a beer in his hand. She'd have been in the kitchen making some boring dinner, or cleaning, frustrated that she had to hold down a job and do all the chores while Joe watched football and got drunk. If they looked a month ago, they'd have seen the same thing, except no Joe and her frustration had morphed into loneliness.

She handed the joint to Kate, then closed her eyes, a little woozy from the pot. She couldn't go backwards, and she shouldn't start resenting the life she'd chosen, one that had given her Sophie. She'd had a fulfilling life. The second time around, she would make new choices.

She slipped the joint from Kate's hand, then took a drag. Starting today, she would make bolder choices and do the things she'd been afraid of before. No more regrets. She blew the smoke from her lungs and looked over at the handsome man. His eyes caught hers, and a thrill ran through her. She wanted him. It had been so very, very long. She gave him her biggest smile.

He smiled back, his whole face brightening. He stood and walked her way. With long legs, broad shoulders, and a blue and white button down rolled up at the sleeves, he looked like candy.

"Hello, I'm Zander."

"Lydia, nice to meet you."

"You are from America?"

"Yes, California."

"Do you mind if I take the seat next to you?"

"No, please do." She swiveled toward the empty seat, then realized she hadn't left much room for his long legs. His jeans touched her knees as he sat. Despite the mellowness coursing through her body, the grain of denim on her skin gave her a shock of excitement.

"Is this your first time here?" he asked.

"Well, it's my first time in this coffee shop, but it's my second time in Amsterdam. My friend Kate and I came when we were in our twenties. This is Kate." Lydia pulled on her friend's sleeve.

"Well, hello there," Kate said, turning from her conversation with the bartender. She looked at Lydia. "Nice job. Go for it."

Lydia turned back to Zander and relaxed into conversation with him. She found it difficult to listen to his words when she kept fixating on his long-fingered hands, his full lips, and the beard she imagined would scruff her cheeks if they kissed. She liked the feel of his jeans and pressed her leg into his, taking in the warmth of his skin beneath the denim.

"You are very pretty." Zander brushed his fingers against her jaw.

Lydia's skin buzzed with electricity at his touch. "Thank you." Heat surged up her cheeks, and she looked down so he wouldn't see the blush. She spied his hand resting against his leg. "You have such large hands and long fingers."

She reached for his hand, and the warmth of it surprised her. She held it palm-to-palm with her own. The tips of her fingers didn't even reach the final knuckle on his. She wanted to wrap his hand around her waist, reach her fingers into his beard, and pull him into a kiss. She dropped his hand. Things were moving too fast, at least in her mind.

Think about everything that went wrong in Amsterdam last time. "Sorry," she said, wringing her hands in her lap.

"Don't be sorry. I like you. You have a lovely body." This time, his finger started where neck met shoulder and trailed down toward the crevice between her breasts. He left his finger on her warm chest for a moment before pulling it away.

"It's the dress," she said. No longer mellow, every cell in her body raced with anticipation. Touch me again, she wanted to scream, to whisper into his ear.

"It is not your very pretty dress. It is you. Would you like to go home with me?"

"No," she blurted, then saw the surprise on his face. She couldn't leave here with him and risk being drawn into some alley like had happened before. A moment of terror gripped her. She'd been so afraid back then. Her fear tonight, lit by the same spark, burned differently. Yes, she feared he would take advantage of her. But she feared more that her old body wouldn't measure up. She looked her age, felt her age, and years had passed since passion had flowed through her veins. What if she wasn't enough?

She turned to Kate for a reprieve and asked the bartender for a glass of water. She imagined the heat radiating from Zander, and that side of her body caught fire. Desire and fear pummeled her, and the mellow undercurrent of the pot asked her to slow down and let things unfold.

"He's pretty cute." Kate leaned her head toward Lydia and spoke in a low voice. "He could be a fine risk."

"I don't think I'm ready," Lydia whispered. "Remember what happened last time we took off with guys in Amsterdam."

"Well, I don't recommend you follow him into any dark alleys. Why don't you take him back to the hotel? We've got adjoining rooms, and that would be on your turf. Do you want me to ask Sam if he knows him?" Kate nodded at the bartender.

"I don't know. I don't think I'm ready. But maybe you could ask him." Lydia stole a glance at Zander. He looked uncomfortable, like he might slip away. She gave him a smile. "Stay. I just need a minute to catch up with my friend."

He gave her that winning smile. "I'll be right back." She watched him head to the back of the bar toward the restrooms, her eyes not straying from his firm ass.

Lydia turned back to Kate. "By the way, the bartender is pretty cute, and he's your type."

"Yeah, you said that before. Thirty years ago, maybe. We're having a conversation about business. I'm helping him strategize about how to continue to attract Americans. I think they should focus on a broader age range. I mean, look at us. We came here thirty years ago, and we're back and still curious about experimenting with hash. They shouldn't cede the market to a bunch of American potheads and conglomerates."

Pink had returned to Kate's cheeks, and her eyes glowed with an interest Lydia hadn't seen since before the hospital. "You should consult with businesses. Look how much knowledge you have to share."

"And have to relive what I went through? No way. It's one thing to talk to some guy when you're getting high, it's another to think about having to do it over and over again. That way lies heartbreak. Besides, I'm used to running things, not teaching. You know the old saying, those who do, do, and those who don't, teach."

Kate might as well have slapped her face. Yes, Kate had started a company. Kate had made a ton of money. Kate had graced the covers of business magazines. But Lydia had a life too. She'd liked teaching and believed it made the world a better place. She'd raised Sophie, and that made the world better too. She bit her bottom lip to keep it from trembling.

"I'm sorry. I didn't mean that." Kate squeezed her hand.

"I think I want to go back to the hotel." She wouldn't complain, wouldn't hold her friend accountable. Just like she'd never held Joe accountable. Damn. Why did life have to be so hard?

"Lydia, I'm sorry. That was a bitchy thing to say. You've contributed more to the world than I have. Your students love you. Everyone loves you, and men are falling all over you. Jordi in Spain, and now this guy. And he's pretty hot." Kate tilted her head toward the back of the bar where Zander had reemerged.

"I think that way lies heartbreak," Lydia echoed Kate's words. That didn't stop the warmth from building in her belly and radiating through her body.

"No, honey. That way lies pleasure, something you've been denying yourself for too long. What if you took a chance? What's the worst that could happen?"

"He could murder me."

"Touché. I'll try to find out if he's a known criminal. Shall we have something else? We haven't tried edibles. They have cookies and space cake."

Lydia, mid-sip when Kate mentioned space cake, burst out laughing then coughed on her water. "Space cake. That's hilarious. No, I better not. I think I've had enough."

Zander had put his hand on her back when she started coughing. "Are you all right?"

"Yes. Kate told me they had something called space cake here. Isn't that funny?"

"I guess so. You eat the cake, then go into space."

That had her laughing again. The laughter popped the bubble of her anxiety. She needed to think less and act more. She'd promised herself that. She swung her knees back toward Zander, bumping into his long legs. "You're funny." She rested a hand on one lean thigh, and her hand burned through denim. She imagined the heat of his skin against her own.

He laid his hand on top of hers and pulled it further up his thigh. With his other hand, he reached for his joint and took a puff, then turned it toward her. "Would you like some?"

"No, thank you. I think I've had enough, and I want to be fully present for whatever comes next." Her words glowed with courage.

"What will come next?" he asked.

Hopefully me, she thought, although she wasn't bold enough to say it. She wanted one perfect night of hot sex and experimentation. She'd done so little of that. She looked at Zander's full lips and could almost taste him. His green eyes raked up and down her body, filling her with desire. He looked confident, experienced. He'd better be as good in bed as he appeared.

Lydia skooched back on her stool and put her knees between his legs. She leaned toward him, placing her hands high on his thighs. High. She started giggling. He squeezed her legs between his. The motion stopped her mid-giggle. His confidence, the strength of his legs, it took her breath away. "Zander, what would you like to do tonight?"

"I would like to make love with you."

A pulse started in her groin and traveled through her body. OMG—he might give her an orgasm with words alone. "Just a minute."

Lydia twisted back toward Kate, leaning into her friend. "Did you learn anything about him?"

"Sam says he comes in here every few weeks. He doesn't know him personally, but we'll be able to track him down if he murders you."

"That's not funny."

"No, it's not. I want you to have a good time tonight. Does he seem like a good guy? You've been talking to him for a while now."

"Actually, he seems nice. And really, really sexy. I think I may go back to the hotel with him."

"Have fun. Can I have the hotel send a bottle of champagne up to your room? It might take the edge off a little."

"That would be wonderful. Thank you. And wish me luck."

The night had cooled when they left the coffee house. Zander guided her with a hand on her lower back as they walked toward her hotel. She asked him more about his job as a computer programmer, asked him about his neighborhood in Amsterdam, asked him about everything that came to her mind. Talking turned her focus away from what would happen when they got back to the hotel.

Fortunately, by the time they arrived, the champagne waited for them in a silver bucket. She went straight toward it, putting off the inevitable.

"Please let me," he said, taking the bottle from her hands that had been nervously pulling at the foil.

She stood awkwardly beside him as he smoothly unwrapped the bottle from its cage and released the cork. He lifted a crystal glass and slowly poured the golden liquid into it and handed it to her before filling his own.

"To a beautiful woman." He lifted his glass.

She clinked hers with his, biting her lower lip in anticipation. The liquid soothed her parched throat. She took another sip, and then another, not knowing what to say or what came next.

"Are you nervous?" he asked.

"A little. I was married for a very long time, and I haven't done anything like this . . ." her voice trailed off. She'd done things like this in the past, not often, but before Joe. It was a lifetime ago.

Zander took her empty glass from her hand and set it down. Then he gently lifted her chin and stared into her eyes. She trembled at his touch.

"I do not want you to be nervous, and I want you to tell me if you want me to stop or want me to leave. But I also would like to kiss you right now. Is that all right?"

Lydia stepped forward into his warm body, her eyes never leaving his. Every cell in her body filled with longing. "Please kiss me."

His lips whispered against hers before coming back stronger. It ignited her. She pressed herself into him. His hands found her back, pulling her closer. As the kiss deepened, he slid his hands down until he gripped her ass, pulling her against the growing bulge in his pants. She moaned.

"I want you very much," he said.

She nodded.

"Will you take off your dress?"

Should she? Women in their fifties shouldn't be asked that.

He must have sensed her discomfort, because he reached for her hand and led her to bed. She sat on the end of it, and he stood in front of it, holding her hand.

"You have a beautiful body. I want to show you that. Is that all right?"

She nodded, then found her words. "Yes. I would like that."

He leaned forward and kissed her again, harder and needier than the first time. One hand slid to the base of her head, while the other trailed over her breast. His hand held a current that electrified her, and she wished her clothes would fall from her body. As he sank to a knee, he kissed her cheek, her jaw, her neck. His hand slid over her breast again, then slipped inside the vee neck of her wrap dress, caressing her.

He gently pulled the dress off one shoulder, exposing the black lace bra she'd bought earlier that day. "Pretty," he said, before slipping the strap off her shoulder and freeing her breast. "Beautiful."

His mouth followed his words, playing her with his tongue and lips. She moaned again, caught in a moment of having everything and still wanting more. She'd lost track of his hands until one slid up her warm thigh. Boldly, she opened her legs to him. He found her, quickly making it past the thin black lace. His thumb rubbed small circles of ecstasy while his fingers explored.

He lifted his lips from her breast, and with the hand that wasn't deliciously inside her underwear, gently pressed her chest back toward the bed. "Relax. I need to taste you." He waited a beat as if seeking her permission.

She leaned back onto her elbows. With both hands, he pulled her underwear from her. She lifted her hips to help, and he dipped his head to meet her. Her head rolled back. It had been a long time since 1996, and even then, these were two different experiences. How could he do so much with his lip, tongue, and fingers all at the same time?

She lost herself in his touch, in her passion, and her body gave in, wracked with pulses as she came hard against him.

"Yes," he said into her, his mere breath almost making her come again. "I want more." He rolled her over and pulled her to her knees before removing her dress. It slid up and over her, leaving her facing away from him and clad only in a bra. Which he quickly unhooked.

He reached for her breasts, caressing them while he laid gentle kisses along her shoulders and pressed his hard erection into the cleft of her ass. His amazing touch made her want to stop time and stay like this forever, until one hand roved down her belly and found her again. She gasped at the pleasure. The thrum of excitement started again, slower this time now that it had been sated once.

"Lean over the bed," he growled, firmly positioning her body. He spread her legs, still caressing her with his fingers. She felt his hot erection against her skin. "Is it okay?" he asked.

"Yes." She hadn't expected her voice to be so loud or so demanding. Yes, she wanted this. Damn. It felt good to say that.

She heard him rip open a condom package. After a moment, he slipped the tip of his cock inside her, then pulled out. He repeated the maneuver. She wanted all of him. She rocked her hips back the next time he entered her and pushed onto him.

"Ah, you want it."

"Yes," she said, her voice husky.

"You will get it, but you must be patient." He pulled away and before she knew it, his mouth was on her again, everywhere.

This had to be one of those moments when her eyes would roll back into her head and she would actually expire from pleasure. Soon he pushed back into her, so slowly. He didn't stop this time, and a long moan escaped her lips.

"When you make that noise, it drives me wild," he said, sliding out then pulling her hips hard onto him.

Captive in his embrace, she came again. He seemed to be everywhere—inside her, caressing her breasts, using those long, strong fingers to explore her body, gently biting her shoulder.

He lifted her from her knees. "Come," he said. He held her hand and led her around the bed, where he moved pillows and pulled back the covers.

Because she'd faced away from him, she hadn't seen him without clothes. His lean, cut body and huge erection almost sank her back to her knees. How had she found this man?

He laid her down and snuggled in beside her, kissing her, gliding his hands across her breasts. They responded, not tired at all. She glanced down at his cock. How did she want it again? But she did. She wanted to taste every inch of him and be as bad as possible tonight.

Chapter 15

Kate

Kate watched Lydia leave the hash bar, hoping she'd get everything she desired and hoping she'd be safe. She should probably follow her back to the hotel and listen for any trouble, but they'd been tied together so closely the past two weeks.

Free from Lydia, she enjoyed the buzz running through her veins in a new way, without the responsibility of ensuring Lydia had a good time. It also released her from the burden of being good herself. Without Lydia, she had the freedom to completely screw up her life after all those years of striving to succeed.

When the bartender returned from waiting on others, she asked for the bill. She'd enjoyed their discussion about the business and may have even provided a few pointers that might help with the American market. But she hated hearing herself drone on and on, spewing her ideas as if she still mattered.

"Thank you for your advice," he said. "I want to implement some of your ideas. May I have your email address in case I have questions?"

She had an electronic business card on her phone, but it went to her company. Where she no longer worked. No doubt they'd changed her password. Every email she'd sent now belonged to other people. That entire part of her life had been severed as if she'd lost an arm or a leg. Or her mind. She reached for a cocktail napkin. "Do you have a pen?"

After she'd paid and given him her dusty personal email, he handed her a cellophane-wrapped bundle. "This is our space cake, as a gift to you for your help. It is quite strong, so be careful."

Kate thanked him and left the bar. She had no idea which way to go, anywhere but back to the hotel. At least wandering the streets gave her mind something to focus on besides her own disastrous life. She meandered down a few different streets until she came across one with a narrow canal. The neighborhood looked mostly residential, and bicycles and flower boxes lined the water.

She found a bench facing the canal. She hated that she'd enjoyed her conversation at the bar. Finding creative solutions to business issues had been her favorite part of her job. For a moment that spark had reignited, although perhaps the weed played a role. Either way, she had to extinguish it. She would not go down that road again. She'd barely survived the first time. She hadn't wanted to survive, still didn't want to. Those jerks destroyed everything. She'd never set herself up for that again. Even thinking about it now ripped her in two.

She slid into the dark comforting thoughts about how they'd wronged her and destroyed her life. How she hated them, but hated herself worse because she'd set the very trap that ensnared her. How she didn't want to go on.

She took the space cake from the brown paper bag and opened the cellophane package. It tasted somewhere between banana and zucchini bread. She savored the cake, heavy with butter and sugar, but it quickly filled her. Halfway through, she couldn't take another bite. She wrapped it up again, stuck it in her purse, and continued her walk.

She eventually came to a busy cross street. On one corner, she spied the twinkling lights of an open business. The din of voices and clatter of dishes reached her from across the water. She crossed the bridge to investigate.

The words *wine bar* graced the awning. That sounded perfect. She'd drown her sorrows. Golden light spilled from the doorway, and she could already taste a deep red vintage on her tongue. It would cut through the cloying sweetness the space cake had left.

Inside, the wine bar smelled of wood paneling and warmth. She took a seat at the bar and quickly asked a blond bartender for the best red.

"Fruity or dark?" the woman asked in a strong accent. She had a pink-cheeked fresh-from-the-fields look that nicely offset blue eyes and platinum hair. Tall and svelte, she seemed to share DNA with all the other beautiful people in this country.

"Definitely dark and dry." Her wine selection perfectly described her emotions.

Kate quickly downed the first glass, then asked for another. Kate had started drinking in her teen years. She liked alcohol, self-medicated with it, but she had never craved alcohol before. Tonight, she couldn't get enough. She asked the bartender for a glass of water after her second wine to force herself to slow down.

The nausea came upon her quickly. She threw some bills on the bar and ran outside, barely making it to the edge of the canal before she started barfing. The violence of her sickness practically threw her to her knees.

She retched over and over, crawling to new spots to get away from her own filth. It made her cry, both from the pain of the exertion and from shame. What a wretched waste of a woman she'd become. A year ago, she'd been on top of the world, married to someone she loved, head of a company she'd built into a powerhouse. She'd been confident. Fierce. Now, on her knees and sick, she had lost it all.

And she never wanted it back, because having it back would open her up to this kind of pain again. Lydia couldn't understand that. Lydia had lived a half-life with her alcoholic, no-good husband. She had a chance to do it over and do it better. Kate would never reach the high she'd already attained. Even if she could, the fall was way too far.

She crawled to the edge of the stone bridge and leaned against it. The cold rock against her back made her shiver but also kept her more alert, a good thing now that wooziness had set in. She still heard voices from the open door of the bar. They were probably talking about her, the typical American who so clearly had imbibed too much. Perhaps they discussed how she'd been alone. No woman, except one clearly unloved and worthless, would go into a bar alone. She wished she spoke Dutch so she could understand their words, hear each strike of a sword against her character.

She heard new voices. Where were they coming from? Footsteps also? Was someone coming to get her? Did they know how horrible she was? She pressed her back into the bridge and pulled her knees close. The footsteps came closer, passing right above her. She held her breath, hoping she wouldn't be heard. The steps and voices faded away.

She should leave, but she had no place to go. An image of the hotel lobby entered her mind. She had no idea where it was and didn't want to be there. People there would know something was wrong with her. If not the desk clerks when she walked in, then Lydia.

Fear enveloped her. She was lost, and she worried about the people on the bridge finding her. The once gentle night grew darker, became ominous. Something bad was going to happen. She scooted down a few feet to a tree planted beside the bridge. She wedged herself as best she could between the tree and cut stones. Hopefully, no one would find her here.

Chapter 16

Lydia

Lydia stirred, snuggled deep in a down comforter. She couldn't remember ever sleeping so well. As her brain crawled out of the fog of slumber, her body awoke, reminding her of the prior night. Zander! She lifted her head and surveyed the room. No Zander. He must have left sometime in the night.

She rolled over in the plush bed, scene of a glorious night. Her body, fully sated, stretched along the king-sized bed. Pale, early morning light filtered in through sheer curtains. She'd need a nap later, but right now, she wanted to savor the morning.

She called room service and ordered coffee. She ran her hands along the soft skin of her arms. Who knew her body could be such a place of pleasure? Even alone in the room, she blushed at the memory of some of the things they'd done. Things she'd read of but never been brave enough to try. Every step of the way, Zander had asked her if she wanted to, if what he did was okay. They took it slow, and it was far better than okay.

She pulled on a silk kimono, the fabric gliding over her tender breasts. Standing at the window overlooking the canal, she found the world changed. The sun shone softer while flower boxes and bicycles glowed with color. She would never again settle.

A knock at the door interrupted her thoughts. She let in a hotel worker with coffee in a lovely silver urn. Lydia poured a cup and added cream. Delicious. Everything was delicious.

Her stomach grumbled, but she ignored the hunger and opted for the pleasure of a bath. She poured the hotel sample of body gel into the tub to create bubbles, then soaked in the steaming water. A whole world of pleasure had opened to her, and she wanted to enjoy every drop.

She soaped up all the places Zander had touched, tried to recall each caress and write it onto her mind so she'd have it forever. Before the water cooled, she left the tub and dried herself with a plush towel. She glanced in the mirror and noticed red, tired eyes. Entirely worth it.

She put on her prettiest wrap dress, feeling as beautiful as the fabric. She slathered on lotion and face cream, dotted her lips with a colorful lipstick and searched for her earrings.

She usually left them on the nightstand, but they weren't there. She opened the drawer in case she'd slipped them in there. She checked her suitcase, then her purse. That's when she noticed the missing money. No, not again.

She raised a hand to her throat, then ran into the bathroom and checked all the drawers and her toiletry bag. Last night, Kate had lent her a gold chain with a beautiful yellow sapphire the size of a fingernail. It had gone with her dress. It had also gone with Zander, along with her earrings and money.

How could a middle-aged woman be so naïve? As ashamed as she was to tell Kate about the necklace, she needed to get it done. Hopefully, she'd understand. When Lydia had left her at the hash bar, she'd thought Kate looked better than she had the entire trip. Maybe talking business with the cute young bartender had revived some of what her friend used to enjoy about life. She hoped so. Lydia supported anything that would help Kate move on from the dark place she'd inhabited lately.

She knocked at their adjoining door, but Kate didn't respond. She found Kate's key-card in her purse, one of the things Zander hadn't stolen. She grabbed her bag, determined to go downstairs for breakfast after she spoke with Kate. Whether from the pot or the great sex, she craved a hearty meal.

She knocked on Kate's door before entering with her card. Her mood plunged when she saw the untouched bed. Kate hadn't been at the hotel last night. For a second, Lydia hoped she'd gone home with the young bartender. But she couldn't believe in pipe dreams. This was Madrid all over again.

She sank into the room's leather chair, head in her hands. Everything turned toward disaster once again.

But it hadn't. She lifted her head. This thing with Kate had happened before, and they'd get through it. Perhaps the wonderful sex had unkinked some of her maternal worry.

An aftershock of last night's passion pulsed through her body. Even though she'd been robbed, Lydia wouldn't have given up her night with Zander for anything. Hell, she'd have paid him far more than he took to learn what sex could be. For the first time, she understood her own passion and needs. It had changed her.

Her thoughts returned to Kate. She needed to find her and then take her back to the US and make sure she started treatment. Unless she'd succeeded in killing herself. If she had, Lydia would have to live with that for the rest of her life. She'd left her friend to go have sex with a stranger. Her friend who needed her. Her friend who might be dead.

She resolved not to melt into a puddle of tears. Instead, she had work to do. She texted Kate. No response. Maybe she would find Kate in a hospital. Perhaps Kate would walk into the lobby looking like death the way she had in Madrid. Lydia might have to walk the streets all day, searching for her friend. She didn't even know where to start. Panic surged through her, wiping away any remaining joy.

She took the elevator downstairs and started toward the check-in desk, in case Kate had changed rooms without telling her, or perhaps the attendant had seen her friend.

She glanced into the restaurant, wondering if she could get something to go. Kate sat at one of the tables. She looked like a junkie. Skinny and dirty, her hand shook as she tried to bring a mug of coffee to her lips.

Sorrow at seeing how truly dreadful her friend appeared fought with rage over having to deal with this again. Rage won. She couldn't make any headway with Kate. She directed her anger inward. Of course she couldn't. She'd taken her friend off on a lark somehow thinking that she, someone with no training whatsoever, could heal her friend. Well, she'd had enough.

She stormed over to Kate. "What the hell? I can't believe you did this to me again."

Kate looked up with troubled red eyes and a ghostly pallor. Coffee sloshed from her cup and soiled the pristine tablecloth. Kate set the mug down with a trembling hand. "Sorry. I had a really hard night."

"We're going home as soon as I can arrange the flight. I will not deal with this anymore." Lydia crossed her arms in indignation.

"Please sit down." Kate gestured to the chair in front of her. "And please stop yelling at me. It hurts."

"I am not yelling." Lydia decreased her volume to a harsh whisper and sat. Kate needed real help, or she would end up dead. My god. The doctor had told her that weeks ago. Why hadn't she listened?

"Were you out there searching for death again?"

"No." Kate wrapped her fingers around her coffee as if to warm her hands. "The bartender from the hash bar gave me some space cake. I think I ate too much." Kate shivered, as if from a bad memory. "Then I stupidly went to a wine bar and drank several glasses of red that I thought tasted lovely at the time, but I couldn't handle it. Even thinking about it now makes me want to barf. I think I had a really bad trip."

"Where were you? You didn't sleep in your bed last night."

"No. I didn't know how to get to the hotel. I was so out of it. I spent the night crouched between a tree and a bridge. I kept thinking people were coming to get me. It was kind of terrifying."

"Oh, my god, Kate. I should never have left you." Guilt replaced fury. Kate's experience sounded horrible. Lydia had feared something like that happening when Kate first brought up the hash bar.

"No, you should have left me. It was a stupid mistake. I had no idea how I'd react to the cake. I think you're supposed to do stuff like that in the bars so they can keep an eye on you. I threw the rest of it out on my way back to the hotel. No more drugs for me."

"That sounds like a good plan."

A tear snaked down Kate's cheek. "I'm so sorry. I didn't mean to scare you. I wouldn't have done that on purpose. Not after Madrid. I promise I won't even drink again for the rest of our trip. I think I've been scared straight."

"Nice eighties reference. I will put you in jail if you do this again. Psychotherapy jail. Which, I believe, you need to go to anyway."

"At the end of our trip, I promise." Kate lifted the coffee again, took a sip without spilling. "Hey, tell me about last night. What happened with you and the hot guy?"

Lydia wasn't sure where to start or how far to go. Heat rose into her cheeks just thinking about Zander. Then she remembered he'd stolen from her. "You won't believe what happened. I had the best night of sex in my life, and then he pulled an Amsterdam on me."

"What does that mean? And congratulations."

"He stole my money, my earrings, and I'm so sorry, but he stole your necklace. The one you lent me."

"But he didn't hurt you?" Kate's look sharpened. Lydia had seen that look before. The fighter in Kate wanted to defend her friend.

"Only when I wanted him to." Lydia couldn't suppress her smile. "I swear it was worth it. Even the humiliation of being robbed. He was amazing."

"Oh, my god. You have to tell me everything."

"There is no way I'm telling you everything. But I promise you, I am never compromising again. I had no idea my body could feel that way. I was beautiful and sexy and powerful. I mean, at this age, who knew?"

"You are beautiful and sexy and powerful. I'm thrilled for you, but we should talk to the authorities about this. I don't care about the necklace, but that guy probably pulls that stunt on lots of women."

"No." Lydia shook her head. "I want to live with the pleasant memories of last night, not drag out the shame part of this. I'd like to think of it as payment for services rendered."

Kate giggled. "Man, those must have been some services for Miss-by-the-books not to want to punish him. Should we warn the coffee shop?"

Part of her wanted to keep everything about Zander locked away in a treasure chest. But Kate had a point. "How about after a shower and a nap, you tell the coffee shop about him? After that, whenever we talk about Zander, I want it to be about his finer qualities."

"I take it his finer qualities were pretty large?" Despite how bedraggled she looked, Kate's eyes sparkled.

"It wasn't that, or at least it wasn't only that. That man's finer qualities included his lips, his tongue, his fingers." Lydia fanned herself with her hands. "I can't talk about this. But you were right. I had settled, but partly because I had no idea what I'd missed. An education is a wonderful thing. Also, I need to order breakfast. I'm starving."

Once they'd ordered, Lydia brought up the trip. "I really think we need to go back to California, and you need to start treatment."

Kate started to protest, but Lydia raised a hand to stop her. "I know last night was a mistake; I believe you about that. But I'm not equipped to give you the help you need, the help you deserve so you can get better. I was terrified when I saw you hadn't slept in your bed last night." Lydia bit her lower lip, trying to keep the tears from spilling down her face.

"I'm sorry, really I am."

Lydia raised her hand again. She needed Kate to understand how her antics affected Lydia. It wasn't only about Kate anymore.

"If I had left my best friend in a bar to go have sex with some stranger," she gasped for air. "If you had ended up dead when I knew you had a problem and shouldn't be left alone—that would ruin me. This isn't just about you. If you die on my watch, then I won't have a life worth living either."

Kate dropped her head into her hands and didn't move. A wave of exhaustion from the stress and lack of sleep swept through Lydia. She loved her friend, and the trip had been great in many ways. It had showed Lydia how much of her life was truly left, and how much she'd missed out on in the past. But the downside risk was unthinkable.

A waiter set down plates of eggs, pancakes, a bowl of fruit, and a selection of pastries. They'd over-ordered in their hunger. Kate hadn't moved, but Lydia started eating, ravenous.

"I'm so sorry for what I've put you through." Kate's voice barely rose above a whisper. "I understand how you feel. Believe me. I understand how unfair this has been." She took her fork and stabbed it into scrambled eggs.

They ate as if they'd walked forty miles in the desert without food. Lydia had thought they'd ordered too much, but it ended up being just enough. She'd never been so hungry. Neither of them spoke during the meal, except to ask for more coffee.

Lydia sat back, hands across her stuffed belly. "I'm going to need a nap today."

"Me too. But first I've got to shower." Kate lifted her arm to her nose. "I stink."

"You don't look so great either. Let's call this a rest day, and I'll try to schedule our flight back to L.A. for tomorrow or the next day."

"I've got a request that I'd like you to consider, but in the end, it's your choice."

Lydia's worry meter turned on. Kate wanted to talk her out of going home. "What is it?"

"We were supposed to go to Bonaire next. It's on the way to L.A., and I'd like you to think about keeping it on the agenda before we go home. Last night was really hard, and I would love to dry out on a warm beach. I promise, no alcohol, no drugs, no disappearing."

The island of Bonaire had cactus and warm breezes, and Lydia felt its pull. It had no big cities, hash bars, or other ways to get into trouble. At least it hadn't thirty years ago. Although Kate seemed to find trouble everywhere. "I don't know. We should probably just go home."

"Just think about it. No rush. It sounds so quiet and peaceful compared to Los Angeles. But again, it's your decision. You can also pull the plug on our trip anytime you want. I haven't been fair to you, and I'm sorry."

Before she made any decision, Lydia needed sleep. She wanted to decide in light of the person she'd become over the last two weeks, not give a knee-jerk reaction from the woman she used to be. "I'll think about it. Let's sleep today and meet in the lobby at seven for dinner. I'll give you my decision then."

Chapter 17

Lydia

The wheels of the plane touched down on a single-lane runway that seemed too narrow for the large, transatlantic airplane. The advantage of flying from the Netherlands to the Dutch Antilles in the Caribbean, was the almost direct flight. Just a quick stop in Aruba, and they landed at their destination.

They'd first touched down in Bonaire thirty years ago. Looking out the airplane window, Lydia saw that the island's main town had sprawled beyond its earlier borders, but the low-slung buildings hadn't changed in character. She'd feared high rises and posh resorts but saw none out the window.

"Are we in the same place we stayed last time?" Kate asked.

"Honestly, I'm not sure. I couldn't remember the name of that place, but this one looks the way I remember it, and you can scuba dive straight from the beach like we did before. I will say, this one definitely looks newer and more upscale.

"Maybe the original got too old, and they tore it down and built something new."

Lydia wouldn't take the bait. Talking about old things had grown boring. She felt younger than she had in years, almost as young as the first time they'd come here. Like then, she had her entire future in front of her.

The muggy Caribbean air hit them the moment they exited the airport. They found a taxi and gave the driver the name of the resort. As he left the airport and turned down the narrow two-lane road, Lydia felt like they'd flown back in time, not just to a different country.

Water puddled on the red dirt beside the road as if it had recently rained. Vacant lots were interspersed with walls hiding houses. As they drove closer to town, pastel buildings began to dominate the landscape. Lydia had forgotten the color scheme of the Caribbean island, but the yellows, blues, and pinks brought the memories back. Tasting the tang of salt in the air, she sank into the cab in relief, glad to be free of hectic cities.

She'd made the right decision in coming here. They'd finally relax. She imagined them leaving the island tan and healthy after days in the sun and a diet of fruit and fish. They could face their lives in Los Angeles after this respite.

The cab turned into the resort, and a man took their bags and led them into the lobby. The term resort belied the simplicity of the open space. Unlike the hotels in Madrid with their marble underfoot and suited attendants at the doors, here terra-cotta floors warmed the lobby and smiling faces beckoned them.

Déjà vu and a sense of ease swept through Lydia. They'd find peace here. The same friendly man who'd met their cab led them to their rooms. Kate stopped short on the cobbled path, and Lydia nearly ran into her.

"This is it. This is where we stayed last time. I recognize the fountain." Kate pointed to a tiled font overflowing with water.

"They've definitely spiffed up the place, but you're right, that's the same fountain."

When they reached their adjoining rooms, Lydia wanted to cry with joy. The simple décor of tile floors and white walls opened onto small terraces with white sand and blue water beyond. She opened the terrace doors wide and stepped toward the sea.

Why had she waited so long to come back here? To go anywhere interesting? She missed Sophie and wished she'd brought her daughter to places like this when she had the chance, before Sophie set out on her own life.

She lifted a hand to shade her eyes and surveyed the bright white sand adorned with lounge chairs and a large hammock strung between two palm trees. An island ringed in white sand and topped by scrubby green brush squatted just offshore. It had been one of their dive sites on their earlier trip. That reminded her, she needed to tell Kate about the dive lessons in the morning. She walked out of her terrace and entered Kate's. Through the French doors, she saw Kate lying face down on the bed. She knocked on the glass.

Kate looked up and smiled, warming Lydia's heart, then she rose and opened the door. "This is fantastic." Kate walked onto the terrace, then out onto the sand.

"I love it here. I can't believe I never came back. Oh, and we have dive lessons at eight tomorrow morning."

"Why? We're already certified," Kate said.

"Well, it's been twenty-four years. I thought a refresher course was in order."

Kate turned to her friend. "You haven't been scuba diving in twenty-four years? But why? You loved it."

Lydia didn't have a good answer. Because she'd focused her life on her family and given up some of the things she'd loved? Because it was expensive? Because she had forgotten how many wonderful experiences existed in the world? "I don't know. I wish I'd kept it up."

"Mitch and I went on quite a few dive trips—the Red Sea, Great Barrier Reef, Belize." Kate turned back toward the ocean. "Although I think I'll like this better. We always went on high-end trips and stayed on fancy dive boats. Do you remember how much fun we had diving here? A couple of times we just walked in from the beach."

"I loved it. And, if I remember correctly, you loved the dive instructor."

"Oh, my god. Erik. I haven't thought of him in years. He was gorgeous. I wonder if he still works here?"

"Well, if he does, please don't do it in the hotel hot tub this time. That was disgusting. It's been almost thirty years and I'm still afraid of hot tubs."

Kate laughed. "I'm not sure I can make promises like that. Are you sure you want dive lessons? I can help you."

Lydia considered the question. She wanted to be brave, not stupid. Twenty-four years was a long time. "I'd really like the refresher. Please do it with me."

"You bet. Can we spend the rest of today lounging in the sun?"

"There is absolutely nothing I'd like more."

When they walked into the resort's dive shop the next morning, Lydia almost gasped. The man behind the counter wasn't Erik, but he was gorgeous. He looked like an ex-surfer who'd aged extremely well, a cross between Rob Lowe and an older Ryan Gosling.

"Holy shit," Kate whispered.

They introduced themselves and learned Pete's name and that he would be their instructor for the day.

"It's nice to meet you," Kate said. "We need a refresher course."

Lydia giggled at Kate's change of tune. Guys like this had been catnip for Kate back in the day. Bonaire had already exceeded her expectations and kept delivering.

Pete took them to the back deck and ran through the equipment, showing them how everything worked. The upgrades in dive equipment over the intervening years meant no more math or charts, which thrilled Lydia.

"Normally we do checkout dives in the pool, but since you ladies have scuba experience, why don't we go for an open water dive? We can walk in from the beach and stay in the shallows while I test you on everything. If it goes well, I'll take you on a little dive."

"We'd love that," Kate said. "Can we book you for dives over the next few days as well?"

"Certainly."

"Can we do a night dive?" Lydia asked, surprising herself. She'd been terrified about diving in the dark last time, but the strange creatures they'd seen had been worth it. She wanted this challenge, wanted to push herself to explore. She wouldn't be so scared this time around.

Soon, Pete led them out to the water. The air between him and Kate crackled with energy, and Lydia hoped she'd spend as much time alone on this trip as she did on their first one. Lydia seemed incapable of convincing Kate she had a bright future ahead of her. Maybe a gorgeous guy would have more luck.

Lydia had learned that lesson well. Hardly an hour went by that she didn't think about the things she and Zander had done. She needed more of that in her life, without the theft. Everyone did.

They walked into the water backwards because of their fins. That should have been a metaphor for something, but Lydia came up empty. She sank into turquoise water just cool enough to refresh. Pete gave them a quick pep talk and a few final rules. Stay with your partner, breathe slowly and regularly, have fun. Life lessons from a scuba instructor.

Lydia held on to her mask and dipped her head in the water, then stretched out in the luxurious blue and flicked her fins. They traveled across a sandy bottom toward a school of silver fish. Soon, corals appeared on the ocean floor. Sea fans waved gently in the current, spongy tubes reached toward the light, and a coral the size of a boulder mimicked the intricate patterns of the human brain. Or maybe the brain mimicked the coral.

She'd forgotten the magical world under the surface of the sea. Traveling horizontally, she floated alongside corals and came face-to-face with fish.

A green and purple parrotfish crunched on fire coral with its beaked mouth. It was one of the few noises to make it beyond the sound of her breath pulling air through the regulator and then releasing bubbles, her background metronome lulling her into an underworld calm.

She had missed so much, the feel of water caressing her skin, the vivid colors of the fish and coral, the certainty of being in a precious new world. She wished her tank of air would last forever, enabling her to stay in wonderland and not have to surface to her life on land.

Whatever else happened over the rest of her life, this would not be the last time she explored the depths of the ocean. She had to bring more meaning and more adventure into her life, starting today.

Ahead, Pete motioned to them to come, then pointed at a crevasse in the rocks. She saw something red moving through the coral, then her eyes focused on a gorgeous octopus. Honestly, she could die happy now.

They swam on, with Pete pointing out the wonders of the sea as if giving a tour of an art museum. A thick green moray eel with needle-like teeth, a school of yellow and purple fish with long noses, and then, as they swam back to shore, a sea turtle. The reptile swam past them, and Lydia looked into its ageless black eye. She wanted to learn the secrets of the world this creature must possess. Her heart filled to overflowing.

The dive reconnected her with her life. As they rose from the water, pieces fell into place. She had stopped working too early. She needed to find a job, something to do to give her life meaning. The thought popped into her head, and she took it as truth.

In her twenties, she'd been desperate to find her future. Now, much needed to change in her life, but amazingly, she had the time and knowledge to make those changes. She hadn't had this confidence back then. She couldn't wait to talk to Kate. Hopefully, she'd had the same experience and could imagine a better future.

The resort's restaurant sat at the end of the pier, marking the dividing line between the sandy beach and the marina full of expensive sailboats. Lydia and Kate took a table at the edge of the open-air building where the view included families frolicking on the beach and boats gliding past.

"I'd forgotten how hungry scuba diving makes you," Kate said, digging into half an avocado overflowing with shrimp.

"Yeah, you looked pretty hungry while you flirted with Pete."

Kate took her eyes off the food and stared at her friend. "Well, he is extremely hot. And I signed us up for the night dive tonight."

"Wow, couldn't even wait until morning?" Lydia joked. "Actually, I'm glad you signed us up. I could dive every day. I forgot how much I loved this."

"Seriously, I can't believe you waited so long."

"Yeah, well that's going to change. Sophie's going to learn to dive at Semester at Sea. I'm hoping this can be something we do together."

"Great idea. I love that she's so adventurous. Have you talked to her lately?"

"Yes. *She* actually called *me* the other day. Talk about a reversal. She wondered why I hadn't been texting as often. I told her that I'd listened to her. She went to Semester at Sea because I smothered her with constant attention. Her words. I told her I wanted to back off and let her live her life."

Kate's hearty laugh cut through Lydia's smugness. "You mean you didn't tell her you were being rammed by a Dutch gigolo?"

Flames roared through Lydia's chest and licked at her cheeks. "My daughter will never know about that."

"I'm sure Sophie is off having plenty of escapades of her own. We did at that age." Kate cocked her head, and a curious look crossed her face. "You know, you might want to talk to her about the importance of speaking up for yourself and not settling, even in bed. Although I'd leave out the detail on how you learned that."

Lydia's arm hairs prickled at the thought. Although Kate had a point. Instead of bothering Sophie about every little thing, maybe she should focus more on the big issues.

"Maybe someday. It does feel good to let her go a little. After Joe died, I focused all my energy on that girl." Lydia sighed, realizing the mistake she'd made. "Looking back, I can see that I was bored and lonely and for some reason, I expected my daughter to fill that void. I wish I hadn't done that." The worry that she'd done irreparable harm to her relationship with her daughter had become a constant in her life.

"Sophie's going to be fine, and I'm sure Semester at Sea will be a great experience for her. Think about it, you love to travel and now you're instilling that in her."

"Well, she chose it, so she's instilling it in herself."

"Give yourself some credit. After all, if you hadn't been bothering her so much, she wouldn't have gone."

Lydia shook her head. "Kids. Believe me, they always put you in your place."

"Sometimes I wish I had kids."

The wistfulness in Kate's voice surprised Lydia. "You always told me you didn't want them. Like seriously, from elementary school until just this moment."

Kate sat back and crossed her arms. "Sometimes I look back at my life and wonder if I should have made different choices. If Mitch and I had kids, would we still be together?"

"Keeping a marriage together is a terrible reason to have kids. I've seen it happen so many times at work. A couple goes through a rough patch in their marriage and decides kids will solve that problem. I guarantee you, kids only magnify the problems in a marriage."

She wouldn't tell Kate she spoke from personal experience. Why give her friend another reason to dislike Joe? But Lydia had always thought Sophie's birth triggered the decline in their marriage. Until then, she had tolerated Joe's drinking and spending all weekend on the golf course. After Sophie, she had to work all week while breastfeeding and caring for an infant every second she was home. She had expected him to help out on the weekends, but for Joe, life never changed. He golfed all weekend with friends, and when she complained, he turned that into an excuse to drink even more. He whined that he needed to drink to put up with her nagging and the baby crying. Not that he hadn't been a good dad, but goddamn it.

She couldn't keep silent. She didn't have to tell Kate everything, but man, she wanted to air out some of this laundry. "When I breastfed Sophie, the doctor recommended I drink dark beer. Evidently, it helps with milk production. Joe sweetly purchased a six-pack of Guinness for me. I drank about half of one on the first day. The next evening, I went to look for the rest of that beer, and Joe had finished it for me, plus he drank the other five."

"Jesus. I love you, but that guy wasn't good enough for you."

"But he gave me Sophie."

"Yes, but next time, choose someone as amazing as you are."

If only words made it so—she sure couldn't. Maybe she'd start a new list for her perfect man, this one jaded by time and experience. First, no alcoholics. Second, they must have their own income. Third, no bores. She wanted someone who didn't sit around and watch sports all day every day. She liked the occasional football game and believed baseball crowned the spectator sports. But seriously, Joe watched whatever the screen showed. Jujitsu. Cricket. Endless talking heads commentating on who knows what. For fuck's sake, she needed someone who would read a book or go on a walk, maybe even go scuba diving.

That's the thing. You never knew what the tradeoffs would be. She wanted a man to give her the security she'd missed as a fatherless child. She'd ended up quite secure, living in the same house for decades. She'd wanted someone who wanted a child, and Joe had granted that best wish ever. But desires on a list at one age didn't stay relevant over the course of a life.

Time to change the subject. She'd spent enough time dwelling on her own issues. "Speaking of choosing, tell me more about your special interest in our dive instructor." Lydia waggled her eyebrows.

"He's definitely hot. Although, I haven't slept with anyone since Mitch."

The server arrived and dropped two plates on the table. Hamburgers, fries, and a half cup of shredded lettuce with an accompanying grape tomato.

"I'm going to inhale this," Lydia said, picking up a fry. "I know I'm usually not the experienced one in our relationship, but you should give it a go. I'm still having sex dreams about Zander."

"I'm thinking about it. We'll see how our night dive goes. There's a group dive on the other side of the island tomorrow morning. Should I sign us up? It would give me another reason to go by the dive shop."

"Definitely. I want to do all the diving I can while we're here. I'm making up for decades of lost time."

"Sometimes I feel that way too." Kate's sunny mood turned sour.

Lydia got it. If she'd known how her life would turn out, she might have made different decisions. But do-overs didn't exist in linear time. "We did the best that we could. We both learned some hard lessons. I'm going to do better next time." She banged the bottom of the ketchup bottle with the heel of her hand. Of course, the viscous red liquid flew out of the bottle, drowning her burger.

"Or, maybe I start my best life tomorrow," she said, glancing at the mess on her plate. Either way, don't let the chance with Pete pass you by. You had a torrid affair with our dive instructor the last time we were here. Do it again. Have some fun." And maybe that will remind you to live again. She didn't add the words to her sentence even though she wanted to. Hopefully, Pete would give Kate a glimpse of what the future could be.

Chapter 18

Lydia

Several days later, Lydia sent Kate off on a solo dive with Pete on the other side of the island. After the dive, Kate said they'd stop for dinner before returning. Lydia guessed she wouldn't see Kate until morning.

Lydia spent a luxurious afternoon reading on the beach. Instead of her usual romance novel, this book followed a woman as she cycled through South America. The ride sounded incredibly tough, but also awe-inspiring. The adventure spark already been lit by her recent underwater explorations grew into a flame.

Challenged by the competing desires of family, love, and adventure, she finally set the book aside and headed for the water. She wanted to tour the world and wished this trip would never end, but she'd been a homebody for so long now. As she sank into the water, she wished it would rinse away whichever part of her she needed to leave behind so she could create a bigger future. She couldn't be tied to home and family and travel the world. And as much as she wanted to, she couldn't afford to travel the world.

She swam as far out in the ocean as she dared. Further from shore, the water cooled and darkened. She treaded, a little afraid of what she couldn't see beneath her. They hadn't seen a shark on one of their dives, but of course they inhabited these waters.

A sliver of her wanted to swim back to shore as fast as possible and keep away from any danger. But some new part of her liked the thrill of forcing herself to tread water and face her fear of the unknown.

How could someone in their fifties want so much? She'd thought this kind of longing disappeared with youth. The wanting to do something great pressed against the fear of doing the wrong thing.

The longer she stayed in the water, still uneaten by a jagged-toothed monster, the more she realized she'd conjured the fear from her own imagination. Fear of the known, not the unknown, was the real terror. Her new desire to travel and the skimpy size of her bank account, the realization that she wanted to work but not in her old job, these things scared her. The ocean suddenly seemed safer than the land and her unknown, impossible to divine, future.

She swam back to shore, only because she didn't know what else to do. After showering, she considered ordering something to go from the restaurant and bringing it back to her room. She hated to eat alone. She always felt eyes on her, pitying the poor woman without a dinner companion.

Of course, if she didn't happen to find someone to spend the rest of her life with, she'd end up eating a lot of meals alone. Did she want to eat them alone in her house in front of the television, or did she want to get out there and enjoy life, try new places, and meet new people?

She forced herself to put on one of her pretty wrap dresses and lipstick. She would try. She might end up feeling self-conscious, but that wasn't deadly.

She strode into the hotel's open-air restaurant on the pier. She glanced at the families and couples in the dining room, then spied an open seat at the bar. An older man on the other side of the bar approached, and she tried on a friendly smile.

"Dinner or just something to drink?" the bartender asked with the soft accent of a local.

"Dinner. What do you recommend?"

"The mahi-mahi. It came in fresh this afternoon and is wonderful on the grill."

"That sounds fantastic. I'll have it. Thanks."

He handed her a menu, and she noticed his huge hands. Probably five or ten years older than Lydia, the thick-set man had balding gray hair and a dark tan. He wore a blue Hawaiian shirt with big-eyed fish swimming in every direction.

"Do you have a drink recommendation?" Lydia smiled at the bartender.

"Have you tried Cadushy? It's a liquor made on the island from cactus and lime. We make a cocktail with it called the Green Bonaire."

"Well, I definitely have to try that. My new mantra is to explore more, and what's more fun than exploring cocktails?"

"Coming right up." He turned to make her drink.

Lydia surveyed the restaurant more slowly. There were a few families, lots of couples, and several larger groups. As far as she could tell, she was the only single. But at least she had a nice bartender to talk to. Being out definitely beat sitting in front of the TV, despite the awkwardness.

"Are you from Bonaire?" she asked when he brought her drink.

"It's been over thirty years since I moved here. I lived and worked in Utrecht, but once I visited Bonaire, I knew I had to find a way to stay here."

"Utrecht is in the Netherlands?" Lydia asked. She knew Bonaire was part of Holland, but didn't know the cities there, other than Amsterdam. Thoughts of Zander's powerful hands flitted through her head, causing her to blush.

"Yes. I worked for a tool and die shop in my hometown. I was just a regular guy. Now I live in paradise."

"I wish I could find a way to live in paradise."

"I'm sure you can. Believe me, if a regular Joe like me can find a way, I'm certain you can."

A regular Joe. Her regular Joe would never have done something like this. Of course, she'd have thought herself incapable of it as well. Until this trip.

"Are you married?" she asked, noticing the ring on his finger.

"Oh, yes. Thirty-eight years. My wife wanted to live here also. She's a nurse, so she didn't have any trouble finding work on the island. We're both happy we made the move."

"That's interesting." Lydia tried to keep the envy out of her voice. This life sounded perfect. His country happened to have an island in the Caribbean, he wanted out of his boring job, and his wife supported his adventure. "You sound like a lucky man."

"Anyone can do it. You just have to stop wanting it and figure out how to make it happen. I've seen hundreds of people, maybe thousands, who think they'd love a life like mine. For some reason, they never pursue it."

"It's hard to change." She felt that down to her very toes. If she knew of some easy path forward where she could check a box for a different life, she'd do it instantly. Heck, she didn't mind working hard if she only knew where to start.

"What do you do for a living?" he asked.

"I'm a retired schoolteacher.

"That's wonderful. That experience can take you anywhere."

"Really?"

"Sure. We have travelers in here all the time, mostly young women, who teach English all over the world."

"Oh, well, I think the operative word there is young." Of course she knew about all the exciting paths open to teachers today. A young woman she'd mentored at her school had taught in Spain and Thailand before settling down and marrying her boyfriend in

Escondido. If opportunities like that had been as easy to come by when she was young, there's no doubt she'd have pursued them.

"I don't see what youth has to do with it. You've got a lot more experience teaching. It seems like someone like you would be in demand." He set a martini glass filled with a chartreuse liquid in front of her.

Lydia took a sip. "Delicious. I can taste the lime. I'm not sure about the cactus."

"It has a few other things in it." He took a shot glass from behind the bar and half-filled it with a green liquid in a triangular bottle. "Try this. It's pure Cadushy."

She sipped the liqueur. "Oh, it's sweet and light. Thank you." Her gratitude extended beyond the tasty beverage. He was right. She must have options. And she needed to at least explore them. Although, she wasn't quite ready to give up on her dream of finding love.

Chapter 19

Kate

Kate's wet skin prickled in the evening breeze. Pete tossed her a towel, and she pressed it to her body. She hadn't spoken a word since they emerged from the ocean. The sight of a giant manta ray gliding between them and the sand below had shaken her.

Many months had passed since she'd seen something so extraordinary in the world. Perhaps years had passed. Her life had become a movie in black and white recently, and suddenly, she saw color again. She shivered with the thought. The ray seemed like an omen of some kind, almost like it had told her she could finally be at peace.

"Are you all right?" Pete asked.

She nodded. Then, she dried herself with the towel and threw a sundress over her suit. She followed him to his van and got in the passenger seat, still thinking about the ray.

When Kate saw the food truck, it snapped her out of her reverie. She laughed. Someone had converted an old double-decker bus into a kitchen below with seating on the top level. They'd parked the bright red bus on a spit of land overlooking the ocean.

As eclectic as the bus, the menu included tuna sashimi on a bun and mango falafel. A constant stream of people flowed by, some driving and picking up to go orders, others walking from a nearby neighborhood.

When their order was ready, she and Pete climbed the narrow stairs to the bus's upper level and sat side-by-side, looking out at the turquoise sea.

"You're American right?" she asked Pete between bites of her sandwich. His Boston accent occasionally came through. "What brought you down here?"

"Well, the dive shop advertised for instructors a few months ago, so I threw my hat in the ring."

"Oh, I thought you lived here permanently. What did you do before you came to Bonaire?"

"I've been a dive instructor in the Caribbean for over twenty years. I tend to travel around quite a bit. Occasionally, I'll stay in one place for a few years, often only for six months. I love getting to know new places."

"Wow. That's an interesting lifestyle." She'd met a few ski instructors like him but found it difficult to fathom a career without security. "Did you always want to do this?"

"Not at all." He got up and moved to the seat in front of her, sitting sideways and stretching his legs along the seat so he could look at her as he spoke. "I graduated from Yale, then Wharton Business School, and then got my dream job at Boston Consulting. And I hated it."

"You're kidding." She tried to imagine him in a suit, but his tan skin and long hair wouldn't shape themselves into a corporate image.

"Nope. I spent all my time traveling, but unlike now, they flew me to exciting places like Cincinnati and Dallas." Sarcasm rang through his voice. "All day, I sat in conference rooms telling people what was wrong with their companies, even though I'd never run my own business."

Kate sat up straighter, bolstered by a memory of her fury at the consulting company the new board had brought in after she took her company public. They acted like she'd built the company from luck and prayers, not from solid experience. She'd fought most of the consulting company's recommendations, not because she didn't appreciate good ideas, but because everything they came up with stripped Indulge of what made it special.

Of course, the new board of directors, a bunch of old white guys, loved hearing the recommendations from the consulting firm's younger versions of themselves. That had been the beginning of the end, she just hadn't seen it.

If she could only go back in time and do things differently. She'd have found a different way to finance her company's growth besides listing it on the stock market. If she went back far enough, would she tell her younger self not to start the company that brought her success and joy but ended in heartbreak? Or maybe she'd have told herself to stay in Bonaire that first time she'd come. A boy fell in love with her back then and asked her to stay. But the world seemed too bright, the opportunities too vast, to be contained on one island.

"How did you decide to leave your job and become a nomad?"

"Nomad, I like that." He chuckled. "I went to Jamaica with my girlfriend in my twenties and went diving for the first time. That was it. I was in love, and not with the girlfriend. I figured if I became a scuba instructor, I'd still travel a lot, but I'd spend my days outdoors, and I'd never have to talk to Chuck in the finance department or Fred in marketing ever again."

"And has it turned out the way you wanted?" Did anything ever?

"Well, sometimes the customers drive me a little crazy, but usually not. They're on vacation, so they are in a far better frame of mind than a bunch of guys who don't know why their companies aren't profitable. Best thing I ever did was quit and move to the Caribbean."

His decision to leave the world behind seemed like an intriguing path she could have taken, but she had one additional question. "Do you ever get lonely?"

His smile brightened to one thousand watts. "Not really. I tend to meet phenomenally interesting people along the way. Like you."

She chuckled. What he lacked in subtlety he made up for in bravado. "You never wanted to settle down?"

He looked out toward the ocean, and she caught gold flecks in his hazel eyes. "I had one girlfriend after I moved down here. We lived together in Puerto Rico for several years. He brought his gaze back to Kate. "But we wanted different things. She wanted a family, and I didn't want kids."

"My ex-husband is about to have his first child with his new wife." She couldn't keep the hurt from her voice.

"Sounds like you dodged a bullet with that one. Unless you wanted kinds."

"No." She chuckled again, aware for the first time that this particular hurt had far more to do with rejection than ever wanting children. "I didn't want them, and he used to say the same thing." If she'd had kids, she wouldn't be able to make her own decisions about her future. She was free to be as selfish as she wanted to be.

"I'm impressed by how happy you seem," she said.

"What's not to be happy about? I get to live exactly the life I want."

"I guess. In your shoes, I'd want to own the dive company, not just work for it."

"Not me. I want to be able to pick up stakes whenever it suits me. Sometimes I want to leave, other times, I stay for a while. But it's always my decision."

Autonomy. That was the important thing. That's what her lifelong effort and struggle had bought her. She had the ability to make her own decision about her life. And she had made that decision. True, she had failed at it so far. And it scared her a little. Maybe more than a little. But the actions she'd taken that led her to this point in her life couldn't be undone, and she was too tired to start over. Besides. Her mother and aunt had both gotten Alzheimer's at sixty. She was fifty-two. The math wasn't in her favor.

Even if she wanted to start over, she didn't have the time. She didn't want to spend the rest of her years languishing. And above all, she didn't want to end up in some home, paranoid half the time, delusional the rest. Perhaps some small part of her thought this journey would change things, but retracing the steps of her youth had led her full circle.

Chapter 20

Lydia

The next morning, Lydia and Kate walked into town to meet their tour guide. As they approached the shop, Kate headed toward the row of Segways parked near the entrance.

"Cool. Are we riding these?" she asked.

"Absolutely not. Unlike you, I'm not trying to kill myself."

"Ouch. At breakfast this morning, you told me you wanted more adventure in your life."

She had said that, but she'd meant big adventure, not learning to ride some death trap while exploring the island. "I've never used one of those, and it doesn't look easy."

"It's not so bad. Mitch and I went on several Segway tours. We even did one ten minutes from home in Santa Monica." She grabbed the handlebars of the vehicle as if she wanted to get on.

"I know you've had about a million more experiences than me. But I have no desire to ride one of those things. We're on a private tour in that contraption." She pointed to a mint green vehicle that looked like the offspring of a bus and a golf cart.

"That looks fun too." Kate left the Segway and headed toward the open-sided cart.

A few minutes later, the vehicle meandered down a narrow two-lane road with the palest blue water a few feet to the left, where it eventually darkened to navy as the sea floor dropped. For a while, homes and other buildings hugged the coast. Soon, they reached unoccupied land, where the arid, desert-like viewscape stretched as far as the eye could see.

Suddenly, the landscape changed, and they entered the salt flats. The road became a thin line between the blue sea and the pink-tinged water covering the salt fields. The wind picked up, eerily lapping at the pink water while waves crashed on the opposite side of the road. Lydia shivered. It was as if she'd entered another place, another planet. She didn't remember being trapped between the lurid pinks and vibrant blues on their earlier trip. The wind blasted her face, and the salt-tinged air scraped her lungs clean. They stopped at a pier that crossed over the road before plunging to the ocean's surface and a large concrete dock. Gleaming white mountains of salt waited to be pulled over the pier and onto a ship bound for the United States, Europe, or Africa.

The far-flung destinations beckoned Lydia. The wind whispered in her ear. She could become someone different. Nothing held her back but her own fears and expectations. For the first time, she didn't want to go home. Ever. She wanted a new life.

She glanced at Kate, also staring out to sea. Did her friend have the same thoughts, or had she sunk back into hopeless images of death and destruction? What about Sophie? Had she left because she needed something bigger than what she had?

Was it Lydia's responsibility to save her friend or guide her now grown child? She'd thought so, the same way she'd shouldered the responsibility for her family when Joe quit trying. But today, standing on a windy spit of land, her heart filled with possibility and the desire to explore her own life.

She wanted to untether herself from the drudgery of saving Kate, who wouldn't fight for herself, and worrying about Sophie, who didn't understand the pain the future held. Lydia had carried the burdens of others from her earliest memories of tending to her emotionally fragile mother. Caregiver wasn't just a role, it was her identity, her security blanket. Who else was she? A tear wound its way down her cheek. It must be the wind in her eyes.

The guide called them back to the vehicle. Lydia reached for Kate's hand as the cart pulled back onto the road to continue the journey.

At the next stop, they saw a line of salmon pink atop a steel-gray lagoon. Flamingos. Lydia remembered them from their first trip. She wished she'd brought binoculars to identify individual birds, but they melded together as if someone had taken a paintbrush to the landscape and added them in.

"Look," Kate said and pointed toward the sky. Two pink flamingos soared above them, then landed in the shallow water a few yards away.

"Oh, my god, they're gorgeous." Lydia kept her voice low, afraid of scaring the birds.

"What are they doing?" Kate asked.

After landing, the birds had dipped their curved beaks in the water and began spinning in slow circles, moving their feet up and down in the shallow waters as if performing a dance.

"They are feeding," their guide said. "They use their feet to stir up the shrimp, then scoop them up with their beaks."

"It's beautiful." Lydia heard the words come out of her mouth, but she had lied. The way the birds spun in a circle with their heads down, fixated on only what lay beneath them, was a metaphor for her life. She had married and had a family, and when it disappeared, she'd been desperate to recreate it. Except maybe she no longer wanted that life. But she didn't want to be lonely. She couldn't imagine anything worse than being lonely.

A few minutes away, their next destination included a series of ochre huts on a stretch of coral next to the ocean. Yellow shame washed through Lydia. She remembered these buildings. The slave huts told of a past almost too horrific to remember. The salt had been produced by enslaved people, first natives of the island and then by those brought here from Africa.

How dare she think her life difficult? She'd envied Kate because she had the money to travel the world, but Lydia had a pension and would never have to worry about being destitute. She'd had every privilege, and the money that put her daughter through college carried that privilege forward.

Kate had already dropped to her knees and crawled inside one of the huts. Lydia followed. With bare floors and bare walls, the huts provided respite against the wind and sun, nothing more.

"Can you believe up to six people slept in these buildings?" Kate asked.

"Can you believe how lucky we are to have been born in a different time and place? We have everything, every opportunity, and I feel like I squander them all." Lydia's anger at herself swept through her body. She had to do more. Be more.

"You think you feel that way? I've squandered everything I ever built."

"Mitch left you. The board took the company away from you. Why doesn't that piss you off? It pisses me off. It makes me want something better for you. And I want to be better also. I want to live a better life. We've only got so many years left. I want them to mean something." The passion in Lydia's words rang off the walls of the tiny hut. She wished they would demolish it and create a new and better world.

"I'm glad that you want more from your life. You deserve that."

"No!" It was all she could do to keep from screaming. "I don't want more, I want to *give* more. Think about the people forced to live in these huts and work in the salt flats all day. What opportunities do their descendants have? Think about our country. So many of my students needed a stable home life or more food in order to learn. That's all they needed, and the richest country in the world wouldn't provide it. I have to make the world better this time around. I have to be better." Lydia's hands shook as if her emotions couldn't stay contained in her skin.

"Wow. That's impressive." Kate sounded depressed rather than inspired.

"You can do that too. You have so much opportunity to do good. You're smart, well-educated, you have money. You can still do great things if you choose to."

Kate deflated, the opposite of what Lydia had hoped. But the words were true. Kate could choose to make a real difference in the world. Instead of rising to the challenge, she sank to the floor and leaned against a wall of the hut.

"What if I gave you my money, and you did something good with it?" Kate's low voice barely reached Lydia.

"What?"

Kate repeated herself. Louder this time. Then she crossed her arms and sat up, challenging her friend to respond.

"You can't give me your money. Besides, this is an opportunity for *you*."

Kate stood, disappointment etched across her features. She crouched in the low space, moving toward the door. Before leaving she turned back to Lydia. "I don't want opportunities; that's your life. I'm giving you the opportunity to fulfill your dreams. You talk a good game but don't want the resources that can help you make the world a better place. If you decide you're serious about saving the world, the offer still stands."

Lydia couldn't scramble out of the hut fast enough. It threatened to suffocate her dreams. She didn't want to be Kate's charity case. She wanted to make a difference. She felt half-formed, caught between who she was and who she was meant to be. How was this possible at her age?

They were supposed to go back to Los Angeles. Lydia had said, Kate needed to get into therapy. Kate had said she wouldn't go. Maybe the best thing to do, for both of them, would be to continue their trip and fight through the impasse.

Four hours later and still seething with uncertainty, Lydia strode into the restaurant on the pier. She'd arrived thirty minutes early for her dinner date with Kate. She headed to the bar where the same thickset man poured drinks. Before he had a chance to say anything, she asked for a Green Bonaire.

"Coming right up."

She hadn't wanted to drink in front of Kate, since her friend had banned herself from drinking to help convince Lydia to continue the trip. But the day had left Lydia so discombobulated that she had to have a drink.

As soon as the bartender set the glass in front of her, she pulled as much of the citrusy green drink through the tiny straw as possible. What on earth was she going to do? She'd come on this trip to help Kate improve her frame of mind but felt like she was losing her own in the process.

"Hey, you're here early." Kate perched on the stool beside her. "I'll have a club soda with lime, she said as the bartender approached.

"Sorry, I wouldn't have ordered this if I'd known you'd get here early." Lydia meant it but also wished Kate hadn't shown up so she could enjoy her drink.

"No worries. I don't mind if you drink. After all, I was the one who tried to off myself with liquor and pills. You are free to drink anything you want."

Kate's blasé attitude didn't match the tension rumbling through Lydia. "I needed to take the edge off. There's something about being here that makes me question my past decisions."

"Like what?" Kate asked. "I mean, not that I don't understand. I question my past decisions every day."

Lydia smirked. Everything revolved around Kate. "Well, like we loved to travel. Why didn't I keep traveling? Why did I think there was only one way to live my life, the way everyone else does?"

"I don't understand. Who did you live your life like?" Kate turned on her barstool so she faced Lydia. The worry line between her eyes deepened.

Lydia sighed, one of the puzzle pieces falling into place. "My mom. I'm afraid I relived my mom's life."

"I still don't understand. Your life has been opposite your mom's. She divorced when you were young and then followed some guy to California as his mistress. You had a happy marriage that didn't end until your husband died."

"I know it sounds opposite, but it's really not. My mom always thought she should be married. My dad left her. As soon as she could, she pounced on another man. She always thought poor Ray would leave his family, but that was never going to happen."

"That's actually quite sad. Although at least her chasing Ray brought you to California. If she hadn't done that, we'd never have met." Kate reached out and squeezed Lydia's hand.

Lydia signaled the bartender for another drink. She'd never thought this deeply about the why behind her actions. She'd always been the good girl. Get married, have kids, become a teacher. Now that foundation had crumbled away. Where did that leave her?

"My mom spent a lot of time sad or angry," Lydia said. "She never got her American dream of the man, the house, the two point five kids. Instead, she had to work and always fell for the wrong guys."

Lydia sighed heavily as the past pushed its weight onto her shoulders. "I spent a lot of years angry at her for failing at family. It became my duty to do better. I wanted everything, the white picket fence, a husband who loved me, a kid to dote on. And I got it. I spent my whole life proving to my mother that I was better at family than she was, and never even asked myself if that's what I wanted."

"But you've been one of the happiest people I know, and it's not like you've had an easy life. If you screwed things up, then what hope does anyone else have?"

The bartender delivered another green cocktail, and Lydia took a long sip. She hoped the alcohol would cool whatever burned inside her. Where had all this frustration come from? "Maybe I just need to do things a little differently this time. I talked to that guy for a long time the other night." She nodded at the bartender. "He had some boring job back in the Netherlands, and he and his wife decided to move to Bonaire and live an adventure. His wife is a nurse on the island, so she not only gets to live in a tropical paradise, but she helps people every day. And when he talks about her, you can see the love in his eyes. Joe never talked about me like that."

"So, do things differently. You've got another shot. And I was serious about what I said earlier. Let me put the bulk of my money in a trust that you can use to make the world a better place."

Lydia struggled to hold herself together. Part of her wanted to burst into tears and tell her friend to stop making plans based on her death. Part of her wanted to strangle Kate. She could use her money today to make the world a better place without Lydia's help.

Lydia jumped off the bar stool. "I've got to go. Would you put the drinks on our bill?" She didn't wait for a response from Kate before she turned and left. She reached the room in seconds, pulled off all her clothes, then stepped into a bathing suit. A wild animal had been caged and sedated inside her, and something woke it up today. She wanted to rip it from her chest, except if she did, she'd go back to being the person she'd always been.

She left her room through the patio and crossed the sand to the water. The lights near the beach only made the sea darker. She shuffled her feet on the way in, hoping to scare away any low-lying creatures.

The cool water reached her knees, her thighs, her waist. It soothed the wildness inside. She dropped into the water until it covered everything but her head. She closed her eyes. How would this end?

"Hey, Lydia. Are you okay?"

She opened her eyes. Kate stood on the beach and unbuckled her belt. Lydia watched her remove each piece of clothing until she wore nothing but a bra and underwear. Then she waded in.

"I'm fine." Lydia didn't want help. She opened her arms wide in frustration and spun away from Kate. As her spin pushed the water, the edges of it glowed bright green. She cupped water in her hands, threw it, and watched the sparkles of light as the drops splashed into the sea. She spun again, faster and harder, pushing the water into a glowing wave. Laughter rang out as she spun again and again and again.

"Bioluminescence," Kate shouted, then her laughter joined with Lydia's. Spinning and dancing beside her, her best friend created her own light spectacular. Just when Lydia wanted to burn everything down, the world showed her its beauty. Why would you ever want to leave a place like this?

Lydia danced and spun and swam until her heaving breath made her quit. She dragged herself back on shore and dropped onto the sand. Kate followed, giving the sea one more splash of light at the water's edge.

"That was amazing." The wonder in Kate's voice matched the emotions running through Lydia.

"Gorgeous. Completely unbelievable." Something in the water freed Lydia to say the words she'd held back in the restaurant. "We're supposed to go back to L.A. next, and I don't want to. This trip is changing me, the way each of our trips changed us in our twenties. Only now, I'm more confused than ever about who I'm supposed to be and what I really want. But you need to get help. I hoped this trip would show you how great

the world is and how much opportunity is in front of us. But that's not happening."
She stopped, mid-rant. Nothing else she had to say mattered. Kate's outlook hadn't
improved, and now Lydia swirled in discontent about the future. She could only help
herself.

"You're right. I wish I could tell you I wanted to live, but everything's just so heavy
right now. I'm exhausted. I mean, I think I've caught up on sleep, at least in terms of
hours, but there's an invisible weight dragging me down. Most days I don't want to
get out of bed. Here, I love diving, so that gets me out. There's something about the
world down there that matches my mood. It feels like a better place for me than up here
where there are people. And memories."

"So, what are we going to do?" Lydia asked.

"I don't want to go back to L.A. either. That's where everything went wrong."

"I don't know that we have an alternative. I can't help you, but I also can't be
responsible for you. I can barely be responsible for myself right now."

Glasses and plates clattered at the nearby restaurant. Slips of conversation floated by,
but the air between them lay still. The flat sea hid its earlier sparkle.

"How did it get so bad?" Lydia asked.

Kate sighed. "It's not as recent as you think. I've always had a dark side. I just never let
it show. Mitch has seen it. I've done some bad things to myself. When I'm angry, when
the hate comes, I hit myself or bang my head against a wall. He hated that. Sometimes
I think he might have left long ago if he weren't afraid of what I'd do to myself."

The shock of the statement made Lydia's skin go cold in the warm air. "How did I
never know?"

"I didn't want you to know. I didn't want anyone to know. And it's not like it's
always there, at least not the really bad part. It comes in waves. It's hard to explain, but
the way I feel about myself isn't all bad. The anger in me drove me, made me succeed. It's
like a hidden sword or an unseen power source. I only turn it on myself occasionally."

"Oh, honey. I had no idea. I'm so sorry."

"Don't be. Normally, I can control it. After Mitch left and then those assholes took
my company away, that's when it got hard. It wasn't the company part that bothered
me. They took my identity away. All the good things the blackness had driven me to
achieve were no longer mine. So, the blackness took over."

Kate's trauma ran far deeper than Lydia had imagined. Her beautiful, confident,
successful friend was mired in something she couldn't escape. Lydia hadn't seen it. And

she definitely didn't have the tools to help Kate deal with such powerful emotions. But she'd do her best to be the friend Kate needed.

"I'm here for you, but as your friend, not your therapist. You must get help immediately. This is so big it feels like it could swallow us both whole."

Kate didn't speak, but her ragged, tear-driven breath surprised Lydia. She scooted closer and wrapped her arms around her friend. "Let's call Dr. Bhavnani in the morning."

Kate nodded her head and mumbled okay.

Chapter 21

Lydia

Lydia and Kate sat side-by-side on the huge jetliner as it left Flamingo International Airport. Kate had asked Lydia to change the original flights so they didn't have to stop in Los Angeles. She didn't want any ties to home now that they'd decided to continue the journey.

Lydia had agreed. She would have agreed to almost anything Kate asked, because she'd started therapy. Well, she hadn't exactly started yet, but she'd called Dr. Bhavnani and gotten a referral. She already had an appointment with Dr. Lin. Lydia had sat on Kate's bed while she made the call. She almost slapped herself in the head when she heard Kate mention online therapy. Kate could have been in therapy this whole time.

Evidently, the pandemic had made it so many therapists now worked via online video calls. She might have to have bloodwork done or go into the office if the psychiatrist determined she needed to treat Kate with drugs, but that would happen after they'd returned from their trip. Kate had scheduled her first meeting with Dr. Lin for their second day in Australia.

"I know I keep telling you this, but I'm incredibly proud of you." Lydia grabbed Kate's hand and gave it a squeeze.

"Thank you for agreeing to continue our trip. I'm not ready to go home." Kate squeezed Lydia's hand in return.

"Me either."

"Champagne?" A flight attendant approached them with a tray of bubbly drinks.

"Yes, please." Lydia glanced at Kate. They hadn't talked about the no alcohol rule. Lydia wanted to be generous. After all, Kate had made the appointment. "Have one," she said. "It's not like you can wander off and get in trouble in an airplane. Besides, it feels like we have something to celebrate."

Kate took a glass from the attendant, but her expression was grim. "Don't get ahead of yourself."

Lydia quieted. Just because Kate had made an appointment didn't mean a cure had arrived. But she had taken a step toward hope, and that seemed worth celebrating. At least it made Lydia want to celebrate.

She tried to put herself in her friend's mind. It would be so much work to get better. Kate would never get her marriage back. She'd never get her company back. Lydia told Kate great opportunities awaited, but Lydia didn't exactly believe that herself.

Every time she thought about her own future, it brought more anxiety than excitement. She needed to give Kate a break and let her figure things out for herself. If she were Kate, she wouldn't want a Lydia hanging on everything she did, judging her, making rules. And at the same time acting weird about things.

She needed to see Kate as an equal, not as the person she looked up to as a model of success, and not as a project. "Hey, I'm sorry about how crabby I got at the bar and in the water the other night. It wasn't my best moment. I was kind of freaking out about the future."

Kate clinked her glass against Lydia's. "Believe me, I get it. I wish you weren't so worried about it. You've worked hard your whole life. You need to enjoy whatever's left."

"Well hopefully, there's a lot left. And I will find a way to enjoy it. But I don't see a clear path right now. A few weeks ago, I'd have told you that as long as I found a husband, everything would be great."

"What if you don't find the man you're looking for?" Kate asked.

"I'll keep looking until I do. Although, I think I'll have to move. All my friends in Escondido were Joe's friends as well. Besides, I know everyone in those circles, and there's no one promising. I need to be someplace new and different. Hopefully, I'll meet someone on this trip." Hopefully wasn't a strong enough word. Desperately was more like it. That had to be what fueled this new anxiety. Each country they visited meant one less to go, her chances diminishing with every plane ride.

"Lydia, I know you hate talking about this, but can I please give you some of my money? Maybe enough to keep you traveling for the next few years."

Lydia shook her head no, pulling away from Kate. She had to stop talking about this. It would make it easier for Kate to leave her if Lydia was taken care of financially. That wasn't what she wanted from this friendship. She wanted the living breathing Kate, not a bank account filled with her money.

"Please. Listen to me." Kate's voice had tinges of desperation. "I have so much more money than you realize. I could give you a million dollars, plus whatever taxes you'd pay on that, and it wouldn't make a dent in my account. You could invest that in something safe that threw off five percent a year. That would be fifty thousand a year in spending money and you wouldn't touch the principal. Use your pension to live on and the other fifty thousand to travel."

"I can't do it. I want you, not your money."

Tears flooded Kate's eyes, threatening to fall. Lydia had rarely seen her friend cry. But the Kate beside her now was not the girl from her youth or the corporate maven from even a year ago. This sad and broken Kate was someone new.

"Everyone has turned their back on me. Everyone but you. You came running when I was hurt. You've stayed with me every day since then, even when I pushed you away. Whether I live to be a thousand years old or die tomorrow, the money means nothing to me. It could buy you the life you want." The tears spilled over, and Kate put her palms to her face.

With her friend bent over and silently sobbing, Lydia struggled to respond. She rubbed Kate's back, hoping it comforted her. She couldn't take the money, didn't want to. Of course, she wished she never had to worry about money again, but that wouldn't resolve her issues. And it would lead to guilt.

Somehow, she needed to figure out her future herself. Kind of the way Kate had to.

Chapter 22

Lydia

"Why did we take a cab to downtown Melbourne; I thought you reserved a hotel in St Kilda?" Kate snapped the question at Lydia.

Even in first class, the incredibly long flight had worn on both of them. Kate had deep dark circles under her eyes to go with her grumpy demeanor. Lydia pushed on, despite the jetlag dragging at her. She wanted only one thing more than a shower.

"There's one place we have to visit first. I've been dreaming about it for decades."

They stood on a busy sidewalk, with cars whizzing past. A streetcar line bisected the road, and the red brick train station sprawled on the far side. Lydia looked at the GPS map on her phone. The cab had dropped them off one block early. "Come on. This way." She darted across a side street with only a few seconds left on the walk timer.

"Whatever," Kate muttered, following her. "Oh, my god. I know where you're going. We're getting hot jam donuts!"

Lydia turned and smiled, then rolled her suitcase right up to the street corner counter. "Two hot jam donuts please."

She handed one of the warm donuts to Kate before savoring her own. A dusting of sugar coated the outside of the pastry and a speck of jam marked one side. She bit into it, and the flavor of warm strawberry jam exploded in her mouth. Suddenly she was twenty-six years old, on an adventure on a hot Christmas Eve. She'd stood on this very street corner eating a donut from this exact store. For all she knew, the same man had served her.

Lydia's emotions roiled the way they had that first time. Back then and now she had taken a risk with no clear future in place. She'd gotten on a plane with a thirst to learn more about the world and meet interesting people.

They'd loved Australia that first time, visiting Sydney and Melbourne before finding St Kilda a few miles down the coast from Melbourne. The Australians partied on the beach and in nearby pubs all day long, and Lydia and Kate made friends they thought they'd keep forever.

Christmas evening, they'd been invited to dinner at a house filled with people their own age. The celebration was as far from the relative-filled formal Christmas dinners in the States as the US was from Australia. They danced and partied with their new friends. People arrived with dishes of food and meat seared on the grill. It was a magical holiday spent in an alternate universe. Everyone spoke a version of her language, and mostly looked and dressed the way she did, but something was lighter here, and much more fun. Maybe she should have stayed.

"That donut was orgasmic," Kate said. "I can't believe you remembered this place."

"Best donut I ever had. Now, let's get on the streetcar to St Kilda. Best town ever."

They made their way across the street to the light rail and got on a modern car heading toward the beach. It whisked them past homes, parks, and stadiums, and then along the blue water of the bay.

"My god, it feels like coming home," Kate said.

"I was thinking the exact same thing. Maybe we should have stayed here back then."

"Life doesn't give you do-overs."

"Maybe we should stay here now." The words popped out of her mouth before she thought about them, but suddenly it opened up new possibilities. She wanted adventure, and she wanted a place to meet new people. She didn't speak a foreign language with any proficiency. "This might be the perfect place to start over."

Kate looked at her, rubbing her bottom lip the way she did when deep in thought. "It might be a decent place for you to start over, if that's what you want."

Had Kate excluded herself because she didn't like Australia, or did she not think she'd be around that long? Lydia decided not to address it. Kate had a therapist now, and the therapist had to help her. Lydia was not responsible for saving her.

They exited at the St Kilda stop. The central part of the town hadn't changed much. Bakeries, cafes, and ice cream shops lined the main street, similar to other beach towns across the world. Lydia led the way to their hotel, a few streets off the main drag.

"Well, this isn't exactly the same level of hotel we've been staying at," Kate said, stopping on the sidewalk outside a nondescript building.

"There weren't a lot of options in St Kilda. Remember, we stayed in a youth hostel the first time we visited." Lydia had worried about the hotel from the moment she'd booked it. They'd paid hundreds of dollars per room at the other hotels they'd stayed at, and this one had been a deal at eighty dollars. It looked like they'd get what they'd paid for, which might not be up to Kate's standards. But they'd arrived, and Lydia was far too tired from the trip to try to find them something else. "Let's give it a try tonight, and if you hate it, we'll move tomorrow."

"I'm sure it will be fine." Kate sighed like she just didn't care.

A flash of anger ran through Lydia. She'd planned the whole damn trip with little help from Kate. If Kate wanted something different, she should have done it herself.

Lydia kept her mouth closed and examined her anger. Joe never planned anything either, maybe because Lydia jumped into that role before anyone else had the chance. Joe also always showed up with long lists of complaints. Kate wasn't that person and had set clear standards. Lydia's anger stemmed from tiredness. She needed to keep her mouth closed. She rolled her bag up the cement ramp, pulled open the glass door to the hotel, and checked them in.

"You can buy soft drinks, booze, and snacks at the check-in desk." Lydia called down to Kate who remained just inside the hotel door as if afraid the basic utility of the place might infect her.

"Come on," Lydia said as she handed Kate a room key. "I know this place isn't fancy, but it will do."

They took the slow elevator up to their rooms. Lydia's stomach sank as she opened the door. Kate would hate this place. Her narrow room held one double bed and a small table that doubled as a desk and nightstand. The linoleum floors and walls without artwork hued the same shade of beige. For some reason, the bathroom had a six-inch step up at the entrance, which would be tricky to negotiate in the middle of the night. At least windows lined the back wall. Lydia pulled the curtains back to view a muddy parking lot, a dirty pickup truck its sole occupant.

She braced herself for complaints and went next door to Kate's room. "It looked nicer online."

"It doesn't matter. I need some sleep. Can we meet up in the morning?"

"That sounds great." More than anything, Lydia wanted a full night's sleep. She couldn't complain about the first-class cabin's lie-flat seats, but she'd binge-watched movies instead of sleeping. The salty food had left her bloated, and she craved nothing more than a gallon of water, a real bed, and eight hours alone.

Under the covers, she longed for the silky sheets and cushy mattresses of the earlier hotels. It had taken so little time for her to become soft, to crave luxuries she could never afford in her real life.

She tossed and turned most of the night on the bed absent even the pillow-top from her home bedroom. The next morning, she needed a strong cup of coffee and a relaxing day at the beach.

She texted Kate. *I'm up & need coffee, can I bring you something?*
Already up. Meet downstairs in 10.

A quick thumbs up, then Lydia pulled herself from bed. Puffy dark smudges formed half-moons beneath her eyes. She dabbed on concealer, then applied eyeliner and lip gloss. She still looked particularly haggard.

She closed her eyes and remembered Jordi from Madrid and Zander from Amsterdam. She wouldn't always love what she saw in the mirror, but others had found her attractive and vibrant. So, she was. This trip had given her truths she'd hold on to as she aged.

Downstairs, Kate looked about as rested as Lydia.

"I'm sorry the hotel isn't up to snuff," Lydia said as they walked toward the center of town. "I so wanted to be in St Kilda, and there weren't a lot of options."

"It's fine. I appreciate you doing all the planning. We had a fantastic time here once. Some of my best memories are from that Christmas. Let's try to recreate that today."

"That's a deal."

The coffee shop they wanted to try had a dozen people in line at the pickup window. Lydia took her place in the back of the line, while Kate wandered to the front and went inside.

"Hey, Lydia, come here." Kate waved to her from the door.

"You can sit inside as long as you order food, and I'm starving."

They sat at a hand-hewn wooden table topped by a small vase containing three Gerbera daisies. Soon they had mugs of delicious coffee in front of them along with a tequila bottle repurposed to hold fresh water and two glasses.

"This is more like it," Kate said as the server set plates of crusty bread topped with avocado and fried egg in front of them. "Today's going to be a great day."

"Agreed. Let's spend it at the beach and then maybe come back here for an early dinner and cocktails."

Nine hours later, they returned to St Kilda's main drag. They found seats at an outside table near where they'd eaten breakfast. They ordered burgers and ice-cold beers.

"The beer is the best part of this day since this morning's coffee." Lydia had hated the day at the beach. She hadn't remembered it being so crowded. Families with screaming kids threw down towels mere inches from theirs, and teens trolled the sand looking for excitement they'd never find. Lydia usually liked kids, she was a teacher after all, but today it had just been too much. She'd expected refreshing water like that in Bonaire, but the bath-warm brew inside the bay failed to cool her off.

She'd looked forward to this day at the beach for weeks. She and Kate once spent almost an entire week lounging on the exact same beach. Then it had seemed new and exciting, something at the opposite end of the world from home. Today, it had seemed as old and worn out as she.

"The beach wasn't the way I remembered it. I felt so old." Kate took a long swig from her pint glass. "Thanks for letting me drink again, though. This is delicious."

"Your behavior is between you and your therapist. It is tasty beer, although I'll stick with a glass rather than that thing." She pointed to the next table over where two couples in their twenties drank from a tube-like contraption that had to hold at least a couple of pitchers worth of beer.

"Have you noticed we're the oldest ones out here?" Kate asked.

Lydia surveyed the other tables. Many restaurants had pulled tables into the pedestrian street where they sat. Kate was right, everyone else looked like they were in their twenties, at the oldest. Lydia heaved out a sigh. Everything about this place bothered her. The hotel sucked, she hadn't fit in at the beach, and now the center of town, which she'd remembered as cute, instead appeared kitsch and touristy. And absolute children surrounded her. She'd wanted something different from this vacation. "I'm definitely not going to meet the man of my dreams here. His kid maybe, but not him."

Just then, one of the foursome at the next table shouted. "One, two, three, drink!"

The kids chugged their beers and one of the guys belched loudly.

"I feel like I'm at a frat party," Lydia said.

"Yeah, although it's kind of amusing. And it's nice to sit here in the shade. Let's have one more beer before we call it a night."

Lydia agreed, but before they'd finished their next beers, the rowdies at the adjacent table, who'd moved on to their next tube of beer, called for an impromptu wet T-shirt contest. The two girls at their table started dancing to the ambient music. Lydia thought it was something by Taylor Swift or maybe Katy Perry. She'd heard it before, but it hadn't made it onto NPR or the audiobooks she usually listened to.

"I wonder if they knew this was going to happen," Kate asked. After all, both the young women managed to show up braless and in thin white T-shirts.

Someone procured a pitcher of water, and the women shared it, squealing as the liquid doused them. They pulled their shirts tight and danced, tits at attention, while the boys cheered and shouted.

Lydia couldn't believe it when two women came over from different tables and joined the contest. More water. More lithe hands running across taut bodies. More perky, bouncy bosoms.

"There is absolutely nothing in the world that can make you feel older than a wet T-shirt contest," Lydia said. All those young boobs made her want to scream in outrage and cry in despair at the same time.

"Can we please pay the bill and leave? I beg you." Kate laughed, which was far more generous than Lydia wanted to be.

They walked back to the hotel, ready to put an end to the day. A blackness descended on Lydia. Perhaps things didn't get better from here.

"St Kilda was supposed to be great. I used to love it so much, and I actually hoped I'd figure out the rest of my life on that beach. Until I went there. If I'm honest with myself, I think I believed I might find someone in Australia. Remember how badly we wanted to stay the first time? I thought . . . oh, I don't know, like maybe there was a life waiting for me here."

It took Kate half a block to respond. "I totally get it. St Kilda seems different, shabbier than I remember. Maybe I'd still love it here if I were twenty-six again. But I'm in my fifties. I don't like it here, and I don't want to stay."

Lydia bit her lip. She hated giving up, on things, or people. But she didn't want to stay either. "Should we go to Costa Rica earlier than we'd planned?"

"Oh, I don't know. We've made it all this way. Let's find someplace else in Australia. Someplace we'd love.

"I'm game for that."

"Let's figure it out tomorrow. I've got my call with Dr. Lin in the morning. Let's stay here one more night and figure out what's next after that.

"That sounds good," Lydia replied, although she wasn't sure it did. She worried Australia was too close to home, culturally, to satisfy her desire for adventure. Something in her DNA had changed, or perhaps she'd buried her true self for so long that, once it was out, her lust for the new and different had taken over.

Chapter 23

Lydia

"Airlie Beach." Kate said, sitting down at the Mexican restaurant across the street from their hotel. "You know, eating tacos in Australia means we're not even trying."

"We're not, or I'm not anyway. I went for a walk this morning and decided this isn't my town anymore. It makes me feel old." Ancient, actually. In Madrid she'd grown younger, but whether a result of all the travel, all the young people, or maybe just the fact that she had reached her fifty-second year, today she'd aged.

That Kate had finally shown some interest in planning the trip, however, brightened the day. She even looked better. Her hair seemed a little shinier, her clothes less schlumpy. Lydia hoped Kate's first therapy session had something to do with her friend's improvement. She craved the details of Kate's seven a.m. meeting with Dr. Lin. She'd have put a glass to the wall had Kate's room been beside hers instead of across the hall.

"Pop in for a cheeky beer or a taco snack," Kate said, reading the menu. "Good god. Did you order?"

"Not yet, but the salads look decent, and I could use a salad. So, where's this beach you're talking about?"

"It's north of Brisbane. You can boat to the Whitsunday Islands at the end of the Great Barrier Reef. It sounds romantic, and since you're trying to find romance, I thought it would be perfect."

Lydia almost choked on her water. "You chose a place where you thought I'd get laid?"

Kate laughed. "It sounds like a great place. We said we wanted adventure, and we can sail around the Whitsunday Islands, go scuba diving, take a crocodile tour, plus it looks beautiful. And it can't be worse for finding you a potential mate than this place."

It sounded like the tables had turned. The original reason for the trip had focused on helping Kate get better. Now Kate had plans for Lydia.

"You seem to be in a good mood this morning." It killed Lydia not to ask about the counseling session.

"I know you're digging. The session with Dr. Lin went fine, but honestly, I'm so tired of talking about myself that I wanted to think about something else. Finding a fun place for us to visit that might also have men our age is way more fun than delving into my dreary life."

"You know, Joe and I went to couples counseling once. It was a terrible experience. We never went back."

"You're kidding. What happened? When was this?"

"I was so angry with him when he kept switching jobs instead of learning the latest software. He said he knew how to do his job, and companies that used the new system just wanted to replace employees with robots. I told him he needed to learn to program the robots. We argued constantly. His drinking got worse. Finally, I told him we needed to go to counseling. Or I'd leave him."

"Holy shit. Why have you never told me this?" Kate perched on the edge of her seat, eyes bright.

"It didn't work. That counseling session was the worst hour of my life. Oh god, I'm sorry. I think I've picked the very crummiest time in the world to tell this story." Why the hell couldn't she shut up? Kate had finally met with her counselor, and now Lydia would ruin it with her awful experience.

"You must tell me this story. I liked Dr. Lin, and I'll meet with her again. But only if you continue with this juicy tale."

Lydia sighed. She might as well rip the rotten memory out. Perhaps some sunshine would heal it. "We sat in this smarmy psychologist's office for an hour. Every question seemed to point the finger at one of us, and it wasn't enough to answer. He had to delve into every response. *How do you think your husband feels when you say that? Did you respond that way because your parents spoke to each other like that? How did you expect Joe to respond to that tone of voice?*" Lydia shuddered at the memory.

"That sounds horrible. Was he one of those guys who hates women?" Kate asked.

"No. He was just as hard on Joe. This guy acted like he hated both of us. When we got out of there, it felt like we'd survived a war. It even brought us closer together for a while."

She and Joe had sat on a bench outside the doctor's building, so mentally exhausted they couldn't make it to the car. Joe had reached for her hand.

"Please. Let's never do that again." She'd been the one to speak the words. He'd chuckled. Things between them got better, probably because they both chose to be nice to each other over sitting through another hour of counseling.

"You're telling me that not going to counseling improved your relationship?" The corners of Kate's lips tweaked in a smile.

"Honestly, it did. We still had plenty of problems, but nothing seemed worse than the torture of counseling."

"I get that. I'd have preferred not to speak to Dr. Lin. I'm a capable woman. I should be able to figure this stuff out on my own." Kate snorted in frustration.

"You have to stay in counseling because I'm making you. But I understand the figuring it out on your own. I felt that way about my marriage. I think maybe it's the way we grew up." She'd had to figure stuff out for herself as a kid. Sometimes her mom helped, other times she stewed in depression or wasn't around.

"You may be right. Our parents pretty much left us alone. I think that's just the way it was with our generation."

"Believe me, that's totally changed. Parents hover over their children in Sophie's generation. Take all that travel you and I did. We almost never called our parents. In Madrid, we had to trek to the main telephone office just to make a phone call."

Kate reached across the table and set her hand on top of Lydia's. "I've seen you tracking Sophie on your phone. How are things going with her?"

Lydia sighed. "Fine. We text and have talked a couple of times. She was right, I held her too tightly. She needs to go experience the world the way we did." The pang in her heart had lessened, but she still wanted to wrap her arms around her daughter and protect her from danger and heartache.

"You've raised a smart girl. She'll be fine."

"I know. And as much as I miss her, I'm experiencing life again as Lydia instead of as Sophie's mom. It's kind of liberating."

"I'm so glad. Now, let's get the hell out of here and go to a place where we can find you a man."

Lydia supposed she should be grateful, but somehow Kate's comment made her feel like a loser. But why? She'd been very clear about wanting someone to share her life.

Coming out of Kate's mouth, it seemed like a petty endeavor. Or an impossible one. Or, maybe, she had other goals to consider.

"I honestly don't know if that's going to happen. The only thing slimmer than the odds of finding someone to share my life with while on vacation are those of finding someone at home."

"I don't know. I think you've done pretty well this trip. What are you looking for in a man anyway?" Kate asked.

Lydia gazed out the plate glass windows where a dark-haired young woman with full sleeve tattoos, tiny shorts, and combat boots wrapped her arms around a redhead with spikey hair and overalls. She'd seen all types come out of the hostel just down the street. The two women kissed, and something tugged in Lydia's belly. "I just want to find love."

Kate's hand closed over hers. Lydia closed her eyes, both to avoid the beautiful couple and to keep the tears inside. "Do you ever wonder what life would have been like if you'd made different choices?"

"Every day." Kate's voice flatlined.

"I mean about love."

"Yes. In Bonaire, I wondered what my life would have been like if I'd stayed that first time. I wouldn't have started Indulge, but I probably would have started some company, or managed a resort, or found something else that I loved to do. I imagine I'd be happy and more fulfilled. It's funny, the way I defined success for myself resulted in failure. If I hadn't been such a snob, would I have found happiness?"

Kate went still. It hurt Lydia to watch the regret on Kate's face and feel it echo in her own body.

"What about you?" Kate turned her dark eyes on Lydia.

"Sometimes I wished I'd stayed in Costa Rica. I was in love with Robert."

"Ah. The surfer. I remember. That was a fantastic vacation."

"Why didn't I take that chance? Why was I so afraid to live a big life? I've thought about that lost opportunity for years, and it probably didn't help my marriage that this other life beckoned."

The two friends sat in silence. Eventually, Kate picked up the menu. "The salads look terrible. How about I order us some tacos?"

Lydia nodded. She had to pull her thoughts out of this dark place. Screw finding love. This trip had taught her more important things. She needed to start thinking about her future in terms of what she'd do next, not who she'd be with. She promised herself not to think about guys for the rest of the trip. It was time for the seventeen-year-old brain to take a break and let the more mature Lydia take over. The one who had something to give to the world, not the one looking for someone to give to her.

Kate returned with two glasses of lemonade. "I was thinking about what you said. I think I left Bonaire because I was afraid that life was too small. There are only so many opportunities on an island. When I remember Costa Rica, I think you were looking for stability, and Robert didn't give you that."

The sword of truth nicked her with its blade. Of course she'd longed for stability, the one thing she'd never had. Growing up with a single mom pining for a married man left her on a stool with a missing leg. She needed a solid foundation. And she had created an incredibly stable, boring life. "Joe gave me that. He allowed me to raise Sophie in a stable home with two parents."

"And now Joe is gone, and Sophie is grown. You didn't do anything wrong. What do you want next? You can still have that big life. You can have whatever you desire." The intensity of Kate's look matched her words.

Lydia gazed at Kate, wishing she could turn those words back on her friend. They both needed to search for their passions. But bringing it up would only remind Kate of her unhappiness. Better to keep her happy in the present and leave the future for another time.

"Maybe I'll find my desire in this Airlie Beach place you found. It sounds nice" Let the next phase of the adventure begin. Her future was out there—somewhere.

Chapter 24

Lydia

Lydia pushed open the door to the Airbnb rental she'd found at the last minute in Airlie Beach. They'd caught glimpses of the water on the taxi ride in, but she didn't have a feel for the place yet. It looked less scruffy than St Kilda, and that had her hopeful.

The apartment didn't reach the standards of the resorts and extravagant hotels of their early journey. They'd had to drag their bags up an outdoor staircase, but the place boasted an excellent view.

"Oh. My. God." Lydia approached the broad glass doors to the balcony as if in a trance. Their building sat high on a hill overlooking a perfect bay. Clouds filtered sun onto the water, sometimes causing it to shine a brilliant gold, other times a steely gray. Hills on green islands dotted the far horizon. Nearer in, on the balcony railing, four perfect white birds with sulfur crests preened, half gazing into the room, half staring toward the sea. "Kate, you have to see this."

"Cockatoos! They're beautiful. Do you have any crackers?"

"Crackers?"

Kate's suitcase thumped to the tile floor. She dropped her tote on top of it and began rummaging through the bag. "Here they are." She pulled out a half-eaten sleeve of cookies and headed toward the sliding glass doors.

"You can't go out there. They might bite you, or you'll scare them away."

Kate slid the door open anyway, albeit quietly. "Polly want a cookie?" she sang, tossing one onto the plastic table.

Lydia held her breath, half afraid the birds would fly in the open door, and half afraid the magical creatures would fly away. One bird hopped onto the table, flared its yellow crest, and tipped his head sideways to examine the cookie. He reached out carefully with his charcoal beak, then snatched the snack and jumped back to the balcony.

The other three birds now faced Kate, expectant looks on their faces. She stepped onto the balcony and laid a second cookie on the table without backing away. The bird farthest away opened its wings and with one flap, landed on the table. He took the offered cookie then flew away, off the balcony and toward the bay.

Two birds watched Kate as she slid a third cookie from the sleeve. The remaining bird held his cookie in his foot, eating by breaking off pieces with this beak. A scattering of crumbs lay on the tile beneath him. This time, Kate held on to the cookie but reached her hand out over the table. One of the remaining birds immediately jumped to the table and took the cookie from her fingers.

"You're amazing. You're a bird whisperer." Lydia kept her voice low so she wouldn't scare the parrots.

Kate pulled out a fourth cookie and held it out to the final bird. He cocked his head back and forth, examining Kate and her treat, but stayed on the railing. The standoff dragged out for one minute, two. Then Kate set the cookie on the table, backed into the condo, and closed the door. Shortly thereafter, the bird hopped to the table, then flew away with his prize. The other two birds quickly followed, leaving the balcony empty.

"That was incredible. I think it's a sign that we've found the right place." Between the awe-inspiring view and the parrot welcome party, Lydia hoped they had stumbled onto a place whose magic would help them figure out the rest of their lives.

"I'd say between the cockatoos and the wine bar I saw on the street beneath us, this may indeed be our perfect location. "Cookie?" Kate asked, holding out the package, a broad smile on her face.

The next morning, a minivan picked up Lydia and Kate and whisked them off to a local estuary for a crocodile safari. Lydia had scheduled their days to include as much adventure and as little downtime as possible. The funk she'd fallen into needed to depart, and a date with crocodiles seemed as good an activity as any to keep her from dwelling on her vague future.

Kate looked a little happier, although Lydia had been afraid to ask if she still felt like killing herself. But she really wanted to ask. Hey Kate, does your shinier hair and brighter eyes mean you're willing to live? Or perhaps, does being in a place of such immense beauty make you realize you should stay? But she wasn't allowed to ask those questions. It wasn't considerate. It would be like someone asking her if she knew what the hell she wanted from her life.

She shook her head as she stepped down from the van. She'd booked the crocodile safari to escape thoughts like these. Her attention turned to the trip leader, a tall man in his fifties wearing waders and something similar to a cowboy hat. He pointed out the restrooms, a cooler full of drinks, and warned them to wear plenty of bug spray.

A few minutes later, they boarded a green, flat-bottom boat with open sides. The boat motored slowly up a waterway. Kingfishers and herons hid among the mangroves. It didn't take them long to see a baby crocodile in the water, sighted by a boy of maybe twelve or thirteen at the front of the boat.

The boy and his parents sat in front of Lydia and Kate and spoke with British accents. The three girls behind them looked a few years older than Sophie. One had an Australian accent, while the other two had to be Americans or Canadians.

The couple with the child reminded Lydia of her own family when Sophie was at that awkward age. The heavyset husband had the red nose of a drinker. The wife wore a skirt and blouse, prim and proper despite her location on a crocodile tour in an Australian estuary. The precocious child spoke at every moment, seemingly in search of his parents' praise.

Of course, she and Joe had never brought Sophie to Australia. In fact, they'd specialized in predictable vacations. They visited Disneyland and Disney World, two places Lydia despised, but Joe enjoyed them and Lydia figured every kid should see them. They went to the Grand Canyon once. She'd planned a vacation in Big Bear so Sophie could learn to ski, but Joe complained the whole time and never left the lodge. Other vacations had been similar, Lydia dragging the family some place she thought they ought to go only to have Joe complain. They'd never traveled before having Sophie either. She'd just assumed they would at some point. He probably hated being dragged on trips as much as she wanted to explore.

She looked out into the bright green mangroves and muddy brown water. An odd ripple caught her eye. "Snake!" she screamed as something slithered through the water.

"Oh, that's a beaut," the guide said, shuffling over to Lydia's side of the boat and causing it to rock. "It looks like a bearded sea snake."

A tremor ran through Lydia. Maybe she wasn't up for this much adventure, especially if their guide was about to dump them all into snake infested waters. She gripped the seat in front of her so hard her knuckles paled.

"It's okay," Kate said. "You're totally safe in here." Her soothing and completely fearless voice helped Lydia relax.

"I really hate snakes."

"I know. You always have. But you've never been hurt by one, and I don't think you will be today. Do you want me to trade places with you?"

Lydia nodded, then half-stood so Kate could scooch into her seat. She took the middle one—away from the water. And the snake. The tour guide droned on about the incredible snake sighting. Four feet long. Venomous. Yuck.

They continued up the river, spotting all kinds of birds. Alligator nests crowned the mud wherever the soil rose out of the water a few feet. Most of the other passengers leaned over the edge of the boat, seemingly fearless.

Fortunately, one of the young women behind them also appeared terrified of the snake and other monsters. She'd screamed just as loud as Lydia. And her friends teased her mercilessly, especially the Australian one. Lydia eavesdropped on their conversation. It seemed like they taught English together and were on vacation. Finally, Lydia's curiosity overcame her.

"Are you all teachers?" she asked, turning around as far in her seat as possible. She directed her question mostly at the snake-scared woman in the center seat. She reminded Lydia a little of herself, with dark hair pulled into a ponytail and brown eyes behind red-framed glasses.

The young woman gave her a big smile, but the Australian answered first. "Yeah, we teach English together in Cambodia."

"I'm a teacher too, or I was one. How do you find a job like that? It sounds interesting."

"It's a great way to see the world," said the woman in the middle seat. "All it takes is passing the TEFL exam, although it helps to have a four-year degree. I've been teaching abroad for two years now."

"It's mostly young people though," the Australian said. She shrugged her shoulders at Lydia.

Lydia turned back to the front of the boat. So much for that idea. She'd have thought her experience would be a bonus, but evidently youth and beauty trumped experience.

"You're an actual teacher?" The question came from a different voice behind Lydia.

She turned back, and the freckle-faced, red-haired American looked at her with questioning eyes. "Yes," Lydia said. "I taught for twenty-five years.

"You'd qualify to teach for an American school. Those are the best jobs. You have to sign a two-year contract, but they come with benefits and other perks. You teach in a real school, not just an English language academy. I'm hoping to qualify for a job like that in the future."

"Huh. Thanks for the information." Lydia turned back to the front of the boat.

Kate elbowed her in the ribs. "Would you actually consider something like that?"

"I don't know." It would open the door to adventure but close so many others.

They didn't see their first big crocodile until their return trip. The guide told them to look in front of the boat on the left, and sure enough, they glimpsed a yellow eye and mostly submerged scales. The guide cut the engine, surrounding them in silence and still air.

"This is Brutus," he said in a voice barely loud enough to be heard. "He's eight and a half feet long and is the king of this river."

The creature glided by the boat, and Lydia could have sworn he stared right at her, although how one could tell with an unblinking eye, she didn't know. His glare challenged her to be brave. She decided to make light of the massive beast.

"That might be a quick way to go." She nudged Kate. As soon as the words left her mouth, Lydia cringed. She hadn't meant to imply Kate commit suicide by alligator. She had only wanted to mouth off about the beast. "Oh, no. I didn't mean that. I wasn't thinking about . . ." She had to shut up. Everything she said made it worse.

Lydia watched Kate's face transform from shock to defiance. She slowly reached over the boat's side and dipped a hand in the water.

"What the 'ell are you doing? Get your hand back in the boat." The guide roared at Kate. "This isn't a joke. You heard the rules before we boarded. I thought I might have to reprimand this one," he pointed to the boy, "but not a grown woman. I will take you back to shore if you do something like that again, and you'll ruin everyone's trip."

"Sorry," Kate said. She didn't sound sorry. Her gaze hadn't left Lydia, and if eyes could sneer, hers would have.

"I'm so sorry. I'm so sorry," Lydia stammered. What the hell was wrong with her? Where had her sense gone, her compassion? "I cannot get my shit together."

Kate finally lifted her gaze from Lydia and sat back against the seat, arms crossed.

Kate made it through the rest of the tour without speaking to Lydia. When the van dropped them off at the condo, Kate huffed up the stairs, then let herself onto the parrotless balcony and sat facing the ocean.

Lydia followed, needing to fix the damage caused by her words. "I'm really sorry," she said, sinking into the remaining plastic chair. Today the sun shone, and the bay glowed turquoise before fading to navy as the shallow bay turned to deeper ocean.

"Don't be. I'd rather you suggest ways for me to off myself than hover over me trying to save me from myself." Kate slumped into her chair, then set one foot then the other on the balcony railing. She didn't look at Lydia but instead seemed to have her gaze trained on the far horizon.

"I still want to save you," Lydia said.

"Well, you shouldn't. I get to determine what I do with my life, and it seems like maybe you should focus more on your own."

"Maybe," Lydia still faced her friend, hoping they would have a genuine conversation. "I hoped your counseling session would help."

Kate finally turned her head toward Lydia. "You hoped one counseling session would change my carefully considered decision? There is nothing in my life I want to go back to. This trip has been a brief, enjoyable step outside my timeline. I'm glad we're getting to spend time together, and I feel like I'm learning more about you, about who you really are and who you want to be. That's interesting. But it doesn't change anything."

The finality in Kate's voice squeezed Lydia's chest, making it impossible to breathe. Tears, however, quickly came to her eyes. "But I want you to live. I want you to keep being my best friend."

"I can give you so much, so many things you keep telling me you won't accept. But I can't give you that."

Silent tears wet Lydia's face. Kate's remained dry. Eventually, Kate turned back to the view. Lydia turned her chair to the ocean as well. For over an hour, they sat sharing space but completely separate in their thoughts.

Lydia would never give her friend what she wanted. The kind of compliance it would take to accept her friend's true desire did not lie within her skin or psyche. She could accept the loss of her husband and her daughter's retreat. She could accept her age, her fears, her emerging desires. But she could not accept Kate leaving this world by her own means.

"What if I want to hold on to you more than you want to let go?"

"Then you'll have to take away my autonomy and have me committed. But I don't think you'll do that."

Committing Kate was a sure way to lose her friendship. And it was something Kate would hate. Something Lydia would hate doing to her. Were the only options truly taking away her friend's freedom or letting her die? Surely, they hadn't reached this crossroads.

Chapter 25

Kate

The next day, Kate woke early since Lydia had scheduled yet another tour. This adventure would take all day as they rode a high-speed catamaran first to a snorkel site, then to an island hike, then to a late lunch at a secluded beach before a final snorkel.

An early morning van ride transported them to a harbor filled with people. An agent from the tour company sorted them into fifteen person groups for each boat and distributed rain gear and life jackets. In addition to Lydia and Kate, their group included a couple in their forties and eleven people from Alabama on a family reunion trip. The Alabamans sported matching red T-shirts and Southern accents.

Kate and Lydia donned their safety gear at the same table as the other couple. The couple appeared put out by the Alabamans, with the woman complaining that they should have booked a private tour. Her diamond-studded Rolex and boulder-sized diamond engagement ring blared money. Her husband had a gym-fit body and his own Rolex. He sighed each time his wife complained, and Kate wondered whether his frustration stemmed from his wife or the noisy Alabama crew.

Kate and Lydia ended up on the last of the plastic bench seats at the back of the boat. Cloud cover, the early time of day, and the speed of the boat had cold air whipping past them. Kate wanted to pull her light jacket closer to her chest but had to keep both hands on the metal rod attached to the back of the seat in front of them as the boat bounced from wave to wave. Occasionally it clunked down with a jolt that ripped through her spine. She tried hard not to knock into the woman beside her on the hardest bumps and ended up half on top of Lydia in the process.

The Alabamans had taken the front rows, leaving Kate, Lydia, and the complaining couple in the worst seats. The woman beside her wasn't about to let anyone forget it and audibly groaned each time the boat slammed them down.

"I don't know why we came on this fucking tour," Kate overheard her tell her partner. Actually, the entire boat likely overheard her, despite the roaring engine and wind noise.

Once outside of the bay, the catamaran raced between islands. Finally, after the boat turned a big circle that threw Lydia into Kate, they entered a gorgeous harbor with aqua water fringed with alabaster sand. The hilly green island stretched around them, sheltering them from the wind. When the guide cut the engine, birdsong followed a moment of silence. They had arrived at paradise.

"It's about fucking time that boat ride ended," Rolex-woman said before huffing in displeasure.

"Do you mind? We've got kids on board." The comment came from a middle-aged man in the Alabama group. The three kids with them sat at the very front of the catamaran.

The woman shook her head and huffed again. The embarrassment of sitting beside this piece of work didn't bother Kate nearly as much as realizing she had acted the same way in the past. The woman acted like the ostentatious wealth she signaled with her jewelry and ridiculous Prada backpack made her better than the people around her. Kate had cringed when she first saw the backpack, as she had a matching $4,400 pack in her closet at home. Surely, she'd never been quite as rude as this woman, although she'd often been far from nice.

Money could change a person. It had changed her. She thought she'd earned it, was entitled to it because of all her hard work. And she had worked hard. But so had a lot of other people, from the women who sewed the garments at Indulge's Los Angeles factory to her assistant, whom she'd run ragged. Had she worked harder than those people? Yet she had reaped almost all the rewards.

Money also changed relationships. She and Mitch used to rely on each other, but once she'd started the business, time became scarce, and money began taking the place of effort. They'd hired a maid, a cook, bought massages instead of giving them to each other. They'd become companions as they enjoyed their newfound wealth. Vacations became like honeymoons, while life at home diminished to fewer and fewer hours. Most of those spent sleeping.

It was easy to miss what was wrong when you weren't around to see it. Kate thought their relationship was tolerable, if no longer passionate. Mitch couldn't tolerate it. She'd have hung on because she had the company to fulfill her. He didn't.

Did the complaining bitch beside her know about the trouble that came with money? Or had she been born into it and never suffered its accumulation? Probably not. Most generationally wealthy people Kate knew would never show off their riches.

"Okay, everyone, listen up." The guide's voice carried above the passenger's din. "This is our first snorkel stop. I'm going to demonstrate one of the ways we can enter the water." She donned her mask, pressed a palm to it, and stepped gently off the edge of the boat.

The three women running the tour impressed Kate. All incredibly buff and tan, they didn't let anything get to them. Not whining kids, a barfing woman, or rude rich people. Kate wished she'd been a little more like them and a lot less keyed up. Who knows what her life might have been like? She'd grown her company into something people loved. She wished she'd spent more time with customers and less with investors.

But all those opportunities had wafted away like silver smoke. Today, she'd swim in an ocean beside an old friend, and tomorrow didn't exist. She held on to the incredible peace that came with ceasing to struggle. She no longer had to make sense of what had happened, bear anger, fight for fairness. She could lay all of that down, let it float away in the cerulean sea.

"John, just sit. We have to let all these yokels get off the boat first." The woman beside Kate intruded into her thoughts.

Kate turned toward her and extended her hand. "Hi. I'm Kate. What's your name?"

The woman glanced down at Kate's hand but didn't touch it. "I'm Miranda."

"I'm the founder and CEO of Indulge lingerie." Kate saw the woman's eyes go big in recognition. "A piece of advice. It's tough going through life as a bitch. Take it down a notch. Maybe even try to be friendly."

Kate stood and pushed Lydia out of her seat. Lydia appeared to choke on something until Kate realized she was trying, and failing, to stifle her laughter. Still, she rose, and they made their way forward.

"I like you," the boat captain said. "Way to give it to the stuffy one." She gave Kate a high-five.

"There's one in every crowd," Kate said. "And it used to be me."

Perfect for swimming, the seventy-five-degree water slid across her body, welcoming her. Unfortunately, she didn't see the spectacular corals or vibrant fish that she expected. She'd read about how climate change had caused the reef to die but hadn't seen its effects before. When she returned to the boat, she asked the captain about it.

"A lot of it's from a hurricane that came through here a few years ago," the woman said. "But it's definitely not the same as it used to be."

Meant to appease tourists, the answer didn't resonate with Kate. She was certain this was climate change in action. How would countries heavily dependent on tourism, like Australia, or smaller ones like Fiji, deal with this catastrophe? She'd read that Australia had closed parts of the Great Barrier Reef to protect it from tourists, but what would protect it from higher ocean temperatures caused by people nowhere near the reef?

Curiosity about the state of ocean reefs and the communities around them prodded at her. She'd do a little research when they got back to the condo. Maybe her money could help.

She took her seat next to Miranda, who refused to look at her. Her husband did look up and cast a grim smile her way. Kate felt a little bad about her comment. It had obviously hit home, but not enough to make her apologize.

The catamaran took to the sea again. They next stopped at a large hilly island for a hike to the highest point. Other boats littered the harbor, and they followed a line of people up through the forest. They emerged at an enormous, terraced overlook. The stunning view filled Kate with awe. Islands stretched as far as the eye could see, each of them green-tipped, surrounded by glowing white sand dipped in sky-blue water. The sky itself hued a mid-day deep cobalt, and a few puffy white clouds crossed its expanse.

"Kate, we have to take a selfie," Lydia said, pulling her to the edge of the overlook. They leaned against a wooden railing, heads touching, and smiled into the camera. When Lydia showed her the picture, it was exactly the way Kate wanted to be remembered.

She returned down the path, feeling like everything had clicked into place. She'd done the things she was supposed to do, from befriending Lydia to starting and growing Indulge to reprimanding the bitch on the boat. The end drew nearer, and peace surrounded her. Lydia had been right. Kate hadn't known she'd needed this last tour of the world, but it gave her the time to revisit the past and leave the world filled with tranquility instead of rage.

She glanced at her best friend, whose chestnut hair blew in the breeze. She had the best heart of anyone Kate knew. Lydia deserved to be happy. Her life hadn't been easy. When Kate first met Joe, he'd treasured Lydia in a way that her other boyfriends hadn't. But that shine had dimmed once they'd married.

Kate had offered him a job managing an Indulge warehouse once when he needed work. He'd shouted that he could get his own fucking job as he walked out the door. Kate rarely visited Lydia at home after that, only for Sophie's graduation party, and once for an uncomfortable Christmas Eve dinner. Instead, they met in the middle, in Orange County for a spa day or Lydia and Sophie would stay with her for a few days each summer. It just made sense.

Somehow, the tension between Kate and Joe made her relationship with Lydia both more strained and closer. Lydia dumped her frustration with her husband into Kate's open ears. But the solutions Kate proffered, divorce or at least separation, Lydia wouldn't consider.

Kate often wondered whether relief or sadness had overcome her friend at Joe's death. The question couldn't be asked. She should have spent more time with Lydia after he died, but the drive to take Indulge public, dealing with the new board of directors, and all of Mitch's bullshit had left her without time or energy. At least they'd reconnected on this trip. Lydia had such a bright future, if only she could see it without dreams of Prince Charming blocking the view.

Lydia would be fine without a man, even if she couldn't see that yet. Thank god she had Sophie. That child had become the focal point of her mother's life. Sophie wanted her independence, and that meant pulling away from Lydia. Kate understood Sophie's desire for independence,;, she'd done the same at her age. Once Sophie became a full-fledged adult, she and her mother would become close again.

Ensuring Lydia's happiness in the meantime had become Kate's last big problem to solve. She'd watched Lydia struggle to figure out the next part of her life. Kate couldn't figure it out for her, but she could definitely make the path easier.

She'd deliver the adventure Lydia wanted. Her attorney had already begun the paperwork to start a foundation. It would be well funded, enabling Lydia to give away the money however she wanted. And if she didn't want that responsibility, she could pick someone to give it away for her. Maybe Sophie. Eventually.

She would also leave Lydia enough money to travel and fill her life with all the adventure she wanted. Lydia would be mad at first, but someday she'd realize the love behind the gift.

Kate couldn't fathom Lydia's desire to marry again. Honestly, she'd slice her own wrist open at the prospect. Still, Lydia seemed to crave the sense of security marriage brought. Her flighty mother had ingrained that into Lydia. If Lydia wanted it, Kate could help. In fact, this final plan had become the most exciting one.

The boat slowed and brought Kate out of her thoughts. They'd arrived at another island, this one made almost entirely of sparkling white sand.

"Welcome to Champagne Beach," the guide said. "It's called that because it's made of almost pure silica, and it bubbles when you step on it. Go explore for a while, and by the time you're hungry, we'll have lunch set up for you on the boat."

Kate and Lydia hung back and let the Alabamans off the boat first. Tension still wafted off the Rolex woman, but Kate didn't give a damn. Miranda would have to find her own way in the world, and she had a lot of searching left to do.

When Kate finally stepped down into the shallow water, it was like stepping onto grains of silk. The other passengers had churned up clouds of sand at the base of the boat's ladder, so she waded up shore to where the water was clear. Sure enough, each time she sank her foot into the sand, hundreds of tiny bubbles fizzed their way to the surface.

"This is amazing! It really is like being in an ocean of champagne." Lydia's excited voice turned Kate toward her friend. Lydia pumped her legs faster and faster until the water boiled around her. "Most. Incredible. Place. Ever."

And it was. But Kate knew she could have been anywhere in the world—as long as she spent this day with Lydia, it would be the most incredible day ever. Each remaining day was precious. And she'd finally figured out how to give Lydia the thing she wanted most.

Chapter 26

Lydia

The rainforest passed by in a whirl as Lydia stared out the SUV's window. Kate drove down the two-lane shoulderless road with pedestrians, bicycles, motorbikes, and cars all vying for space.

"I can't believe you can take a major airline to the west coast of Costa Rica. We spent all day trying to get here from the capital when we were young."

"I can't believe you haven't been back to Costa Rica since then. It's been the global center for ecotourism practically since we were twenty. And, if I remember correctly, you almost didn't go home the first time."

Lydia sighed. She'd carried the truth of that memory for a quarter of a century. Once, she'd had a chance at a different life. She could have stayed in a tropical paradise with the love her of life. Back then, she'd chosen safety, and Joe. She wouldn't have those same regrets if life gave her a second chance. "Did you know I looked into the visa requirements to move to Australia?"

Kate glanced at her, mouth agape. "You mean now? When we were just there?"

"Keep your eyes on the road!" Lydia screeched, as a dog scampered in front of the car.

Kate slammed on the brakes, causing the dog to stop and stare at them. As they rolled slowly by the animal, it glared at Lydia and barked. A nervousness ran through her, as if the dog had tried to tell her something.

"Are you going to move to Australia?" Kate asked. "I loved Airlie Beach."

"Me too. I don't think I'll do it. It's mostly a tourist town, and I don't know that I'd want to be surrounded by people always leaving. But I bet there are other coastal towns that have a higher percentage of locals. I really loved it there."

"I did too. St Kilda didn't work out this time, but that Australian magic of being in a slightly parallel but better universe returned in Airlie Beach."

"I felt it too. It's similar to Southern California, only people are nicer and it's more relaxed. I didn't want to leave."

"We didn't have to. We can do whatever we want. It's not like anyone is waiting at home for us. We can go back." Kate turned the blinker on, then maneuvered into the gravel parking lot of a red and yellow restaurant called Pollolandia. "Seriously, Lydia. If you want to go back to Australia, I'll turn the car around right now."

The earnestness in her friend's voice made Lydia tread carefully. Kate hadn't shown this intensity since before she went to the hospital. Lydia shook her head. Kate hadn't gone to the hospital, she'd been taken there after trying to kill herself. Did this intensity about Australia mean Kate wanted to be there? Did it mean she wouldn't kill herself if they went back? Something about her friend's overeager behavior chilled Lydia.

"How much did you like Australia?" she asked. She couldn't comfortably probe any deeper.

Kate put the car into park and turned the engine off. "This is about you, not about me. For once in your life, think about what you want. Stop caring for everyone else. The people around you have their own lives. All those years with Joe, you tried to get him to stop drinking, but that wasn't what he wanted. You wanted Sophie to stay close, so you mother-henned her, but she signed up for Semester at Sea anyway. You've known me long enough to understand that my life is my own. My decisions are my own. I love you, but not because you want to save me. I love you because you're fantastic, and I wish you'd realize that and stop compromising for everyone else."

The humid jungle air became stifling. Kate didn't understand that if you focused on yourself and made decisions based on what you wanted instead of what others wanted, it made you responsible for what happened. If things didn't work out, she had no one to blame but herself.

But so what? Was she really going to do something that couldn't be undone? That was Kate's desire, not her own. "I want to go to Tamarindo. I can always go back to Australia."

Speaking those sentences shifted her perspective. She had always been the good girl, the one who lived her life the way you were supposed to in order to earn safety and security.

She didn't need to earn things from people anymore. If she screwed up, she screwed up. It wasn't like her life would turn to crap because of it. She'd always seen life as a road from which you dare not deviate. You drove from point A to point B.

She looked outside the car window. Pollolandia. Chicken land. A shop that sold fried chicken with a ridiculous name. She laughed. Were they supposed to be here? Who knew?

Who cared? Maybe she needed to worry less about the future, not more. She could stop at Pollolandia, some other place down the road, Australia, wherever. Maybe point B didn't matter. Perhaps being on the road gave life meaning.

She made her decision. "Let's go. There's a beautiful surf town waiting for us."

"Atta girl," Kate said, turning the car back onto the road.

Thirty minutes later, they turned off the main road and began driving down the coast. Because of the hills and dense jungle, they only occasionally spied water peeking through green trees, but the land grew even more lush. Lydia inhaled salt-tinged air, and a breeze had palm fronds dancing silver and green.

"It's so much more developed now," Lydia said as they passed another gated resort.

"Yeah, and we're not even to Tamarindo yet. It's the biggest city on this part of the coast."

Going against reality and the passage of years, Lydia had hoped it would look the same. When they'd visited before, Tamarindo had been a sleepy surf town with more palapas than concrete buildings.

Close to their destination, they passed a chain grocery store in a large shopping center geared toward tourists. They could barely see the beach between walls guarding private houses and restaurants. Still, she occasionally caught sight of beige sand and a green sea beyond the walls. The area teemed with restaurants and hotels. Pedestrians and parked cars crowded the street.

Finally, Kate turned the car down a long paved driveway flanked by cream-colored cement walls, planters, and a tile sign bearing the name of the resort they'd booked. Lydia had found a place posh enough for Kate to enjoy, and from what she could tell on Google Maps, it might have sat on the exact location of the palapa they'd stayed in years earlier.

They drove up to the grand entrance, and attendants whisked their doors open and carted their luggage away before Lydia had a chance to shove her sunglasses to the top of her head. They sauntered through wide double doors framing the ocean beyond and attendants offered them cool glasses of fresh juice. After they checked in, different attendants showed them to enormous rooms on the third floor with gorgeous views over the luxury pool and bay beyond.

Despite its carefully curated beauty, the grand resort seemed sterile compared to their tiny condo in Australia with its welcoming parrots and trudge up the stairs. The drive in had looked familiar, if built-up, since her last visit. But when Lydia stepped onto the balcony, she would have sworn she'd never set foot in Tamarindo before. The resort had carved its idea of paradise into the place she'd once loved.

Disappointment washed over her. She'd most looked forward to revisiting this location, but now she didn't think she could get away fast enough. She went next door to Kate's room.

"It's really changed," Lydia said when her friend opened the door.

"I think I hate this resort. I would have preferred a hut on the beach or maybe something a little nicer, but not this. You've cured me of fancy resorts."

"They ruined our beach. If we stay here, I'm afraid I won't remember the real thing."

"Oh, sweetie. This is the real thing. This is what we do to the world." Kate wrapped her in a hug.

Lydia began to cry. She hadn't intended to, heck, she didn't even know she was sad. But she let herself cry on Kate's shoulder for everything she would never see again.

"Hey, it's going to be okay. I promise, everything will be okay." Kate rubbed her back and held on to her until Lydia's sobs quieted.

"I'm sorry, I don't know why I'm so emotional."

"Probably because we've flown halfway around the world and back. We've been on the road for weeks, and even before that, things sucked. I'm usually a bitch after a two-hour flight. For you to shed a tear or two after all of this," she waved her hand out to the balcony and everything that lay beyond. "I'd say it's about time."

"Maybe I need a nap."

"Even better, why don't we go down to the pool and order some kind of snack with lots of tropical fruit, and a limeade."

"That sounds perfect." If she filled her body with good things and added a little warm sun, maybe she'd recover her equilibrium.

"And while we're there, I'll find us more suitable lodging."

While it made her happy that Kate wanted to take care of the trip details, it wouldn't work. "I'm afraid this place is nonrefundable." She looked around the luxurious room. "It will be fine."

"You let me worry about that," Kate said. "Now go change."

Once she eased into the lounge chair, her perspective shifted. She had finally returned to the northwest coast of Costa Rica. The sultry air caressed her skin, the humidity relieved by a refreshing ocean breeze. In the past, when someone had asked her to name her favorite place in the world, she mentioned Tamarindo. The resort's manicured lawns and azure infinity pool didn't match her memories, but the air hadn't changed.

Next to her, Kate tapped away on her laptop, and soon a sweaty glass of tart limeade appeared by her side. The flavor pulled her back to that earlier time of palapas, cold beer, fresh-picked limes, and muscles tired from learning to surf. A couple of beach bums from California had ended up here and opened a surf school. Kate had been a natural, but Lydia needed more help. Help that came in the form of a kid from Florida.

Robert had haunted her dreams for almost thirty years. His tanned skin, easy smile, eyes the color of the sea. Even today, she warmed at the thought of him. They'd quickly moved from the surfboard to sharing a palapa. Days became filled with adventures, canoeing down jungle rivers, snorkeling near offshore islands, visiting hot springs on the side of a volcano.

Nights brimmed with the kind of love Lydia had only dreamed about. A wild boy bent on adventure toppled the girl who planned everything out and followed every rule. She became freer, more spontaneous, a better version of herself. And he thought the sun rose and set because of her. For the first time, the only time, she understood what it meant to have someone fall deeply in love with you. He fell so far that he'd been willing to sacrifice what she loved most in him to be with her.

The day he said he'd do anything, go back to the States, get a real job, leave surfing and paradise behind, was the day she knew she had to leave. She would not change this creature built on that curious combination of adrenaline and peace. He made paradise real, and she'd rather live with the memory of paradise than the reality that she'd destroyed it by allowing him to be less.

Of course, the thought that she might be the one to change taunted her as well. She wanted the home and the baby, security, and a job. He'd spun tales of how Costa Rica promised that as well, how more people would come and they could build a future in paradise. Looking at the luxury that surrounded her now, she probably should have believed him.

Gazing back at life, paths that once seemed overgrown with jungle and passion looked strangely clear. The straight and fast and safe path she'd trod had petered out somewhere in the suburbs. Now she got to start anew, cut a new trail. Where would she walk and with whom?

Looking back might drown her. Lydia sat up on the lounge chair instead. "I'm getting philosophical. I think I need a piña colada."

"I'm sure they're wonderful here, so order up. Tomorrow, we're leaving." Kate shut her laptop and looked over at Lydia.

"Why? Where are we going? I'm not ready to leave Costa Rica."

"I'm not either. I booked us a house overlooking Playa del Coco. It's a little farther north, but it's got a beautiful bay and no big resorts."

"That sounds fantastic, but how did you get out of the booking here?"

"You let me worry about that." Kate waved at a nearby waiter and ordered Lydia's drink. "I also booked us massages in an hour to help us recover from the plane ride. Maybe we can walk into town after that and see how much it's changed.

It took a few tries to find a place to eat where they could hear each other talk. Every beachfront location blasted the latest hits. Even the place they'd found pulsed with beats from competing restaurants on either side. They sat at a high-top table under a few palm fronds meant to resemble a real palapa and ordered shrimp cocktails.

Most of the clientele were thirty years younger and far firmer than Lydia. Strangely, two tables of grizzled old men framed the entrance. At a table near theirs sat one of the cutest couples Lydia had ever seen. They'd pressed their chairs close together and constantly whispered in each other's ears. Occasionally, they'd hold their hands up to the light where shiny gold bands glinted.

"Look at them." Lydia nudged Kate. "They have to be newlyweds."

"Good for them. I wish them great luck," Kate said in her least sincere voice.

"Oh, come on. They're so cute. Just because it didn't work for you doesn't mean it won't work for them."

"You mean marriage?" Kate's eyebrows rose so high Botox wouldn't have stopped the forehead crease.

"Yes. It might work for them. We can root for them anyway." Lydia said as a waiter approached.

"Would you ladies like anything else?"

"Yes," Kate said. "Please send a bottle of your best champagne to the couple at that table." She pointed to the newlyweds.

"You do know how to be sweet," Lydia teased. "Marriage was a lot of fun in the beginning."

Kate rested her head on a hand and stared out across the beach. "It was nice at first. In fact, it was good for a very long time. Mitch and I used to be on the same track. But somewhere, probably as I got more and more involved in the businesses, we grew in different directions. The excitement of creating a great company and making things people loved engulfed me. I had to learn so much every day just to keep my head above water. Marketing, distribution, sales, real estate, finance. I studied it all. And I think Mitch resented the time it took. I used to spend that time with him."

"And you thought hiring him would help?" Lydia still remembered when she'd met Kate for lunch in Beverly Hills and Kate had told her she'd become Mitch's boss. It had seemed like a horrible idea. Joe would have divorced her then and there.

"I told you, that was his idea."

"Yeah, because you paid him more than he'd ever make on his own."

"I did. I paid him a lot more. And gave him stock options. I set him up for his current life of wealth. The one he's now sharing with another woman." Kate sat up a little straighter. "You know what? That doesn't hurt anymore."

"What do you mean?" Lydia noticed a change in her friend. Kate looked almost joyous.

"I don't care that Mitch is with another woman. It doesn't hurt anymore." Kate looked at her hands as if searching for something missing, then rolled her shoulders. "There's no pain left at all. I think we evolved away from each other. We had a lot of good years before that, times when we made each other better. I couldn't have started Indulge without him, but we reached a point where we didn't need each other anymore, and frankly, we just weren't that interested in each other."

"Huh. I had good years with Joe too. When we first married and when Sophie was young. He coached her first soccer team, stuff like that. I'm not sure we ever really evolved though. We hit a cul-de-sac in the suburbs and never grew beyond that."

"But that's what you wanted, right? Safety and security. There's nothing wrong with that."

Lydia considered Kate's question. Something pinged in her brain, and with that came clarity. "I think I'm supposed to evolve now. That's what this trip has taught me. I can no more recapture the woman I was when I married Joe than I can recapture the girl that sat on this beach thirty years ago. I'm learning how to be the woman I'm about to become."

She stood, suddenly so full of energy she had to move. This trip was never about starting over, it was always about progressing. She just hadn't known it until that very moment.

They needed to pay the bill and go for a walk on the beach. Lydia's revelation called for motion and continued discussion. She still didn't know the where or the how, but she finally understood the why.

"Excuse me," a woman at her shoulder said. "We wanted to thank you for the champagne, that was so nice."

Lydia turned to see the cute dark-haired woman with green eyes and her muscled and buzz-cut husband. "You're newlyweds, aren't you?"

"Yes ma'am. We got married on Saturday."

"I recognize a Southern accent when I hear one. Where are you from?" Lydia asked.

"Huntsville, Alabama. My name is Leah. TJ here is from Raleigh, North Carolina, but we're both stationed at Camp Pendleton right now."

"You're both Marines?" Kate asked.

"Yes ma'am," the woman answered.

"Thank you for your service," Lydia said. "And you guys are about the cutest couple ever."

"Is this your honeymoon? Where are you staying?" Kate asked.

"We're at the Hurricane Hotel," TJ said, then laughed. "It may not be luxury, but we're making the name work." He wrapped an arm around his wife, his black skin contrasting with her bronze tan.

A current of their happiness sparked in Lydia. She'd been so keyed up over the past few weeks, but now, deep in her core, new confidence sprang up that the future would not just work out but would be great.

She glanced at Kate, wishing she could pass on this current of joy, but she couldn't. Somehow, Kate needed to find her own way. Maybe tonight's realization that her marriage had run its course would help. Perhaps nothing would help enough. That would permanently break Lydia's heart.

Stop interfering. Love her. Enjoy her. Stop trying to change her.

Lydia returned her focus to the couple. "I hope you have a wonderful life together. Keep evolving as people so you stay interesting. And evolve together, so you can stay together."

"Yeah," Kate said. "We both learned that one the hard way. How much longer will you be in Costa Rica?"

"Four more days," Leah said.

"Then back to reality." TJ squeezed Leah tight and looked into her eyes when he said it.

"Well, you two have a wonderful time here," Lydia said, grateful to see love in bloom.

Chapter 27

Lydia

The next morning, Lydia practically threw herself into the Jeep, excited to be leaving the resort behind. It surprised her when Kate pulled up to the Hurricane Hotel and Hostel.

"I've got to run in for a second. Be right back," she said, before leaving Lydia sitting alone. The small, shabby hotel sat around the corner from the beach. What a bummer. She hoped the couple had their own room.

"Spill it," Lydia said, the second Kate got back.

Her grin grew Cheshire cat big. "You were right about not being able to cancel our room. However, I was able to convince the resort to turn the reservation for our two rooms into a suite for the rest of the week. And I just dropped off the key to Leah and TJ."

"Ah!" Lydia screamed, then wrapped Kate in a hug. "You are the best."

"I also bought them dinner and a couples massage. Plus, with the room they get breakfast every day, and champagne, roses, and chocolate await them there now. I haven't felt this good about anything in a long time."

"You should feel good. You're a fucking fairy godmother," Lydia said. She loved seeing Kate's broad smile.

"Now that we've got the newlyweds taken care of, let's go see our new digs."

They drove the winding roads of Costa Rica back up the coast. Lydia basked in the tropical air, her window down and a fresh breeze lifting her hair from her neck.

Kate turned off the road to Playa del Coco right before reaching town and climbed a ridge. They entered a housing development where the rental manager met them at a one-story house that stretched along the private roadway.

The manager opened the front door and stepped aside for them to pass. Lydia had barely made it inside before she stopped and gasped.

Kate almost ran into her back. "What? Why'd you stop?"

Transfixed by the view, Lydia neither moved nor spoke. A wall of glass greeted them across an expansive but homey living area. A deck led from the cabana doors to an infinity pool. Beyond that lay a perfect half-moon bay guarded by green hills. Further still, the blue ocean stretched all the way back to Australia.

"Oh." Kate sighed. "This is magnificent. I can't believe it looks as good as it did online. Maybe better."

"It's the most beautiful place I've ever seen." Lydia said. When she finally pulled her eyes from the view, she noticed the travertine floors and sweeping ceilings covered in tongue-in-groove hardwood. The living area opened onto a kitchen with granite countertops and hardwood cabinets. An open-plan dining room shared the incredible view.

"Ladies, please let me show you around." The manager walked them through the house before leaving. Entire master suites anchored each end of the home, with large bathrooms and stunning views. Smaller rooms were tucked between the masters and the living space.

"What on earth are we going to do with four bedrooms?" Lydia asked. Somehow the ridiculously large space felt homey, but it was still too much.

"Who knows, maybe we'll have visitors. It doesn't matter anyway. It's all ours. We can move from room to room if we want. We do have to do all the cooking, although I imagine we'll eat out a lot."

"I don't know. I may never leave that view." Lydia walked onto the patio and kicked off her shoes. She stepped onto the top step of the deep blue pool. "The water is perfectly cool, and I think we'll have gorgeous sunsets."

A bright yellow bird flitted past and landed on a nearby banana plant with a stalk of tiny green bananas. The bird, once Lydia looked at it closely, was mostly lemon yellow, with a cloak of black feathers covering its wings and back.

The bird stared into Lydia with its shiny black eye. Was it trying to tell her she'd finally found home? She could live here and never set foot in Escondido again. Sophie could visit her here. She could find a meaningful life here in a paradise that had already etched itself into her soul.

She stepped from the pool onto the warm slate deck, then sank into a lounge chair facing the bay. A few minutes later, Kate set an icy glass of water on a table beside her and then poured herself into the next lounge chair.

"I wish we didn't have to go to the store tonight. I swear I could stay in this chair forever," Kate said.

"I truly love it here. Thank you for finding this place."

"I'm glad you feel that way. I know we were supposed to go home at the end of the week, but the minimum booking on this place was two weeks."

"That is wonderful news." Lydia sank deeper into the chair, stretching out so she took up the most room possible. An awning kept the sun at bay while a breeze swirled the air around her.

She fell asleep, then woke to memories of dreams of helping kids down at the beach. They sat in child-sized plastic chairs in rows on the sand, while she stood at the head of the class writing English words on a whiteboard with different colored markers.

In town that evening, they ate at an outdoor table with their toes in the sand. Sailboats and skiffs made their way toward the bay as night started to fall. The tables around them filled with tourists and locals. They ate plates of rice and beans with freshly grilled fish and drank bottles of Imperial, the local beer.

On their walk through town after dinner, the local crowd came out in force. Young people dressed for a party spilled out of open-air bars. Makeup free and wearing shorts, Lydia didn't feel out of place. Contentment flooded her. She didn't need a man and didn't need to appear young. Her chest filled to bursting with the joy of being alive, just as she was, in this buzzing place on this spectacular night.

They made their way to a modern grocery store where they loaded up on local coffee, eggs, and fruit. Two weeks in paradise. She would find the answers to her future in that time. Change rumbled through her bones as she evolved from mother/teacher/caretaker into a new woman with new priorities.

Kate kept checking her phone. At dinner, during their walk through town, and even in the grocery store, she'd turned from Lydia and read and responded to messages. When they got back to the house, Kate's phone beeped again. She grabbed it and slipped into another room while Lydia put away the groceries.

"What's going on?" Lydia asked when Kate returned.

"A lot. I'm in touch with my banker and lawyer back home trying to sort some things out, and there's other stuff going on."

"Other stuff? Like with your therapist?"

A long pause ensued. "No. Not like with my therapist. I meet with her once a week and we talk. That's it. My life is my life, and I thought you were going to stop interfering in that."

"My bad." It irked Lydia that after weeks together she still didn't know if Kate was any better. She couldn't do anything about it, but how could someone not want to live on a night like this? She lamented that her friend had been injured so badly.

Kate looked at her phone as it pinged again. "Lydia, there's something I have to tell you."

The seriousness of Kate's tone worried Lydia. She tried to divine how bad her next words would be.

"You might want a drink. Or to sit down or something."

"Kate, what the hell is going on?"

"I found Robert."

"Who? What?" Confusion bubbled up from deep inside her. Hope? Fear? Anticipation? She couldn't name it, but that didn't stop it from knocking her off balance. She grabbed onto the cool marble of the kitchen counter to steady herself.

"Robert. Robert Barnes. The surfer you fell in love with thirty years ago."

"You found him?"

"Yes. It was easy. I can't believe you never looked him up."

"I couldn't. I was married." Searching for him online had occurred to her many times over the years. She'd never done it. It seemed too close to cheating. Or maybe it would have led to her leaving her husband to recover a deeper kind of love.

Confusion crossed Kate's face. "Looking someone up isn't cheating. But nonetheless, I found him. And I invited him here."

"What?" The counter could no longer hold her up. She staggered to the couch and sat.

Kate sat beside her and took her hand. "I'm sorry. I didn't mean to upset you. I thought you'd be excited."

So many feelings sped through Lydia, so many questions. She grabbed for one. "Is he married?"

Kate took a deep breath and seemed to relax. "I'm sorry, I should have started with that. He's never been married."

Curiosity took over. "Really? I wonder why."

"Maybe he never got over you."

Heat rose from Lydia's sternum to her cheeks. "No. That can't be. That was so long ago." A new tremor started, this one finely tuned to hope.

"Maybe it's time to find out. He just landed. He'll be here in under an hour."

"What? Now?" Her world spun, a tornado fed by fury at Kate for springing this on her, and some new kind of anticipation-fear-joy. But mostly fed by worry. How did she look? Would she have time to shower? Should she put on makeup or was that trying too hard?

The feelings welled up and exploded out of her. "Why didn't you tell me about this? You're always bitching at me about interfering in your life. How long have you known about this? What am I supposed to do now?"

Kate leaned away from the tirade until Lydia stopped. "I'm sorry. I thought this would make you happy. You've been talking about men and getting married since we left Los Angeles. I thought that maybe the one guy you really loved was the answer. I should have included you. I see that now."

"I loved Joe! Why couldn't you ever believe that? We had a lot of wonderful years. I'm prouder of my family than anything I've done. You always devalue that. Maybe he wasn't as handsome or well-off as Mitch, but he was a good man for many years. He was an excellent father. And at least he kept his dick in his pants and didn't leave me for a younger woman!" Lydia screamed the words, rage and frustration lighting a sudden hatred of her friend.

"That was low." Kate's calm voice didn't match the bright pink spots on her cheeks.

"What the fuck am I supposed to do now?" Realization washed over Lydia. "You brought him here so you could leave me. You're trying to set things right so you can ride off into the sunset, but what you'll actually leave behind is a bloody mess of a body and a big empty space. Is that what this is? Did you think Robert would fill the hole you're planning to punch in my heart?"

Kate said nothing, but she didn't look away. One tear leaked out of the corner of her eye.

"I can't do this anymore." Lydia fled to her bedroom and pulled out her suitcase. She shoved clothes into it, not folding, not caring. She didn't care at all. She ran her fingers under her eyes to wipe away the flood of tears.

The soft pad of feet stopped outside the room. "I'm sorry Lydia. I'm doing my best. This is who I am." Kate sounded small, and broken.

Lydia turned to face her. "This is only part of who you are. I've seen the whole Kate, and she's a much stronger woman."

"She's gone."

"Only because you don't want to reclaim her. Clearly, I can't help you with this, but I won't become your last project."

"The fuck you won't." Cold anger shone through Kate's eyes. "I get to decide how I leave things. I don't care whether you meet with Robert or not. That's your call. But he's on his way. You can't go anywhere because I have the car keys, and there aren't any flights out tonight anyway."

"You're a bitch."

"I'm aware. Also, just so you don't accuse me of holding anything else back, I'm in the process of creating a foundation and leaving you in control of it. You're welcome to pass that responsibility on to anyone else. Maybe Sophie would be interested. And I'm leaving you a million dollars, plus the taxes you'll owe on that in my will. I don't care what you do with it, but it's yours whether you want it or not." Kate crossed her arms, reminding Lydia of a petulant child. One who'd just ripped her heart clean out of her chest.

"And then what?"

"And then I'm gone."

"When? How? Where? You might as well prepare me since you've got everything else laid out." Anger and desperation fought inside her.

"You really want all the details?"

"Why not? Bring it on." Lydia spread her arms wide and puffed herself up. She'd take on this load. The only way forward was through, at least according to the poster in the teacher's break room that she'd stared at year after year.

Kate froze. Lydia wondered if she'd truly thought this far ahead.

"I'd prefer not to tell you, so you won't try to stop me."

"Yeah, sure." She stared at her friend. What a ridiculous, deadly game. They'd reached an impasse. They stood on opposite sides of a chasm they'd never cross. "I'm leaving tomorrow."

"Please stay." Kate broke Lydia's gaze and looked at the tiled floor. "I'll leave if you want."

"Where is Robert staying?"

"I told him he could stay here. The place is so big, and it's already ten o'clock. But if you'd like, I can call some of the other hotels to see if they have a room."

Lydia sat on the clothes-covered bed, suddenly exhausted. "I can't deal with you anymore. We're going to fix all of this. I don't want your money. You and I will sit down and figure out what to do with it, but it will not be my responsibility."

"Okay." Kate seemed to surrender.

"You go put away the rest of the groceries. I'm going to take a shower. I honestly don't know what to do about Robert, but I guess it's okay for him to spend the night here." Lydia surrendered as well. This war had no winners.

Lydia scrubbed herself clean, focusing on soap and skin and not on her intruding thoughts. It was all too much. Kate foisting her departure plans on Lydia. Inviting Robert to their retreat. Hell, finding him at all. And not telling her any of it, just expecting her to be fine with everything. The way she'd always been fine with everything everyone dumped on her.

Thoughts spun through Lydia's head. *Keep drinking, even though Lydia asked you not to. Don't worry about giving Lydia the teaching assignments she asked for, she won't care. Take off for six fucking months and tell your mother it's her fault. Don't worry about it. She'll be there when you need her.*

Lydia was so goddamned tired of being everyone else's doormat. And now she had an ex-boyfriend about to show up, and she had no idea what to do about it. Staying angry gave her control, but hope fluttered in her chest.

She dried her hair, debated makeup, and went with the barest slip of foundation and a touch of lip gloss. And what should she wear? She didn't want to be in this position. Not without time to prepare. An ache started deep in her chest. If she only had a chance to do things differently, to do them her way. But she didn't.

The doorbell rang.

All her worries fell away, replaced by urgent curiosity. She forced herself not to run into the living room. Voices wafted toward her, Kate welcoming someone. Then a male voice she would have recognized anywhere. While deeper and a little rougher, as if sandpaper had worn it down over the years, his voice still maintained a friendly, laid-back cadence.

She stepped into the room, and her heart stopped beating for a moment as she took him in. Gray now lightened his hair, but he'd maintained his sun-bronzed skin, now etched with faint lines around the sea-blue eyes she used to drown in. He looked fantastic, all broad shoulders and trim waist. And if his stomach no longer lay flat against his hips, it added a softness to him, the same rough and tumble that had softened his voice had smoothed the once rock-hard curves of his muscles. He looked perfect.

"I can't believe it's you." The words burst from her lips. She stood, rooted in place wanting to run to him and afraid to approach all at once. He opened his arms.

"Lydia." His voice caught. "It's been too long."

She flew across the room into his embrace. The years melted away as he wrapped himself around her. She was twenty-eight and in love. She was fifty-two and madly in love with the people they'd been then. Perhaps her future had arrived in a package from the past.

"Can I make you two a drink?" Kate asked, her voice soft. "Lydia, maybe you can show Robert to his room, and then I'm going to turn in."

Lydia pulled back from Robert. "It is fantastic to see you."

"You too. I never thought I'd get a second chance." He reached out and stroked her jaw.

She wanted to lean in and kiss him the way she used to. But so much time had passed, she needed to learn about him all over again, learn the second half of his life. "I'll have an Imperial," she said to Kate. "The taste takes me right back to my first time here." She looked into Robert's eyes, and all those earlier memories flashed before her—his eyes in the ocean, in her bed, reflecting the glow of a beach bonfire. So many good times.

"I'll have one too," he said.

Lydia briefly thought about showing him to her room instead of his, but she wanted to do this right. Besides, she'd left clothes strewn everywhere and her suitcase still sat half-packed atop the bed. Instead, she led him to the room closest to hers.

"Wow, ocean view. Impressive." He set down his duffel and walked toward the window.

"The house is amazing. You won't believe the view come morning. All this is courtesy of Kate. She made quite a killing with her company."

"I can't wait to learn all about it. Although, I mostly want to know what you've been doing since I saw you last. I do know you married and had a child."

That startled her. "How do you know that?"

"I have to admit, I've looked you up a time or two over the years. I always wondered what might have been. I was so stupid back then. I should have found a way for us to be together, and I've regretted it ever since."

"Wow." His words slammed into Lydia, completely discombobulating her. "Let's go get that beer and sit out on the lanai and catch up."

"I'll be right there. Just let me wash off the airport grime."

Lydia remained dazed as she left his room. In the kitchen, two sweating bottles of beer sat on the granite countertop, but Kate had disappeared. Lydia opened the doors to the back, set the bottles on a coffee table, and sat on the outdoor sofa waiting for Robert.

A soft wind blew in from the ocean. The harbor, awash with the lights of anchored boats, matched the deep blue sky and starlight above. It was perfect and beautiful and even a little frightening, not knowing what the future held but sensing its potential.

"Hey," a soft voice said.

She'd heard him pad through the house, but still, his voice made her jump. The air around them had turned electric.

He sat beside her and took a long swig from his bottle. "So, tell me what you've been up to."

And she did, filling in the gaps of the intervening years. Her marriage, her career, and her incredible daughter. She asked him the same. He'd stayed in Costa Rica for a couple of years after she left but admitted to eventually growing up. He'd returned to Florida and started an insurance company, putting his dusty finance degree back to work. When she asked, he admitted to having girlfriends but never finding the right one.

"I always compared them to you. No one ever measured up."

The thought made her sad. Had he really let potential happiness pass him by? "That makes me feel a little guilty."

"That wasn't my intent. I had a serious girlfriend or two, but never wanted to spend my life with them, and I did enjoy single life. I do think that if I had grown up a little earlier and been ready to put the Costa Rica dream behind me when you were ready to settle down, things would have been different."

She needed to turn the conversation back to more solid footing. "Did you really just pick up and leave when Kate reached out to you?"

"It took me half a second to make the decision. I've come back here from time to time over the years. I was actually glad when Kate told me you relocated up here from Tamarindo. That town has unfortunately lost its charm. I usually stay one beach further up at Playa Hermosa. I'd love to take you to my favorite restaurant there."

"That sounds good." Cue the awkward silence. She looked down at their knees, not quite touching on the sofa. How much space divided twenty-five years? She returned to his gaze, unable to see the blue of his eyes in the dark night. "I'm not sure exactly how this is supposed to go."

"Me either. Let's take it one day at a time. It feels a little awkward to be staying here, but Kate said there was plenty of room."

"There is." Lydia thought of the huge king bed with her clothes strewn across it. She wanted to be strewn across it as well, with Robert, but not tonight. Not until she knew him better.

"Hey, have you ever been to Nicaragua?" His question came out of the black night.

"No. Why?"

"Honestly, one of my favorite places in the world is this little palapa that serves as a restaurant and bar on the shore of Lake Nicaragua. Let's go there tomorrow. I know a guy who will drive us. I'll take you and Kate, and we can get to know each other again."

Lydia sighed, a wave of relief passing all the way to her toes. She'd try all this again tomorrow. All the stress from her argument with Kate and worry about Robert's arrival receded, leaving nothing but a starry night and a twinkling bay. "That sounds perfect. Thank you."

"No worries. I'll see you in the morning." He leaned forward and pressed his lips to her cheek. The soft movement took her breath away, exactly like it used to. She kept still, despite her lips longing to press against his. Happiness, memories, anticipation, they all fueled a smile that lit up every cell in her body. Tomorrow would be a great day.

Chapter 28

Lydia

Kate tried to beg off going to Nicaragua with them the next morning, but Lydia wouldn't let her. She needed Kate to relieve the stress of being alone with Robert. That relationship needed to unfold gradually and without too much pressure.

After talking with him by the pool, she'd gone to bed hoping for a good night's sleep. Instead, she thought of him nonstop, memories from earlier years caressing her body the way his hands once did. She tried to touch herself the way he had, but it only relieved some of the stress. A mere wall separated them; had he heard her? Was he engrossed in similar memories? She touched her own body again, hoping to find her way to satisfaction and then sleep. It must have eventually worked, because she woke up to the sun streaming through her window.

Now, two hours later, they sped through a forest in Nicaragua. The rain that had assaulted them as they crossed the border receded, and a blue sky beckoned them forward. Soon they caught sight of an enormous, slate-gray lake. They pulled off onto a side street and a friendly blue and white building under a thatched roof greeted them. In front of the palapa, a green lawn stretched toward the lake's shore. They spilled from the car, and Robert took each of their hands and pulled them toward the water.

"Do you see the volcanoes?" he asked.

Sure enough, two giant volcanoes sprouted from the lake.

"Are they in the water?" Kate asked.

"Yes. Both volcanoes are on a single island in the middle of the lake. I've been out there before. It's a nature reserve."

"I almost feel like I could swim to them," Kate said, as she kicked off her flip-flops and waded into the water.

"I wouldn't try it," he said. "They're farther away than they look, and the lake is known for its crocodiles and bull sharks."

"Really?" Lydia asked. "Kate, get back here. Bull sharks are mean."

Kate turned and threw Lydia a raised eyebrow and a wicked smile.

"Not here, and not now." Lydia put on her schoolmarm voice. How could Kate even joke about such a grotesque suicide? Lydia shuddered, picturing blood in the water.

"I'm going to order us breakfast," Robert said. "Does everyone want coffee?"

They sat at a card table covered with a checkered plastic tablecloth and ate simple, delicious food. Black beans, rice, eggs, and tortillas, all smothered in a spicy salsa. Gusts of cool air blew in from the lake. They ate quickly but then lounged. Lydia wanted to sit there all day, enjoying the breeze, the conversation, and the sense of adventure. In fact, she might never need to go anywhere again.

Three young men worked in the restaurant, and they had to be brothers. Lydia guessed they ranged from sixteen or seventeen to one in his mid-twenties. They looked so alike, they seemed like triplets born a few years apart. At one point, the youngest brother moved a large pink hog from across the gravel drive to the lawn in front of the lake. Later, he brought them a baby alligator to hold. Lydia wanted nothing to do with it, but Kate immediately picked it up and began stroking its olive scaled back.

The tiny sharp teeth next to Kate's soft wrist made Lydia shudder again. Would she ever look at her friend without thinking about death? She turned back to Robert who regaled them with stories of dozens of tiny islands further north in the lake, many of them topped by a single fancy home.

"You still love it down here, don't you?" Lydia asked.

"Definitely. I make it down here every year or two. Someday, I hope to retire down here. I have to say though, with Tamarindo and the rest of Costa Rica overrun with tourists, I'll most likely settle here in Nicaragua."

"On the lake with the alligators and bull sharks?" That hardly seemed a peaceful retirement.

"No, over on the coast. It's not much different from Costa Rica back in the day."

"That does sound nice," Lydia said. "How long until you think you'll retire?" She pictured a simple life, a modest house with an ocean view. Her dream of teaching children on the beach wafted through her mind.

"Oh, I'd say it'll be at least another ten to fifteen years. I've got a good life in Florida. I'd love it if you would come visit."

Lydia smiled at him. She didn't have much of an opinion of Florida other than retirement homes and extreme politics. She'd hate that. Especially for ten or fifteen years. A month ago, the offer would have promised the security she thought she needed. Now, she craved adventure. She pushed the thoughts aside. They had just found each other again. Last night and this morning, they'd regained an ease around each other that filled her with quiet joy. He brought a light into her life that she'd missed. She needed to pace herself and enjoy this, not look for ways to destroy something that hadn't even begun.

That evening, after they'd returned to Costa Rica, Robert took Lydia to his favorite restaurant. Kate begged off, saying she wanted to turn in early. She clearly wanted to give Lydia and Robert a chance to rekindle their relationship. Lydia wanted that as well.

The day's conversation had flowed easily, remembering the things they'd done together and explaining the things they'd done since. She enjoyed him. The relaxed cadence of his voice put her at ease. The way his attention shone on her, how he hung on her words when she spoke, told her he saw her. A pang of memory of all the times Joe had talked to her while turned toward the TV sliced through her. Quickly, she replaced those memories with better ones from her marriage. She'd chosen her earlier life, and it had been a good one. Now a new horizon awaited. Her gaze wandered over Robert, and she wondered what Sophie would think of him.

Every time her eyes found his hands, she saw the younger version of Robert. The long fingers that knew her so well. His body had softened, but the planes and angles remained the same. She had fit into them once.

The restaurant had hardwood tables set in the sand. A breeze kept the insects at bay, and someone had strung twinkle lights between the palms. Skinny, long-eared cats roamed table to table begging for handouts.

Their drinks, a pina colada for her and a margarita for him, came in fishbowl-sized glasses and went down smoothly. They ate cool ceviche while a man played guitar in the corner.

Their entrees arrived, the freshest of grilled fish atop rice and fresh vegetables. Robert reached across the table and took her hand. He swiped his thumb across her palm the way he used to. "Thank you for coming to dinner with me tonight. I haven't seen you in so many years, and yet this feels as familiar as yesterday."

She squeezed his hand. "It does. It's like all those years happened in a different dimension." Her heart leaped in her chest, the way it had so many years before. "I missed you."

The temperature on the beach seemed to rise a few degrees. The candlelight on the table caused a flicker in his eyes that looked like passion. A spark in her chest caught and grew until her whole body flamed.

Lydia ate what she could, but her mind had moved on from food. She had so many needs beyond hunger. She wanted to reclaim more of that woman from years ago. She could tell this passion ran both ways, and it lit her on fire.

When the server asked if they'd like to see the dessert menu, she quickly said no.

"Are you sure?" Robert asked. "We could share a banana split."

Lydia giggled. Memories of bananas and ice cream and love from years earlier slid through her. "I'd prefer a walk on the beach if that's okay?"

Robert paid the bill, and they headed into the dark night where they heard the waves gently lapping against the shore. She took his hand in hers and pulled him away from the twinkle lights.

When she finally stopped in the wet sand and turned, he was right there. He stepped into her embrace, and she raised her head as he lowered his. Their lips touched and transported Lydia back in time. Back to a hunger she had long forgotten that had nothing to do with food. She wanted him. Not wild Zander sex, not exactly. Instead, she wanted to be part of him, to meld with another person the way they had once fused their bodies and minds together.

As they kissed, every cell in her body zoomed faster. He ran his hands along her bare arms, raising the skin in tiny prickles. He wrapped his arms around her and pulled her tighter to him. Feelings resurrected from another life rushed through her again. She finally pulled away to breathe, lest she lose herself altogether.

"Nothing has changed," he said, his voice rough with passion. "I've dreamed about this so many times, and it's even better than I remembered. I still love you."

The world stopped spinning. The words scared her, yet she could have uttered them herself. This had been missing for so many years. This is what it was like to want someone with every cell in your body, and to have someone want you that badly in return. These cool ocean breezes and fiery kisses were life, or at least what life was supposed to be.

Could her issues resolve so easily? The right man finally shows up, and poof, like a fairytale, all your dreams come true. At least all of them except the one where your best friend didn't live happily ever after. Real life crashed down around her. But she didn't want real life. She wanted the fantasy, so she leaned into Robert and whispered, "I love you too." And pressed her lips against his.

They returned to the rental house, and she led him to her room. She'd put her clothes away and made the bed, secretly hoping things would work out. And they definitely worked out. She briefly swooped back to the awkwardness of her teens. How do you take your clothes off in front of a boy? But then her older, smarter self stepped in, and she kissed him again and let him disrobe her.

His skin, hot and smooth against hers, made her dizzy with need. They practically tumbled into the bed, into each other. The similarities and differences the years had dealt them filled her with wonder. So much was the same, but her passion was older and smarter. She could give better than she used to and understood how to get what she needed.

The first time was longing. Then they held each other and kissed. They explored their new/old bodies, gently, thoroughly. The heat came on like a sunrise, slowly, and then brighter and warmer until it lit up the room. She wanted to be with him forever. Never let him go, never leave this room. Never lose him again.

Chapter 29

Lydia

Balancing her identity as a mother and a friend became more difficult as Lydia plunged into love. She deserved it and found it selfish at the same time.

She and Robert slid into a time warp where they recreated their earlier lives. They spent hours at the beach where Lydia watched Robert surf. She hadn't ridden a board since she left the country. The cold water and dangerous waves of Southern California couldn't compare with Costa Rica. Not that she'd tried. She couldn't bear the thought of surfing without him.

As he had before, he encouraged her to try again. He steadied her board, told her when to stand, encouraged her after the inevitable fall into the water. Despite his encouragement, the years told her this wasn't her sport. Hopping up to your feet then standing on a wobbly piece of fiberglass while trying to catch a wave to take you to shore was a young woman's game. Creaky knees and underprepared muscles took the fun out of the sport.

Robert had always surfed, so had never lost the ability. He made it look as difficult as washing the dishes or vacuuming a rug. They did snorkel together and even went scuba diving once. That time Kate joined them, but usually she remained at the house or went for a spa day at a local resort.

One day, Lydia woke up before Robert and padded into the kitchen. The full pot of hot coffee signaled Kate had arisen as well. She poured herself a cup, noticing that Kate must have been to the market the day before because an unopened jug of almond milk sat on the refrigerator's top shelf.

When she peeked across the living area, she spied Kate lounging beside the pool as the day gently moved from gray to full light.

"Hey, it's been a while," Lydia said, stepping onto the patio.

Kate turned to look at her. "Yes. You seem to be having a wonderful time."

"I'm in love. It's weird, it feels like I've always been in love with him, despite all the years between then and now." Lydia slid into the lounge chair beside Kate. "Do you want to come to the beach with us today?"

"And watch Robert surf for a few hours? No thanks."

"If you change your mind, let me know. It would be nice to have someone to talk to." Lydia thought about the comment. She did like to watch Robert surf, although sometimes she wished she had something else to do. When she got bored, she could always take a dip in the ocean.

"You could take a book." Kate lifted a paperback from her lap. "I've got several I can lend you."

"No, thanks. I like to watch him." And it would seem rude to read while he did his favorite thing. Although, a time or two it reminded her of watching one of Sophia's sporting events. She loved seeing her daughter compete, but hanging around a pool waiting for a child's few seconds of swimming made for a long and boring day.

"I'm thinking about leaving soon," Kate said.

Kate's words hung in the air between them. She hadn't specified what that meant, and Lydia was a little afraid to ask. Unfortunately, she had to. "Are you going back to L.A.?"

"I think I'm done with Los Angeles. I've listed my condo with a realtor, and there's already an offer on it."

"Don't you have to go back to move your stuff? Where will you live?"

"I've hired someone to pack up the place. I actually did that when we were in Australia. It's amazing what you can pay people to do. They've sold or donated most of the furniture already. My realtor brought in new furniture to stage it properly."

"You don't even want to say goodbye to the condo? You lived there for years." Lydia didn't bring up the fact that Kate hadn't mentioned where she'd move next.

"Good god, no. Mitch and I bought that place together. I'm honestly happier never seeing it again." Kate seemed to dismiss the conversation with a wave of her hand.

"Are you happy?" Lydia asked. The question sat between them, unanswered.

Lydia tried again. "Are you still going to therapy with Dr. Lin?"

"Yes."

Lydia heard the coffee grinder spin in the kitchen. Robert must be up and hadn't checked whether someone had made coffee already. Well, he'd lived on his own for a long time. He probably wasn't used to other people doing things like that. For some reason, Robert being awake annoyed her. Probably because she needed more time with Kate.

"We'd planned on going to the Arenal Volcano together before Robert arrived. Do you still want to do that?"

"Why don't you and Robert do it?"

"Because I want to do it with you like we did the first time we were here."

Kate paused a long time before answering. Lydia worried Robert would come out and ruin their conversation. Finally, Kate crossed her arms and sighed. "I guess I would like to see it. We've already got two rooms, so there's no reason Robert can't join us. Unless you don't want him to." Kate turned to Lydia, her gaze a challenge.

"That sounds perfect."

"Hey, ladies. What do we have going on today?" Robert said, coming onto the patio in nothing but a worn pair of board shorts.

Lydia moved her feet for him as he sat on the end of her chaise. He had a large cup of black coffee in his hands, so he must have figured that out.

"We were just talking about our trip to Arenal. Are you up for that?"

"Sure, I love that place. The ziplining is great, and some of the big ecolodges have hot springs with swim-up bars."

"You'll be happy to know that the place we've booked does indeed have a swim-up bar." Kate's tone teased Robert. Lydia wouldn't have been so nice. Who cared about a swim-up bar when she wanted to spend time with her friend? She shook her head. She'd definitely woken up on the wrong side of the bed.

"Hey, Robert, I think I'm going to take a day off from the beach and stay here and do laundry and catch up on a few things," Lydia said.

"Why don't we both do that? We can go to the beach a little later. Or, if you're tired of watching me surf, and believe me, I would be tired of it, we can do something else fun."

Oh, sweet man. Every time she felt the slightest pinch of discomfort with their relationship, he proved what a good guy he was. His attitude was old, and new, and wonderful.

Another night, another candlelit dinner, with the beach breeze lifting her hair from her shoulders and a blue-eyed man across the table who loved her. And she loved him too, the way she did in her twenties, with abandon. Back then she'd thought only about the present joy until she'd had to think about leaving.

She'd had more time then, a long vacation of hot summer weeks where she fell so deeply she never really got over him. Would she have turned that love on her husband if she hadn't already spent it on Robert, or did being with him teach her how to love, so she could stay with Joe into the long cold fall? It must be the latter. Robert filled her with enough love to last most of a lifetime.

And here he was again. He smiled at her, lines crinkling the corner of his eyes. "You look pensive. Is anything wrong?"

"Nothing is wrong. I was thinking about how in love we were when we were younger."

He reached for her hand and squeezed it. "I still love you that much. Maybe I always have. I don't want to lose you again."

Her mind raced over familiar territory. She hadn't wanted to lose him back then but couldn't find a way for them to be together. Now it would be easier to be with him. She no longer searched for the security of a husband and family. Lydia smiled to herself. She had certainly started this trip looking for that, but she'd shed that idea along the way. She'd tossed it aside in Bonaire or Australia, the way she'd left behind clothes that didn't fit right.

And yet, it had come back to her like an old friend, or a sweatshirt too ratty to wear in public but you couldn't bear to give away. She could relax into knowing she'd have a partner for the next part of her life. "Where would we live?"

"Well, you're retired, and I own a business in St. Petersburg. It would probably make the most sense if we lived in Florida. Of course, only if you like it there. I think you would. It's beautiful, and the beaches are wonderful."

"They're not bad in California either, especially for a surfer." Why had she said that? She didn't even know if she wanted to stay in California, regardless of whether she was with Robert. She'd sounded so defensive. Why couldn't she just be happy?

"I agree. Although I hear the rents are pretty high. But I will go where you want. I might be able to sell my business." His eyes turned a darker cobalt, as if reflecting dimmer thoughts.

She'd hurt him or made him feel inadequate. She hadn't meant to, she'd just voiced her thoughts. St. Petersburg might be a wonderful place. It didn't seem fair that he would assume she'd move. And she didn't know much about Florida. It had never made the list of places she wanted to visit.

Escondido, St. Petersburg, they sounded mundane compared to the global exploring she'd pursued over the past weeks. If she could have whatever she wanted, she'd keep traveling with Kate forever and have Robert show up on occasion for romantic love. Kind of like a love booster shot.

Where had these ridiculous thoughts come from? She had the chance for a do-over, the opportunity to settle down with the one big love of her life, and now she trifled with it as if she hadn't spent decades longing for exactly this.

"I want to be with you too," she said, squeezing his fingers. "And this time, we will find a way to work it out."

His shoulders visibly relaxed, and the overhead lights twinkled in his once-again sea-blue eyes. Those small changes showed her she meant everything to him. It didn't matter where they lived, as long as they lived together. She needed to get over herself and her newfound independence. That might be great short term, but over the rest of her life, what on earth would surpass spending it on someone she loved deeply?

"I like this. I like you. I want to be with you." Warmth, even excitement, flowed through Lydia as she made up her mind to commit to this man. Her life unfolded before her, lazy days of comfort, hot nights of slow love. A life she'd always wanted, searched for, and when her life turned into something else, longed for. Now she had everything she'd always wanted.

Chapter 30

Lydia

The next day, they set off for Arenal. Kate drove them past farms, coffee plantations, and through mountain towns. They traveled on the Interamerican Highway, the fabled stretch of road that extended from Alaska to the southern tip of South America.

When they finally turned off the highway, it pulled at Lydia to keep going. It wanted her to travel all the way to the end, to see incredible sights, meet fascinating people, continue the journey. Maybe someday she and Robert could drive that road together, exploring the world until they reached the end.

Her mind couldn't seem to settle. Perhaps that's why she wanted to stay on the long road. She wanted so much it threatened to burst her open. She wanted Kate to want to live. She wanted to find a meaningful life. She wanted love. She wanted to learn and to teach.

The car wound up a mountain. After a sharp turn, the vista opened. Before them, a huge shimmering lake spread to the base of a volcano. The perfect cone shone vibrant green at the base and turned black as the mountain rose above the surrounding hills like a giant beast. It had grown so tall that, like Jack's beanstalk, clouds obscured the top. It just might stretch all the way to heaven.

Kate careened into a large pull-out area and stopped the vehicle. They all got out and walked to the concrete barrier. Sun-speckled blue water, a slash of green jungle, and then a lava rock mountain that disappeared into clouds.

"This might be the most beautiful view I've ever seen." Lydia whispered. It didn't seem real, and she wished she could reach out and touch it to ensure its existence.

"I feel like it's looking back at us, like it knows what we're thinking." Kate's voice filled with awe.

Lydia understood. The mountain went beyond beautiful into the realm of magic.

"It's pretty, but I don't think it has any special powers," Robert said.

"I doubt the locals would agree with you." Kate didn't take her eyes off the mountain, but displeasure laced her reply.

"I do think places can be more than the rocks and sand they're made from," Lydia said. Life was bigger than mere humans understood. She needed to leave room for a little magic in her life. Robert didn't seem to understand this. If everything was black and white, it snuffed out hope. Colors, texture, and sound created interest, which created legends, which recreated the past and laid the groundwork for the future.

"Let's go." Kate jangled the keys and headed for the car, giving Robert the side-eye in the process.

Lydia put an arm around him and pulled him to her, her eyes still locked on the volcano. "It is truly beautiful."

"You're what's beautiful." He pulled her around to face him and kissed her waiting lips.

Carved out of the jungle on the volcano's side, the resort stretched across acres of green lawn and tropical plants. Individual cabins dotted the grass, each with a sliding glass door opening onto the mountain. Not that they could see it. Fog socked in everything except the surrounding rainforest.

When they reached their cabin, Robert grabbed Lydia in an embrace and shuffled her toward the bed. She kissed him. A small fountain made of black volcanic rock trickled inside the room, and the king-sized bed beckoned, but it could wait. Other things couldn't.

"Hey, I'm going to go spend some girl time with Kate. Is that okay?"

"Are you getting tired of me already?" He smiled but came in for another kiss.

Lydia gave him a quick peck before backing away. "Of course I'm not tired of you. But we've spent so much time together lately. I feel like I'm losing touch with her, and she's really struggling right now."

"She can't be struggling too much if she can afford this place." He swept his hand around the room. "I wish you'd let me pay for the places we stay."

Prickles of anger raced up her spine. "Robert, I love you, and frankly, I don't give a damn who pays for what, although I certainly couldn't afford to stay in a place like this.

But Kate is dealing with some big issues right now. Her whole life fell apart, and I want to be there for her."

She debated telling him about the suicide attempt. Maybe then he'd take her seriously. But that wasn't her story to tell. He'd just have to believe her. "I'll be back later. Take some time for yourself."

She hated leaving when he wanted her to stay. He'd come all this way to be with her. But they couldn't spend all their time together. She tried to imagine a future in some house she'd never seen in Florida, Robert at work and her whiling away her days trying to find something important to do. The image wouldn't come.

The wet grass soaked her shoes as she made her way to the next cabin over. Lydia walked through the open glass door into Kate's cabin and found her friend splayed across the bed, eyes closed. "Hey, are you up?"

Kate's eyes sprang open. "I'm completely awake." She looked around the room. "Where's Robert?"

"Back at the room. I told him I wanted some alone time with you."

"That's great. I know we just spent three hours in a car together, but I miss you. And Robert gets on my nerves a little."

"I can tell."

"Sorry. He did twenty-five years ago as well. I'd forgotten how he fawned all over you. I'm sure it feels great when that attention shines on you, but it makes me feel a little left out." She shook her head. "But that's not important. How are things going between you two? It seems as hot and heavy as it did back in the day."

Lydia lit up with happiness at the question. "It is amazing to be fawned over. I haven't been the center of someone's world since Sophie hit the preteen years. Although it feels a little more like a fantasy than reality. I mean how long can this go on? It's hard to picture what our future together might be like."

"Interesting. I think we had this exact same conversation decades ago. But actually, I want to spend some time talking about the future."

"Okay." Lydia dragged the word out, not liking the conversation's turn.

Kate grew serious. "We have to be able to have this discussion without getting mad at each other."

Lydia sank into a rattan chair beside the bed. Her friend needed her, so she'd listen. Just like Robert needed her, so she'd acquiesce. A pang of longing hit her. She wanted to be alone, completely on her own. She'd spent her life tying others to her, so she'd have the security she'd craved as a child. For the first time, she wanted to let them all go.

She turned her gaze to the friend who needed her. She would listen, like always, would help however she could. Despite that moment of pure clarity about what she truly wanted, she stuffed that strange loner woman who'd appeared back down into her heart. "Tell me what you're thinking."

"I have more money than anyone could possibly use. You got mad at me when I said I'd leave it in a foundation for you, but something should be done with it. Please help me figure that out."

The old Lydia wanted to scream, to tell her friend to spend the money or save it, she didn't care, as long as they didn't have to confront the reason Kate wanted to get rid of it. Instead, she chose not to argue. Maybe the weeks of travel had beaten her into submission. Maybe she needed to move on.

"Why do you want to start some new foundation? Aren't there plenty of groups doing good work that you could donate to?"

"But I thought you—" Kate must have seen the anger wash over Lydia's face. She stopped speaking. The silence in the room grew heavy.

Kate sighed. "You're right. I'm trying to foist my issues on you. I like your idea of donating the money to existing organizations. Do you have any suggestions?"

Lydia relaxed into her seat. "I've got a few. Where's your laptop?"

Two hours later, they decided to venture to the pool bar to celebrate. They'd figured out how to give away millions of dollars. After Kate's attorneys carried out her instructions, her money would help an organization that built libraries in poor areas of the world in an effort to educate girls. They also funded female entrepreneurs through another organization and contributed to global water quality through a third. The heady power of making a difference had been exhilarating, like a drug, only better.

Lydia stopped by her room and found it empty. Her shoulders sank in relief that Robert had found something to do. It wasn't like she didn't enjoy his company, but they'd spent so much time together recently. Hanging out with Kate, she didn't have to worry about her own future. Only Kate's.

She slipped into a swimsuit and wrapped a patterned sarong around her hips. Kate arrived, and they crossed a long expanse of grass to the lodge's pool. The water meandered through tropical landscaping, with plenty of coves where people could hide. A hot-spring-fed waterfall crashed into the swimming pool at one end, with the water gradually cooling before leaving the pool on the opposite side. The bar sat in relatively cool water at the pool's edge. The barstools didn't break the surface and the palm frond roof protected customers from sun and showers.

"This is paradise." Lydia floated in lukewarm water and gently paddled toward an empty seat. She swirled, letting water caress her skin. Everything in her life would work out the way it should. She had loved working with Kate, figuring out how to use money to make the world a better place.

She stopped swirling and faced Kate who pulled herself onto a bar stool. "Thank you for letting me be a part of that. I'm so excited about all the good your money will do. Little girls will read, women will work, health will improve. It's amazing."

"It is a pretty good feeling." A genuine smile lit Kate's face, although Lydia glimpsed ruefulness beneath it.

She wanted to pull that sadness out of her friend, drown it in the pool, and then throw it into the volcano. But she couldn't force happiness on Kate. At best, she could be an example, and she would always let her know how much she loved her. "You are an amazing person. I know you're struggling, and I know I don't have the solution for that. But what you did today was extraordinary. It will make a huge difference in the lives of people across the world."

"It definitely feels like the right thing to do. Now get up here so we can have our celebratory drink."

Lydia sat on the barstool next to Kate. A server came by and asked for their drink order.

"Do you have any champagne?" Kate asked.

"I will have some brought down from the main lodge."

"Champagne. That's fancy." Lydia nudged Kate with her shoulder.

"Today feels momentous. I've given away over ninety percent of my wealth."

"Do you think you should have held more back? Are you worried?" Lydia asked. Kate had donated a staggering amount. It almost seemed like they'd played with Monopoly money, the numbers were so big.

"No, I'm not worried at all. In fact, every dollar we spent left me feeling a little lighter. I never realized the burden of money before. Don't get me wrong, I appreciate living my life without worrying about making ends meet, but I started my company because I loved the idea of making beautiful, comfortable clothing for women. The men who run it now only care about money. Today, it feels like I've divorced them."

"Well, that's a great reason to celebrate. They were a bunch of assholes." Lydia smiled when Kate chuckled at her words. She watched as a golf cart drove up to the pool and a hotel worker jumped out with a bottle of Moët, then passed it down to the bartender.

Once they had full glasses, Lydia raised hers toward Kate. "To good deeds and good divorces."

"To us," Kate said, clinking her glass against Lydia's. "This has been a fantastic world tour. Thanks for taking it with me. Again."

"I'm not sure if it was more fun the first time or the second time around."

"I vote for the first time," Kate said.

The first time, they'd been so young. They'd been blessed with energy and the beauty of youth, but Lydia had learned so much about herself on both trips. They had bookended different phases of her life. But this trip had more gravitas, partly because she was wiser and partly because she worried about her friend.

"It's funny how I'm ending both of our Costa Rica jaunts with the same questions." Lydia couldn't stop thinking about Robert, both how much she loved being with him and how much she still wanted a big life.

"That's definitely crossed my mind. What do you think you'll do?" Kate asked.

"I don't know. I'm not ready to go back to my boring life in Escondido, but I honestly don't think St. Petersburg would be that much more exciting."

"Do you still want to get married? Finding the right man was a big deal for you when we started this journey."

The question flummoxed Lydia, and she'd been thinking about it for days. She had wanted a man, a husband. Somewhere along the way, she'd shed that need without even noticing it. Yes, eventually it would be nice to grow old with someone, at least that's what you were supposed to want. But she wasn't ready to grow old yet. The trip had given her new energy akin to a runner's high, and she wanted to keep going, to keep exploring, and definitely to keep using her skills to help others. She was a teacher, but she no longer wanted to teach in American classrooms. Instead, when they looked at the organization setting up libraries in rural communities in Africa and Asia, she'd dreamed about teaching there. The world still had much to show her, and she had something to give in return.

"I think your silence is an answer," Kate said.

"I really do love Robert, and this seems like a second chance for us, but I just don't know." Lydia swallowed a gulp of champagne. That strange desire to be completely on her own bubbled back up. She took a deep breath. Finally, time was on her side. Nothing needed to be decided today. Things would work out.

"You've got a great head on your shoulders. I have no doubt you'll figure out what's best for you," Kate said.

"Thanks. I love you, you know. And I truly appreciate the opportunity to travel with you again. I know you're unsure of the future, but I personally hope this is something we can do for years to come."

"Come here." Kate wrapped her in a savage hug, almost pulling her off the submerged barstool.

Lydia embraced her friend. Underneath Kate's skin, somewhere deep inside her, Lydia sensed a tremor, as if her heart beat at a different pace. Or maybe some monster lived inside her that she couldn't expel. Again, Lydia wanted to save her friend, wanted to reach down inside her and find that creature, wring its neck, and drag him into daylight. Then she'd pummel him until nothing remained.

Kate tried to pull away from the hug, but Lydia wouldn't let her. "If you decide to fight this thing, I'm here for you. Whatever it takes."

At that, Kate went limp and cried silently into Lydia's shoulder. Lydia closed her eyes and gently rocked her, the way she'd rocked Sophie as a child. She never solved Sophie's problems either, even when she tried. If she'd learned that earlier, she would have a better relationship with her daughter, but at least she'd learned it now.

Eventually, she loosened her grip. Kate seemed smaller than she had just minutes ago. Smaller than she'd ever seemed.

"Do you want to head back to the room and rest?" Lydia asked.

"No. Not really. I'd rather sit here with you in this warm water, in a tropical country, and drink champagne."

"Yeah, me too. Let's take our drinks over to the steamy part of the pool."

They waded away from the bar. A few more people had arrived. Families with children played in the shallows or near the built-in slide. Two couples sat at the bar.

Lydia and Kate soaked near a waterfall of steaming liquid arriving straight from the bowels of the volcano. The day had grown even foggier, making it difficult to determine steam from cloud. Tiny droplets shone on Kate's hair as if she'd become a water goddess emerging from smoke.

"Are you excited about tomorrow?" Lydia asked. "I hear the ziplining is amazing. I've never done it before."

"I may back out and spend my time wandering around the mountain. But you should definitely go. I hear they are some of the highest and longest zip lines anywhere."

"Oh, I wish you'd go."

"No thanks. Have fun with Robert. I'm looking for something a little more low-key."

Lydia would have never used the term low-key to describe Kate. At least not in the past. She couldn't help worrying about her friend, but Kate wasn't her responsibility. Earlier in the room, she'd mentioned talking to her counselor again. Hopefully, they'd made some progress.

"Fine. But we're having dinner together in the lodge tonight? Right?" Lydia asked.

"You bet. In fact, I should probably head back soon to get ready."

"Yeah. Me too. I wonder where Robert went. I thought maybe we'd see him down here. Come on, do one more lap of the pool with me and then we'll leave."

They wandered around the beautiful pool with its white concrete floor decorated with smooth black lava. Walls and eddies made for constantly changing temperatures. They saw children and parents, lovers and friends, but no Robert. Lydia finally gave up, and they headed back to their cabins.

That night, they met for dinner in the grand room of the lodge. The peaked hardwood ceiling had to be forty feet high. The room had filled with guests who created a constant background hum. Wide doors opened to the cooling night.

They drank lime and guaro cocktails, and the earlier soak in the hot springs along with the local firewater left Lydia immensely relaxed. Staff in starched shirts brought them sushi served on slabs of pineapple, followed by thick steaks with perfect grill marks.

Robert had returned to the room just before they left for dinner. He said he'd needed to run some errands in town, although what he needed and what town he could have possibly visited eluded her. She didn't ask, happy to have had the time with Kate.

The conversation flowed easily, and at one point he had taken her hand, and she had reached for Kate's. Love surrounded Lydia in that moment, and she couldn't believe her luck. Life was amazing and fulfilling and she couldn't get enough of it. From here on out, she'd greet every day she had left with enthusiasm and love, grateful she'd been given so many second chances.

She dropped their hands and gazed around the room at the happy, tired faces. A lull in the noise and the distant call of parrots made the moment perfect. She could stay here forever. Even better, she wanted to explore different places forever. She had to put that first as she moved forward with her life.

She smiled at Kate, who returned her grin. She turned to Robert.

"I love you," he said, all sincerity and happy gaze.

"I love you too. I'm the luckiest woman in the world." Contentment flowed through her veins.

Robert stood, then grasped the edge of the table as he dropped to one knee.

"Oh, my god." Kate's voice flew past Lydia's shoulder.

Lydia sat frozen. She couldn't move at all. She just stared at him. Her boyfriend? Her lover? She didn't even know what to call him yet.

He pulled a ruby-colored velvet box from his pocket and lifted the lid. A diamond set in a gold band sparkled under the lights. This should have been everything she ever wanted. Her gratitude for his love buoyed her as much as it threatened to drag her down. It was just too soon. But if she didn't say yes, she risked losing him again.

"Lydia, I kneel before you more in love with you than ever. I fell in love with you years ago, and it was a love I never got over. You are the most incredible woman I have ever met, and I've already spent far too much of my life without you. Would you please do me the honor of becoming my wife?" His sea-blue eyes gazed at her with love and tenderness, imploring her to say yes.

"I, well. I didn't expect this."

"Look, a proposal!" some woman screeched from the crowded dining room.

Time slowed like syrup. "I love you," Lydia said, putting all of her heart into the words.

Robert set one hand on her knee. The other stretched the ring box toward her. In the background, seemingly in a world apart from the intense stare the two of them held, she heard a chant. "Say yes. Say yes." The entire room focused on them.

"Please say yes." Robert's voice almost broke her heart. Wasn't this exactly what she wanted? If she could have picked a man to live out her days with, it would have been him.

"Yes. I will marry you."

The entire room released its breath in one collective cheer. Before she knew it, Robert had jumped from the floor and pulled her from her chair. His embrace lifted her feet, and he spun her in a circle. "She said yes," he announced.

Even with her feet back on solid ground, emotion almost toppled Lydia. She grabbed the back of her chair with both hands to steady herself. Robert took the ring out of the box and reached for her hand, but she feared letting go.

An awkward dance ensued. He pulled at her wrist, while she white-knuckled the chair. Finally, Kate broke in. "Honey, why don't you sit down? You look a little unsteady on your feet. Plus, you're making a scene."

Lydia turned and glared at her friend, but Kate's eyes shone with laughter and love, not the admonishment Lydia expected. She followed up on the sound advice and plopped into the chair. Robert reached for her hand and began to slide the ring up her third finger. The ring barely fit over the first knuckle. He pushed it, metal sinking into skin, but the ring wouldn't budge.

Lydia squeezed his hand. "It's okay. We can get it sized correctly. She slid the ring off her finger and slipped it onto her pinky, where it fit perfectly.

He raised her hand toward the ceiling, and the room erupted in claps and hoots. Kate flagged a server and ordered a bottle of champagne.

"It looks like we have something else to celebrate today," Kate said.

Lydia thought back to that first bottle of champagne in the warm swimming pool. After they had done such important work. Her heart longed for that sense of satisfaction. She closed her eyes and breathed. Tonight was about Robert. He loved her and wanted to be with her. It was more than she could have asked for.

She opened her eyes and caught him bowing to the crowd. He loved this the way a bride loved being the center of attention at a bachelorette party. He'd never been married before. The second time around, Lydia had expected it to be low-key.

He finally sat down. She took his hand and tugged him toward her, planting a big kiss on his lips. This was going to be wonderful. It had to be.

Chapter 31

Lydia

They'd drunk champagne, returned to the room, made love. They'd done all the things they perhaps should have done so many years ago. But they hadn't back then, and now the clock read five in the morning and Lydia lay in bed, wide awake, wondering about it all. Robert lay inches away, but their bodies didn't touch.

She hadn't had so many lovers. She'd had a serious boyfriend in high school. Serious back then, but definitely not serious over the course of her life. They'd had sex, but never actually slept together. In her early twenties, she'd dated Mario, a hot Italian from New York City. They slept tangled up like cats after sex. Her gut told her he had too deep an appreciation for women, and she'd broken up with him after she and Kate returned from Amsterdam.

There had been a few other guys, none of them worth remembering. Except Robert. Then she'd met Joe. He loved to sleep with an arm around her. She'd curl into him, safe in his cocoon. Even when it was too hot to sleep, or she was too disappointed in him to cuddle, he'd reach a foot out to touch her in his sleep. She doubted a lot of things about him, but never his love.

She couldn't remember how she and Robert slept in their twenties. She didn't remember this buffer of space. Experimenting, she moved a hand toward him, rested it gently against his hip. He moaned slightly and rolled away from her, never waking.

Why did this trouble her? It was as if she sought reasons their relationship wouldn't work.

She rose quietly and threw on some clothes, then slipped out of the room and headed toward the lodge for coffee. She paused as she passed Kate's cabin. For a moment she thought she'd knock on the door, but she wasn't ready to face her yet. Despite Kate setting her up with Robert, she didn't think her friend approved of their getting married, at least not yet. Or maybe that was Lydia's own voice talking.

The coffee helped. She sat at a corner table in the massive dining room watching bleary-eyed tourists load up on caffeine, eggs, and fruit. She avoided looking at the spot where she'd become engaged the night before. She tried to keep the memories of the awkward and embarrassing moment at bay.

She loved this man, she truly did. He was everything she needed, sweet, stable, and madly in love with her. The Robert of today checked every box on the perfect husband list she'd made in her twenties. He hadn't made the cut back then. Joe had. That should teach her about lists.

If only they'd had more time together. They'd only been back in touch for two weeks, enough time to fall in love but perhaps not enough to plan a future. How strange that she feared commitment this time around.

Fidgety, she jumped up from the table and headed back to the cabin. Thankfully they'd planned to ride an allegedly scary zip line with amazing views today. She needed to quit thinking for a while and just spend more time with him. Her heart knew things her mind wanted to second-guess.

Standing on a platform, strapped to a zip line, Lydia had a lot to second guess. Trees shrouded the partner platform on the opposite side of a wide ravine, and it looked like the long silver rope that had become a form of transportation just disappeared into jungle and fog.

"Relax," said the guide holding onto her. "And don't be afraid to brake."

Right. The "brake" happened to also be the metal bar she clung to in fear. Supposedly it would slow her down if she turned it, creating friction on the silver rope, but anything other than hanging on for dear life wasn't going to happen.

"Here you go," he said, then gave her a gentle push. She closed her eyes as she sailed out over the platform. Not seeing her surroundings scared her more than watching the jungle floor drop away. She opened her eyes. A jolt of exhilaration hit her as the landscape slid by. The lake glittered below, and above, the volcano hid in its foggy shroud. This must be what it felt like to fly. She wanted to shout to the heavens, squawk like the flock of parrots clamoring below. She was as powerful as a god and nothing but a tiny speck of humanity all at once. She'd never felt so alive.

The ride ended too soon, but fortunately, they'd just started and many ziplines waited for them on this mountain. The guide released her, and she took an unsteady step before finding her footing.

She turned to watch Robert come down next. Unlike Lydia, he actually whooped as he slid down the line. He came in fast, and the guide had to work hard to slow him down before he hit the barrier at the end of the platform.

As soon as they'd unhooked him, she ran to him. "That was so much fun! Thank you." She embraced him and squeezed him hard. "Thank you for bringing me here. This is fantastic."

"Of course. I'm glad you like it."

"Like it? I love it." She squeezed him again, then pulled him toward the side of the platform, excited to see where they'd go next.

"You have changed from that shy girl I knew all those years ago."

Had she heard a hint of wistfulness in his voice? Maybe he had some doubts about their future also. "I have changed," she said carefully. "I'm not so shy anymore, and I know who I am and who I want to be." They treaded thin ice, something rarely seen in a jungle. She hoped he wouldn't ask who she wanted to be.

He didn't. He just gave her a strange look, then turned away and looked toward the incoming zipliner.

She wondered, not for the first time, how they would make it work long term. "Hey, Robert. How would you feel about me teaching abroad?"

"What?" His look of confusion didn't match the clarity in her heart.

"I've been thinking about becoming an English teacher in a foreign country, a poor country that needs more teachers. What do you think about that?" Lydia watched Robert's cheeks flame red.

"When? Before we get married? Or after?" Shock coated his too loud voice.

"I'm not sure. I haven't thought it through." Of course, she had. She just hadn't realized it. Just like before. The guilt that had buried itself in her belly unfurled, seeping into her blood and bones. She loved him. She hurt him. Twice.

"You don't want to get married, do you? You're going to leave me again."

"Folks," the guide said. "It's time to hike to the next line. Please follow me."

Lydia stayed on the platform until only she, Robert, and the trailing guide remained. Then she followed the others onto a path through dense jungle. Fitting.

"I do love you," she said, turning her head as she walked. "I love you so much, it hurts to even think about this. But at fifty-two years old, I'm finally ready to live a big life. The kind of life you talked about when we met."

"I can tell you from experience, that kind of life doesn't work out. I thought I could have everything. I could chill on the beach, spend my days teaching people to surf, and come home to the girl of my dreams. But she left me because she wanted more stability."

Lydia focused on the jungle ahead, glad he couldn't see the tears welling in her eyes. The easy path would be to take it all back. Apologize. Marry and move to Florida. But she knew it wouldn't work the way she'd known tying him down wouldn't have worked twenty-five years ago.

"I offered her more stability back then." Robert's voice wafted over her shoulder, an angry, brewing storm. "That wasn't good enough for her either."

"You would have resented me if I'd made you change your life for me."

"Maybe not. You assumed that. You didn't give us a chance then, and now it's déjà vu all over again!"

How could she want to cringe, laugh, and cry all at the same time? She had no real response. She wanted everything. She wanted someone to love her. She wanted to travel the world. She wanted to teach in a place where she had something to learn. Lydia made her way around a large tree and almost ran into the woman in front of her. They'd arrived at the next platform.

One by one, the tourists were shackled to the metal rope and sent on a ride from one ridge of the rainforest to another. Robert breathed heavily behind her, but she couldn't turn around to face him. Not yet.

The caretaker in her wanted to tell him everything would be all right. They'd find a way to work it out. A bigger part of her knew that was unlikely. So, she faced forward, followed instructions, and soon flew through the air again.

For a few seconds, the ride freed her from the worries of real life. Instead, she glided on the edge of fear and fantasy. It ended too soon. Like a five-year-old, she wanted to shout *again, again*.

When they'd unhooked her, she turned to watch Robert. He whooped, surely a good sign. As soon as he was off the ride, she wrapped him in a hug. He tried to back away, but she held him fast. Slowly, he relaxed into her.

"I love you," she whispered into his ear. Then she pulled back and looked him in the eyes. "I love you." She'd said it loud enough for people to turn and stare, but she didn't care about them. She only cared about Robert.

"But you won't marry me."

"Not right now. There are things I want to do with my life."

He sighed. "I think I said those exact words to you years ago, early on. I changed my mind too late back then." His voice grew grave. "I wish I'd made a different choice."

"Part of me worries I'm making the wrong choice. But this is something I need to do. I want my life to be full of meaning. I want to make a difference. I've never dreamed so big before." Her whole body zinged with possibilities. She wanted to run into her new future, hell, she'd zipline there if they'd let her.

"You amaze me," he said. "I can't believe we're letting this go again. But I won't hold you back."

"Thank you." She grasped him in a desperate, joyous hug. "This time, let's not let it completely go. Let's keep in touch. Who knows what the future holds?"

"That's a promise." He released her from the hug but held onto her hand as they walked toward the path at the edge of the platform. "When are you taking off on this adventure?"

"I don't know. I need to plan it first."

"You're welcome to stay with me in St. Petersburg while you plan."

She looked into those blue eyes that she'd managed to both hold onto and let go. "Thanks for the offer, but I think I'm going to figure out where Sophie's next port is and fly there to tell her the news."

She pictured a globe taut with strings. She'd be on one side of the world, tied with bright string to Sophie in another location and to Robert in a different one still. She thought about Kate, her string gone gray. She hoped with all her heart Kate would keep her string attached. Without it, the world would be a much darker place.

Chapter 32

Kate

Kate had waited until Lydia and Robert left on their zip line tour to depart the lodge. She'd heard about the hanging bridges of Mount Arenal. Photos showed metal grates stretching between the verdant ridges of the volcano, hundreds of feet above the jungle floor. The chain link sides of the bridge reached chest high.

She parked in a busy parking lot then walked the entire loop trail. Six hanging bridges, each showcasing a spectacular view. She looked down on the lake they'd driven by on their way in. When she turned toward the volcano, clouds cloaked its peak the way they had since their arrival.

She'd expected lots of tourists on the trails. Tour groups of ten to twenty people dotted the paths, but few solo travelers hiked between the crowds. She'd waited so long for the perfect time and the ideal location.

It had taken weeks, but finally she'd arranged everything. With Lydia's insightful help, she'd distributed the vast majority of her wealth to organizations that would make a difference in the world. She'd created a trust that would leave a million dollars to Lydia.

She'd thought about writing goodbye letters, but in the end didn't see the point. Of the people she'd reach out to, one had been with her for weeks. The other, Mitch, she just didn't care about enough to make an explanation worthwhile.

At the end of the route, she ate an orange she'd brought. She'd found the perfect bridge on her walk, one long enough that if she waited for the right timing, no one would be able to reach her in time to save her. Its height guaranteed death, unlike the booze and pills she'd tried the first time.

She sat quietly on a bench, wanting to spend a little more time in the beauty of the jungle. It made her sad to think of death. The last few weeks with Lydia had at times been terrible, but they'd also been magical.

Still, no real future lay ahead. She'd never go back to Los Angeles. She hated everything about her life there. She wished she could take back certain decisions she'd made. She shouldn't have taken her company public. But if she hadn't, she'd still be on that hamster wheel of work and worry. The person she'd become, engrossed in business and not living her life, wasn't anyone she'd ever wanted to be.

She and Mitch should have divorced years earlier. That she was blindsided and unaware of their problems clued her in to how messed up her life had become. How could you live with someone completely oblivious to the fact that they no longer loved you, and worse, had fallen in love with someone else? She'd never outlive the shame of that.

So, she'd decided not to. Instead, she smothered the sparks of joy that had lit the last few weeks. There were so many more reasons to throw herself off a bridge than to live. She'd get Alzheimer's like her mom and her aunt, and no cure existed. What a frightening, horrible disease.

But also, she'd set a course. She'd made a decision, and the one thing she prided herself on most was her ability to accomplish every goal she set. She couldn't tolerate this person who had ruined her life and had no prospects for the future. She stood, dropped her orange peel in a nearby trash can, and headed back onto the trail.

She found the longest bridge again, one so high in the jungle that the clouds shifted like something alive. At times she saw nothing but white. Other times they cleared and opened a space where verdant plants far below became present. They looked like such a soft cushion from this height.

She stood in the middle of the bridge alone and in thought. The things she didn't want still outweighed the things she craved. She had failed. She wasn't a person who failed.

A tremor ran through her body. It could be the bridge swaying in the light breeze. It could be the battle raging between her heart and her head. It could be the fear of the fall.

A single plan left to carry out, and all the worry and heartache and sadness of the past months would disappear. That shiny vision prodded her on. Nothingness pulled at her, a thick rope beckoning her to the jungle below. The tiniest strands of a spider's web clung to her and begged her to stay: the sound of the ocean, the echo of her friend's voice telling her she had a lot to give.

She touched her face where tears mingled with damp air. She couldn't go forward, and she wouldn't go back. The lonely howl of lost souls filled her as she reached for the railing.

Epilogue

The heat sank into Lydia's bones as she swung her leg over the moped. She steered the vehicle out of the school's parking lot and through the streets of Can Tho, Vietnam. Eight months later, it still shocked her that she'd ended up in a city so beautiful.

She spun into the restaurant's circle drive and parked near the door. Excitement welled in her as she entered the huge space. She made her way to the enormous pagoda, open to impressive gardens and a spectacular view of the Mekong River.

"Lydia, over here." Kate waved at her from a table, then trotted over to embrace her.

"It's so good to see you." Lydia hugged her friend, never wanting to let go. "Thanks for coming to visit."

"It's your turn next time," Kate said, leading her toward the table.

"Absolutely. How are things going with the tourism project in Timor Leste?"

"It's going well. I'm surrounded by wonderful people who work hard to balance the influx of visitors without losing the charm that makes the place different from a thousand other destinations. And the scuba diving is spectacular."

"Well, with your help, I'm sure they'll find that balance," Lydia said. Kate had been a dynamo since volunteering for the Peace Corps in the small Asian country. She'd thrown herself into her job helping the government with business development.

But the job had helped her also. The morose Kate had disappeared under a dark tan and graying hair cut short to lop off the part she'd dyed in the past. This Kate practically glimmered with life force, the way she used to, although the hardened lines around her eyes hinted at the struggles she'd overcome. Lydia thought she was lovelier this way, with her beauty shining through the cracks.

"How did Robert's visit go?" Kate asked.

"It was good. He liked it here."

"But not enough to move?"

"No, but that's okay." She loved Robert, but it had taken her a while to realize she loved the idea of him more than the actual person. She'd imagined him into the perfect man when no man reached perfection. She'd see him when she could. Maybe when they retired, they'd live together on a Nicaraguan beach. Until then, she'd focus on the joy she'd found teaching and exploring. Plus, many fish roamed the sea. "I haven't exactly been lonely here."

"Nice." Kate's grin dimpled her cheeks. "How's Sophie?"

"Back at school. Still shocked her mother is on the other side of the world. Although she's changed her major to environmental studies." Some combination of her Semester at Sea program, growing up, and maybe even having her mother strike out on her own, had changed Sophie. She understood the immensity of the world and wanted to be a part of making it better.

When Lydia had told her she had accepted a teaching position in Vietnam, Sophie had beamed with pride. It still gave her chills to remember that she'd impressed her child.

"How has so much changed in the past year?" Kate asked.

"I think we were too immersed in our own problems. Living in the US encourages that. But then all of us, even Sophie, got out and saw the world. It changed us. For the better."

"I'll say. I was a mess. Literally, a basket case."

"You just went through a really hard time. How are you now?" Lydia still didn't understand whether it was better to ask or let Kate give the update on her own time, but she seemed so much better now that she gave it a shot.

"I'm still in therapy every week. It helps. I'd always known about that dark side of my psyche—I thought I was the darkness. Somehow, when I was about to let go, I found the part of me that wanted to hang on. It's a lot to unwind, and it's rarely fun to hash through those feelings, but I'm better. I don't think I'll ever drop quite that far again. I hope not."

"Well, if you're ever feeling particularly low, call me. I'll be there in a flash."

"Another five-country tour?"

"Maybe." Maybe it took them five tries to get it right. But they had.

The sinking orange sun lit the silt in the Mekong River, turning it from sandy brown to brilliant gold. The air around them glowed with possibility. Lydia reached for Kate's hand as the golden moment and a tantalizing future drew them into the next, best part of life.

THE END

❦

Other novels by Kathryn Dodson

Tequila Midnight

Hired to find a tycoon's daughter, a hard-drinking woman needs more than tequila to survive the night.

The Podcast Chronicles

She traded suits for mom duty, but she'll risk everything to save the Colorado mountain paradise she loves.

Portrait of Deception

A photographer on the brink of fame. A dictator with a fatal agenda. A terrifying trap she may not escape.

Afterword

Mental illness is a serious issue. The mental illness depicted in this novel was meant to represent the journey of one woman. While she was reluctant to receive care, I sincerely hope that anyone with similar feelings seeks help. If you are struggling, it is okay to share your feelings and you are encouraged to do so. In the United States, help is available by phone when you call or text 988.

Acknowledgements

Thank you for finding this novel and reading it to the end. Lydia and Kate's journey is ultimately a story of friendship. I've been fortunate to have a number of close friends who've helped me along my path at various points in my life. These include Lisa Ulrich Hoffman, Cara Williams, Libby Estrin, Colleen Knutson, and Lisa Rudloff. I'm also lucky to have a number of writing friends who help make my books the best they can be. A special thanks to my partner in all things bookish, Jocelyn Lindsay. I'd also like to thank my critique partners Sydney Clark and Claudia Armann who read an early version of this book—their comments made *Five Tries to Get It Right* a much better novel.

My best friend for the past thirty years has been my husband Tom—he makes everything possible. I also owe a big thanks to Jack who's off on his own journey.

About the author

Kathryn Dodson grew up writing and riding horses in far West Texas. She graduated from SMU in English/Creative Writing and went on to get an MBA from Thunderbird and a PhD from Clemson.

She has worked on both sides of the US/Mexico border and has held jobs with governments, chambers of commerce, and other businesses. Now she spends her days writing about interesting women in fascinating places.

Join Kathryn for updates and extras at www.KathrynDodson.com.

If you enjoyed ***Five Tries to Get It Right***, here are additional novels by Kathryn Dodson you may enjoy.

Tequila Midnight

Hired to find a tycoon's daughter, a hard-drinking woman needs more than tequila to survive the night.

The Podcast Chronicles

She traded suits for mom duty, but she'll risk everything to save the Colorado mountain paradise she loves.

Portrait of Deception

A photographer on the brink of fame. A dictator with a fatal agenda. A terrifying trap she may not escape.